PENGUIN BOOKS

THE KRAKEN WAKES

John Wyndham Parkes Lucas Benyon Harris was born in 1903, the son of a barrister. He tried a number of careers including farming, law, commercial art and advertising, and started writing short stories, intended for sale, in 1925. From 1930 to 1939 he wrote stories of various kinds under different names, almost exclusively for American publications, while also writing detective novels. During the war he was in the civil service and then the army. In 1946 he went back to writing stories for publication in the USA and decided to try a modified form of science fiction, a form he called 'logical fantasy'. As John Wyndham he wrote *The Day of the Triffids* and *The Kraken Wakes* (both widely translated), *The Chrysalids*, *The Midwich Cuckoos* (filmed as *Village of the Damned*), *The Seeds of Time*, *Trouble with Lichen*, *The Outward Urge* (with 'Lucas Parkes'), *Consider Her Ways and Others*, *Web* and *Chocky*, all of which have been published by Penguin. John Wyndham died in March 1969.

THE
KRAKEN WAKES

JOHN WYNDHAM

This Book Belongs To:

Em. Catuford

PENGUIN BOOKS

PENGUIN BOOKS

Published by the Penguin Group
Penguin Books Ltd, 80 Strand, London WC2R 0RL, England
Penguin Group (USA) Inc., 375 Hudson Street, New York, New York 10014, USA
Penguin Group (Canada), 90 Eglinton Avenue East, Suite 700, Toronto, Ontario, Canada M4P 2Y3
(a division of Pearson Penguin Canada Inc.)
Penguin Ireland, 25 St Stephen's Green, Dublin 2, Ireland (a division of Penguin Books Ltd)
Penguin Group (Australia), 250 Camberwell Road, Camberwell, Victoria 3124, Australia
(a division of Pearson Australia Group Pty Ltd)
Penguin Books India Pvt Ltd, 11 Community Centre, Panchsheel Park, New Delhi – 110 017, India
Penguin Group (NZ), 67 Apollo Drive, Rosedale, North Shore 0632, New Zealand
(a division of Pearson New Zealand Ltd)
Penguin Books (South Africa) (Pty) Ltd, 24 Sturdee Avenue,
Rosebank, Johannesburg 2196, South Africa

Penguin Books Ltd, Registered Offices: 80 Strand, London WC2R 0RL, England

www.penguin.com

First published by Michael Joseph 1953
First published in Penguin Books 1955
This edition published 2008

008

Copyright © John Wyndham, 1953
All rights reserved

The moral right of the author has been asserted

Printed in England by Clays Ltd, St Ives plc

ISBN: 978-0-141-03299-3

www.greenpenguin.co.uk

MIX
Paper from
responsible sources
FSC
www.fsc.org   FSC™ C018179

Penguin Books is committed to a sustainable
future for our business, our readers and our planet.
This book is made from Forest Stewardship
Council™ certified paper.

CONTENTS

CONTENTS

Rationale

THE nearest iceberg looked firmly grounded. Waves, with the whole fetch of the Atlantic behind them, exploded upon it, just as they would upon solid rock. Further out there were other large bergs, also stranded by the falling tide, and looking like sudden white mountains. Here and there among them smaller ones were still afloat, with the wind and the current driving them slowly up the Channel. That morning there were more, I fancy, than we had ever before seen at one time. I paused to look at them. Blinding white crags in a blue sea.

'I think,' I said, 'that I shall write an account of all this.'

'You mean a long one, about the whole thing? A book?' Phyllis asked.

'Well, I don't suppose it will ever be a printed book, with stiff covers and a cloth binding – but still, a book,' I agreed.

'I suppose a book is still a book, even if no one but the writer and his wife ever reads it,' she said.

'There's a chance that someone else might. I've a feeling it ought to be done. After all, we know as much about the whole thing as anyone – in a general way. The specialists know more about their particular bits, of course, but, between us, we ought to be able to put together quite a picture.'

'Without references or records?' she questioned.

'If anyone ever *does* read it, then he'll be able to have the pleasure of digging out the documentation – what's left of it. My idea is simply to give an account of how the whole thing has appeared to me – to us.'

'Stick to "me" – you can't do it from two points of view,' she advised.

She huddled her coat more closely round her. Her breath clouded in the cold air. We regarded the icebergs. There seemed to be even more than one had thought. Some of those further out were only visible because of the waves breaking on them as they wallowed along.

'It'd help to pass the winter,' Phyllis conceded, 'and then, perhaps, when the Spring comes . . . ' She let the thought tail off, unfinished. At the end of some reflection she said:

'Where will you begin?'

'I've not got as far as thinking of that yet,' I confessed.

'I think you ought to start with that night on board the *Guinevere* when we saw – '

'But, darling, no one has ever proved that they had anything to do with it.'

'An account, you said. If you are going to need proof of everything, you might as well not start at all.'

'What about that first dive?' I suggested. 'The thing does connect up pretty closely from there.'

She shook her head.

'People – if anyone does read it – can disregard what you put in if they don't like it – but it doesn't help anybody if you go leaving out things that *might* be important just because you're not absolutely sure.'

I frowned.

'I've never been really convinced that those fireballs were – Well, after all, the word coincidence exists because the things do.'

'Then say so. But the *Guinevere* is the proper place to begin.'

'All right,' I conceded. 'Chapter One – An Interesting Phenomenon.'

'Unfortunately, in several ways, we are not living in the nineteenth century. Now, if I were you I should divide the whole thing into three phases. It falls naturally that way. Phase One would be – '

'Darling, whose book is this to be?'

'Ostensibly yours, my sweet.'

'I see – rather like my life since I met you?'

'Yes, darling. Now, Phase One – Gosh! Look at that!'

A large berg, thawed below and undercut by the water, began to turn over with a monstrous deliberation. A great, flat ice-face smacked down, sending spray high into the air. The berg kept on rolling, slowed, hung for a moment, and then started to roll back. We watched it loll lazily this way and that with decreasing swings until it settled down, presenting an entirely new aspect.

Phyllis returned to the matter in hand.

'Phase One,' she repeated firmly, and then paused. 'No. Before that you want a sort of key question, with a page all to itself.'

'Yes,' I agreed, 'I'd thought of – ' But she shook her head, thinking. Presently:

'Got it!' she said. 'It's by Emily Pettifell, whom I don't suppose you ever heard of.'

'Quite right,' I told her. 'I'd thought of – '

'It was in *The Pink Nursery Book*,' she said. She pulled a gloved hand out of her pocket, and recited:

I shook my head. 'Too long. And, if I may say so, don't you think *The Pink Nursery Book* is a trifle out of key?'

'But the last two lines, Mike. Just right.' She repeated them:

– *But, Mother, please tell me, what can those things be*
  That crawl up so stealthily out of the sea?

'I'm sorry, darling, but it's still "no," ' I said.

'You won't get anything more apposite. What were you thinking of?'

'Well, I had in mind a thing of Tennyson's.'

'Tennyson!' she exclaimed, painedly.

'Listen!' I said, and took my turn at recitation. 'Not one of his major poetical works,' I admitted, 'but even Tennyson was young once.'

'My last couplet was more appropriate.'

'In words and at the moment, but not in spirit. Besides, mine may even come true in the end,' I told her.

We ding-donged a bit about it, but, after all, it is supposed to be *my* book. Phyllis can write her own if she likes. So here goes:

Below the thunders of the upper deep;
Far, far beneath in the abysmal sea,
His ancient, dreamless, uninvaded sleep
The Kraken sleepeth: faintest sunlights flee
About his shadowy sides: above him swell
Huge sponges of millennial growth and height;
And far away into the sickly light,
From many a wondrous grot and secret cell
Unnumber'd and enormous polypi
Winnow with giant fins the slumbering green.
There hath he lain for ages and will lie
Battening upon huge seaworms in his sleep,
Until the latter fire shall heat the deep;
Then once by men and angels to be seen,
In roaring he shall rise and on the surface die.

ALFRED TENNYSON

Phase One

I'M a reliable witness, you're a reliable witness, practically all God's children are reliable witnesses in their own estimation – which makes it funny how such different ideas of the same affair get about. Almost the only people I know who agree word for word on what they saw on the night of 15 July are Phyllis and I. And, as Phyllis happens to be my wife, people said, in their kindly way behind our backs, that I 'over-persuaded' her: a thought and a euphemism that could only proceed from someone who did not know Phyllis.

The time was 11.15 p.m.; the place, latitude 35, some 24 degrees west of Greenwich; the ship, the *Guinevere;* the occasion, our honeymoon. About these facts there is no dispute. The cruise had taken us to Madeira, the Canaries, Cape Verde Islands, and had then turned north to show us the Azores on our way home. We, Phyllis and I, were leaning on the rail, taking a breather. From the saloon came the sound of the dance continuing, and the crooner yearning for somebody. The sea stretched in front of us like a silken plain in the moonlight. The ship sailed it as smoothly as if she were on a river. We gazed out silently at the infinity of sea and sky. Behind us the crooner went on baying.

'I'm so glad I don't feel like him; it must be devastating,' Phyllis said. 'Why, do you suppose, do people keep on mass-producing these decadent moanings?'

I had no answer ready for that one, but I was saved the trouble of trying to find one when her attention was suddenly caught elsewhere.

'Mars is looking pretty angry to-night, isn't he? I hope it isn't an omen,' she said.

I looked where she pointed at a red spot among myriads of

white ones, and with some surprise. Mars does look red, of course, though I had never seen him look quite as red as that – but then, neither were the stars, as seen at home, quite as bright as they were here. Being practically in the tropics might account for it.

'Certainly a little inflamed,' I agreed.

We regarded the red point for some moments. Then Phyllis said:

'That's funny. It seems to be getting bigger.'

I explained that that was obviously an hallucination formed by staring at it. We went on staring, and it became quite indisputably bigger. Moreover:

'There's another one. There can't be two Marses,' said Phyllis.

And sure enough there was. A smaller red point, a little up from, and to the right of, the first. She added:

'*And* another. To the left. See?'

She was right about that, too, and by this time the first one was glowing as the most noticeable thing in the sky.

'It must be a flight of jets of some kind, and that's a cloud of luminous exhaust we're seeing,' I suggested.

We watched all three of them slowly getting brighter and also sinking lower in the sky until they were little above the horizon line, and reflecting in a pinkish pathway across the water towards us.

'Five now,' said Phyllis.

We've both of us been asked many times since to describe them, but perhaps we are not gifted with such a precise eye for detail as some others. What we said at the time, and what we still say, is that on this occasion there was no real shape visible. The centre was solidly red, and a kind of fuzz round it was less so. The best suggestion I can make is that you imagine a brilliantly red light as seen in a fairly thick fog so that there is a strong halation, and you will have something of the effect.

Others besides ourselves were leaning over the rail, and in fairness I should perhaps mention that between them they appear to have seen cigar-shapes, cylinders, discs, ovoids, and, inevitably, saucers. We did not. What is more, we did not see eight, nine, or a dozen. We saw five.

The halation may, or may not, have been due to some kind of jet drive, but it did not indicate any great speed. The things grew in size quite slowly as they approached. There was time for people to go back into the saloon and fetch their friends out to see, so that, presently, a line of us leant all along the rail, looking at them and guessing.

With no idea of scale, we could have no judgement of their size or distance; all we could be sure of was that they were descending in a long glide which looked as if it would take them across our wake. The fellow next to me was talking know-all about St Elmo's fire to a partner who had never heard of St Elmo and didn't feel she had missed anything, when the first one hit the water.

A great burst of steam shot up in a pink plume. Then, swiftly, there was a lower, wider spread of steam which had lost the pink tinge, and was simply a white cloud in the moonlight. It was beginning to thin out when the sound of it reached us in a searing hiss. The water round the spot bubbled and seethed and frothed. When the steam drew off, there was nothing to be seen there but a patch of turbulence, gradually subsiding.

Then the second of them came in, in just the same way, on almost the same spot. One after another all five of them touched down on the water with great whooshes and hissings of steam. Then the vapour cleared, showing only a few contiguous patches of troubled water.

Aboard the *Guinevere*, bells clanged, the beat of the engines changed, we started to change course, crews turned out to man the boats, men stood by to throw lifebelts.

Four times we steamed slowly back and forth across the area, searching. There was no trace whatever to be found. But for our own wake, the sea lay all about us in the moonlight, placid, empty, unperturbed ...

The next morning I sent my card in to the Captain. In those days I had a staff job with the EBC, and I explained to him that they would be pretty sure to take a piece from me on the previous night's affair. He gave the usual response:

'You mean *BBC*?' he suggested.

The EBC was younger then, and it was necessary to explain almost every time. I did so, and added:

'As far as I've been able to tell, every passenger has a different version, so I thought I'd like to check mine with your official one.'

'A good idea,' he approved. 'Go ahead, and tell me yours.'

When I had finished, he nodded, and then showed me his entry in the log. Substantially we were agreed; certainly in the view that there had been five, and on the impossibility of attributing a definite shape to them. His estimates of speed, size, and position were, of course, technical matters. I noticed that they had registered on the radar screens, and were tentatively assumed to have been aircraft of an unknown type.

'What's your own private opinion?' I asked him. 'Did you ever see anything at all like them before?'

'No. I never did,' he said, but he seemed to hesitate.

'But what – ?' I asked.

'Well, but not for the record,' he said, 'I've heard of two instances, almost exactly similar, in the last year. One time it was three of the things by night; the other, it was half a dozen of them by daylight – even so, they seem to have looked much the same; just a kind of red fuzz. Both lots were in the Pacific though, not over this side.'

'Why "not for the record"?' I asked.

'In both cases there were only two or three witnesses – and it doesn't do a seaman any good to get a reputation for seeing things, you know. The stories just got around professionally, so to speak – among ourselves we aren't quite as sceptical as landsmen: some funny things can still happen at sea, now and then.'

'You can't suggest an explanation I can quote?'

'On professional grounds I'd prefer not. I'll just stick to my official entry. But reporting it is a different matter this time. We've a couple of hundred witnesses and more.'

'Do you think it'd be worth a search? You've got the spot pinpointed.'

He shook his head. 'It's deep there. Over three thousand fathoms: that's a long way down.'

'There wasn't any trace of wreckage in those other cases, either?'

'No. That would have been evidence to warrant an inquiry. But they had no evidence.'

We talked a little longer, but I could not get him to put forward any theory. Presently I went away, and wrote up my account. Later, I got through to London, and dictated it to an EBC recorder. It went out on the air the same evening as a filler, just an oddity which was not expected to do more than raise a few eyebrows.

So it was by chance that I was a witness of that early stage – almost the beginning, for I have not been able to find any references to identical phenomena earlier than those two spoken of by the Captain. Even now, years later, though I am certain enough in my own mind that this was the beginning, I can still offer no *proof* that it was not an unrelated phenomenon. What the end that will eventually follow this beginning may be, I prefer not to think too closely: I would also prefer not to dream about it, either, if dreams were within my control.

It began so unrecognizably. Had it been more obvious – and yet it is difficult to see what could have been done effectively even if we had recognized the danger. Recognition and prevention don't necessarily go hand in hand. We recognized the potential dangers of atomic fission quickly enough – yet we could do little about them.

If we had attacked immediately – well, perhaps. But until the danger was well established we had no means of knowing that we *should* attack – and then it was too late.

However, it does no good to cry over our shortcomings. My purpose is to give as good a brief account as I can of how the present situation arose – and, to begin with, it arose very scrappily. . . .

In due course the *Guinevere* docked at Southampton without being treated to any more curious phenomena. We did not expect any more, but the event had been memorable; almost as good, in fact, as having been put in a position to say, upon some remote future occasion: 'When your grandmother and I were on our honeymoon we saw a sea-serpent,' though not quite. Still, it was a wonderful honeymoon, I never expect to have a better: and Phyllis said something to much the same effect as we leant on the rail, watching the bustle below.

'Except,' she added, 'that I don't see why we shouldn't have one nearly as good, now and then.'

So we disembarked, sought our brand new home in Chelsea, and I turned up at the E B C offices the following Monday morning to discover that in absentia I had been rechristened Fireball Watson. This was on account of the correspondence. They handed it to me in a large sheaf, and said that since I had caused it, I had better do something about it.

There must, I think, be a great many people who go around just longing to be baffled, and who, moreover, feel a kind of immediate kin to anyone else who admits bafflement along roughly similar lines. I say 'roughly' because it became clear to me as I read the mail that classifications are possible. There are strata of bafflement. A friend of mine, after giving a talk on a spooky experience, was showered with correspondence on levitation, telepathy, materialization, and faith-healing. I, however, had struck a different layer. Most of my correspondents assumed that the sight of the fireballs must have roused me to a corollary interest not only in saucers, but showers of frogs, mysterious falls of cinders, all kinds of lights seen in the sky, and also sea-monsters. After I had sifted through them, I found myself left with half a dozen which might possibly have reference to fireballs similar to those we had seen. One, referring to a recent experience off the Philippines, I identified with fair certainty as being a confirmation of what the Captain of the *Guinevere* had told me. And the others seemed worth following up, too – particularly a rather cagey approach which invited me to meet the writer at La Plume d'Or, where lunch is always worth having.

I kept that appointment a week later. My host turned out to be a man two or three years older than myself who ordered four glasses of Tio Pepe, and then opened up by admitting that the name under which he had written was not his own, and that he was a Flight-Lieutenant, RAF.

'It's a bit tricky, you see,' he said. 'At the moment I am considered to have suffered some kind of hallucination, but if enough evidence turns up to show that it was *not* an hallucination, then they're almost certain to make it an official secret. Awkward, you see.'

I agreed that it must be.

'Still,' he went on, 'the thing worries me, and if you're collecting evidence, I'd like you to have it – though maybe not to make direct use of it. I mean, I don't want to find myself on the carpet. I don't suppose there's a regulation to stop a fellow discussing his hallucinations, but you can never be sure.'

I nodded understandingly. He went on:

'It was about three months ago. I was flying one of the regular patrols, a couple of hundred miles or so east of Formosa –'

'I didn't know we – ' I began.

'There are a number of things that don't get publicity, though they're not particularly secret,' he said. 'Anyway, there I was. The radar picked these things up when they were still out of sight behind me, but coming up fast from the west.'

He had decided to investigate, and climbed to intercept. The radar continued to show the craft on a straight course behind and above him. He tried to communicate, but couldn't raise them. By the time he was getting the ceiling of them they were in sight, as three red spots, quite bright, even by daylight, and coming up fast though he was doing close to five hundred himself. He tried again to radio them, but without success. They just kept on coming, steadily overtaking him.

'Well,' he said, 'I was there to patrol. I told base that they were a completely unknown type of craft – if they were craft at all – and as they wouldn't talk I proposed to have a pip at them. It was either that, or just let 'em go – in which case I might as well not have been patrolling at all. Base agreed, kind of cautiously.

'I tried them once more, but they didn't take a damn bit of notice of either me or my signals. And as they got closer I was doubtful whether they were craft at all. They were just as you said on the radio – a pink fuzz, with a deeper red centre: might have been miniature red suns for all I could tell. Anyway, the more I saw of them the less I liked 'em, so I set the guns to radar-control and let 'em get on ahead.

'I reckoned they must be doing seven hundred or more as they passed me. A second or two later the radar picked up the foremost one, and the guns fired.

'There wasn't any lag. The thing seemed to blow up almost as the guns went off. And, boy, did it blow! It suddenly swelled immensely, turning from red to pink to white, but still with a few red spots here and there – and then my aircraft hit the concussion, and maybe some of the debris, too. I lost quite a lot of seconds, and probably had a lot of luck, because when I got sorted out I found that I was coming down fast. Something had carried away three-quarters of my starboard wing, and messed up the tip of the other. So I reckoned it was time to try the ejector, and rather to my surprise it worked.'

He paused reflectively. Then he added:

'I don't know that it gives you a lot besides confirmation, but there are one or two points. One is that they are capable of travelling a lot faster than those you saw. Another is that, whatever they are, they are highly vulnerable.'

And that, as we talked it over in detail, was about all the additional information he did provide – that, and the fact that when hit they did not disintegrate into sections, but exploded completely, which should, perhaps, have conveyed more than it seemed to at the time.

During the next few weeks several more letters trickled in without adding much, but then it began to look as if the whole affair were going the way of the Loch Ness monster. What there was came to me because it was generally conceded at EBC that fireball stuff was my pigeon. Several observatories confessed themselves puzzled by detecting small red bodies travelling at high speeds, but were extremely guarded in their statements. None of the newspapers ran it because, in editorial opinion, the whole thing was suspect in being too similar to the flying-saucer business, and their readers would prefer more novelty in their sensations. Nevertheless, bits and pieces did slowly accumulate – though it took nearly two years before they acquired serious publicity and attention.

This time it was a flight of thirteen. A radar station in the north of Finland picked them up first, estimating their speed as fifteen hundred miles per hour, and their direction as approximately south-west. In passing the information on they described them simply as 'unidentified aircraft'. The Swedes picked them up as they crossed their territory, and managed to spot them visually, describing them as small red dots. Norway confirmed, but estimated the speed at under thirteen hundred miles per hour. A Scottish station logged them as travelling at a thousand miles per hour, and just visible to the naked eye. Two stations in Ireland reported them as passing directly overhead, on a line slightly west of south-west. The more southerly station gave their speed as eight hundred and claimed that they were 'clearly visible'. A weather-ship at about 65 degrees North, gave a description which tallied exactly with that of the earlier fireballs, and calculated a speed close to 500 m.p.h. They were not sighted again after that.

The reason that this particular flight got on to the front pages when others had been ignored was not simply that this time there had been a series of observations which plotted its track; it lay more in the implications of the line that had been drawn. However, in spite of innuendo and direct suggestion, there was silence to the east. Ever since their hurried and unconvincing explanation which followed the first atomic explosion in Russia, her leaders had found it convenient to feign at least a temporary deafness to questions on such matters. It was a policy which had the advantages of calling for no mental exertion while at the same time building up in the minds of the general public a feeling that inscrutability must mask hidden power.

And since those who were well acquainted with Russian affairs were not going to publish the degree of their acquaintanceship, the game of aloofness was easily able to continue.

The Swedes announced, with careful lack of particularizing, that they would take action against any similar violation of their sky, whoever might be the violators. The British papers suggested that a certain great power was zealous enough in guarding its own frontiers to justify others in taking similar measures to protect theirs. American journals said that the way to deal with any Russian aircraft over US territory was to shoot first. The Kremlin apparently slept.

There was a sudden spate of fireball observation. Reports came in from so far and wide that it was impossible to do more than sort out the more wildly imaginative and put the rest aside to be considered at more leisure, but I noticed that among them were several accounts of fireballs descending into the sea that tallied well with my own observation – so well, indeed, that I could not be absolutely sure that they did not derive from my own broadcast. All in all, it appeared to be such a muddle of guesswork, tall stories, third-hand impressions, and thorough-going invention that it taught me little. One negative point, however, did strike me – not a single observer claimed to have seen a fireball descend on land. Ancillary to that, not a single one of those descending on water had been observed from the shore: all had been noticed from ships, or from aircraft well out to sea.

For a couple of weeks reports of sightings in groups large or small continued to pour in. The sceptics were weakening; only the most obstinate still maintained that they were hallucinations. Nevertheless, we learnt nothing more about them than we had known before. No pictures. So often it seemed to be a case of the things you see when you don't have a gun. But then a flock of them came up against a fellow who did have a gun – literally.

The fellow in this case happened to be the USN Carrier, *Tuskegee*. The message from Curaçao that a flight of eight fireballs was headed directly towards her reached her when she was lying off San Juan, Puerto Rico. The Captain breathed a short hope that they would commit a violation of the territory, and made his preparations. The fireballs, true to type, kept on in a dead straight line which would bring them across the island, and almost over the ship herself. The Captain watched their approach on his radar with great satisfaction. He waited until the technical violation was indisputable. Then he gave the word to release six guided missiles at three-second intervals, and went on deck to watch, against the darkling sky.

Through his glasses he watched six of the red dots change as they burst, one after another, into big white puffs.

'Well, that's settled them,' he observed, complacently. 'Now it's going to be mighty interesting to see who squeals,' he added, as he watched the two remaining red dots dwindle away to the northward.

But the days passed, and nobody squealed. Nor was there any decrease in the number of fireball reports.

For most people such a policy of masterly silence pointed only one way, and they began to regard the responsibility as good as proved.

In the course of the following week, two more fireballs that had been incautious enough to pass within range of the experimental station at Woomera paid for that temerity, and three others were exploded by a ship off Kodiak after flying across Alaska.

Washington, in a note of protest to Moscow regarding repeated territorial violations, ended by observing that in several cases where drastic action had been taken it regretted the distress that must have been caused to the relatives of the crews aboard the craft, but that responsibility lay at the door not of those who dealt with the craft, but with those who sent them out apparently under orders which transgressed international agreements.

The Kremlin, after a few days of gestation, produced a rejection of the protest. It proclaimed itself unimpressed by the tactic of attributing one's own crime to another, and went on to state that its own weapons, recently developed by Russian scientists for the defence of Peace, had now destroyed more than twenty of these craft over Soviet territory, and would, without hesitation, give the same treatment to any others detected in their work of espionage. . . .

The situation thus remained unresolved. The non-Russian world was, by and large, divided sharply into two classes –those who believed every Russian pronouncement, and those who believed none. For the first class no question arose; their faith was firm. For the second, interpretation was less easy. Was one to deduce, for instance, that the whole thing was a lie? Or merely that, when the Russians claimed to have accounted for twenty fireballs, they had only, in fact, exploded five or so?

An uneasy situation, constantly punctuated by an exchange of notes, drew out over months. Fireballs were undoubtedly more numerous than they had been, but just how much more numerous, or more active, or more frequently reported was difficult to assess. Every now and then a few more were destroyed in various parts of the world, and from time to time, too, it would be announced that numbers of capitalistic fireballs had been effectively shown the penalties that waited those who conducted espionage upon the territory of the only true People's Democracy.

Public interest must feed to keep alive; without fresh nourishment it soon begins to decline. The things existed; they buzzed through the air at high speed; they blew up if you hit them; but, beyond that, what? They didn't appear to *do* anything – at least nothing that anyone seemed to know about. Nor did they do anything to fulfil the sensational role they had seemed to promise.

Novelty waned, and an era of explaining-away set in. Presently we were back to something very like the St Elmo's fire position, for the most widely accepted view was that they must simply be some new form of natural electrical manifestation. As time went on, ships and shore-stations ceased to fire at them, and let them continue on their mysterious ways, noting merely their speed, time, and direction. They were, in fact, a disappointment.

Nevertheless, in Admiralty and Air Force Headquarters all over the world these notes and reports came together. Courses were plotted on charts. Gradually a pattern of a kind began to emerge.

At EBC I was still regarded as the natural silting-place for anything to do with fireballs, and although the subject was dead mutton for the moment I kept up my files in case it should revive. Meanwhile, I contributed in a small way to the building up of the bigger picture by passing along to the authorities such snippets of information as I thought might interest them.

In due course I found myself invited to the Admiralty to be shown some of the results.

It was a Captain Winters who welcomed me there, explaining that while what I should be shown was not exactly an official secret, it was preferred that I should not make public use of it yet. When I had agreed to that, he started to bring out maps and charts.

The first one was a map of the world hatched over with fine lines, each numbered and dated in minute figures. At first glance it looked as if a spider's web had been applied to it; and, here and there, there were clusters of little red dots, looking much like the money-spiders who had spun it.

Captain Winters picked up a magnifying-glass and held it over the area south-east of the Azores.

'There's your first contribution,' he told me.

Looking through it, I presently distinguished one red dot with a figure 5 against it, and the date-time when Phyllis and I had leant over the *Guinevere's* rail watching the fireballs vanish in steam. There was quite a number of other red dots in the area, each labelled, and more of them were strung out to the north-east.

'Each of these dots represents the descent of a fireball?' I asked.

'One or more,' he told me. 'The lines, of course, are only for those on which we have had good enough information to plot the course. What do you think of it?'

'Well,' I told him truthfully, 'my first reaction is to realize that there must have been a devil of a lot more of them than I ever imagined. The second is to wonder why in thunder they should group in spots, like that.'

'Ah!' he said. 'Now stand back from the map a bit. Narrow your eyes, and get a light and shade impression.'

I did, and saw what he meant.

'Areas of concentration,' I said.

He nodded. 'Five main ones, and a number of lesser. The densest of the lot to the south-west of Cuba; another, six hundred miles south of the Cocos Islands; pretty heavy concentrations off the Philippines, Japan, and the Aleutians. I'm not going to pretend that the proportions of density are right – in fact, I'm pretty sure that they are not. For instance, you can see a number of courses coverging towards an area north-east of the Falklands, but only three red dots there. It very likely means simply that there are precious few people around those parts to observe them. Anything else strike you?'

I shook my head, not seeing what he was getting at. He produced a bathymetric chart, and laid it beside the first. I looked at it.

'All the concentrations are in deep-water areas?' I suggested.

'Exactly. There aren't many reports of descents where the depth is less than four thousand fathoms, and none at all where it is less than two thousand.'

I thought that over, without getting anywhere.

'So – just what?' I inquired.

'Exactly,' he said again. 'So what?'

We contemplated the proposition awhile.

'All descents,' he observed. 'No reports of any coming up.'

He brought out maps on a larger scale of the various main areas. After we had studied them a bit I asked:

'Have you any idea at all what all this means – or wouldn't you tell me if you had?'

'On the first part of that, we have only a number of theories, all unsatisfactory for one reason or another, so the second doesn't really arise.'

'What about the Russians?'

'Nothing to do with them. As a matter of fact, they're a lot more worried about it than we are. Suspicion of capitalists being part of their mother's milk, they simply can't shake themselves clear of the idea that we must be at the bottom of it somehow, and they just can't figure out, either, what the game can possibly be. But what both we and they are perfectly satisfied about is that the things are not natural phenomena, nor are they random.'

'And you'd know if it were any other country pulling it?'

'Bound to – not a doubt of it.'

We considered the charts again in silence.

'People,' I told him, 'are continually quoting to me things that the illustrious Holmes said to my namesake, but this time I'll do the quoting: "When you have eliminated the impossible, whatever remains, *however improbable,* must be the truth." Which is to say that if it is no terrestrial nation that is doing this, then – ?'

'That isn't the kind of solution I like,' he said.

'It's not the kind of solution anyone would like,' I agreed. 'And yet,' I went on, 'it does seem somewhat far-fetched to suggest that something in the deeps has been following an evolutionary line of its own, and has now blossomed out with a well-developed technology. That appears to be the only remaining possibility.'

'And slightly less credible even than the other,' he remarked.

'In which case, we must have eliminated a possible along with some of the impossibles. The bottom of the sea would be a very good place to hide – if one could manage the technical difficulties,' I said.

'Undoubtedly,' he agreed, 'but among those technical difficulties happens to be pressure of four or five tons per square inch in the interesting areas.'

'H'm. Perhaps we'd better think some more about that,' I conceded. 'The other obvious question is, of course, what do they seem to be doing?'

'Yes,' he said.

'Meaning, no clue?'

'They come,' he said. 'Maybe they go. But preponderantly they come. That's about all.'

I looked down at the maps, the criss-crossing lines, and the red-dotted areas.

'Are you doing anything about it? Or shouldn't I ask?'

'Oh, that's why you're here. I was coming round to that,' he told me. 'We're going to try an inspection. Just at the moment it is not considered to be a matter for a direct broadcast, nor even for publication, but there ought to be a record of it, and we shall need one ourselves. So if your people happened to feel interested enough to send you along with some gear for the job . . .'

'Where would it be?' I inquired.

He circled his finger round an area.

'Er – my wife has a passionate devotion to tropical sunshine: the West Indian kind, in particular,' I said.

'Well, I seem to remember that your wife has written some pretty good documentary scripts,' he remarked.

'And it's the kind of thing EBC might be very sorry about afterwards if they'd missed it,' I reflected.

*

Not until we had made our last call and were well out of sight of land were we allowed to see the large object which rested in a specially constructed cradle aft. When the Lieutenant-Commander in charge of technical operations ordered the shrouding tarpaulin to be removed, there was quite an unveiling ceremony. But the mystery revealed was something of an anti-climax: it was simply a sphere of metal some ten feet in diameter. In various parts of it were set circular, porthole-like windows; at the top, it swelled into a protuberance which formed a massive lug. The Lieutenant-Commander, after regarding it awhile with the eye of a proud mother, addressed us in the manner of a lecturer.

'This instrument that you now see,' he said, impressively, 'is what we call the Bathyscope.' He allowed an interval for appreciation.

'Didn't Beebe – ?' I whispered to Phyllis.

'No,' she said. 'That was the bathysphere.'

'Oh,' I said.

'It has been constructed,' he went on, 'to resist a pressure approaching two tons to the square inch, giving it a theoretical floor of fifteen hundred fathoms. In practice we do not propose to use it at a greater depth than twelve hundred fathoms, thus providing for a safety factor of some 720 pounds to the square inch. Even at this it will considerably surpass the achievements of Dr Beebe who descended a little over five hundred fathoms, and Barton who reached a depth of seven hundred and fifty fathoms . . .' He continued in this vein for a time, leaving me somewhat behind. When he seemed to have run down for a bit I said to Phyllis:

'I can't think in all these fathoms. What is it in God's feet?'
She consulted her notes.

'The depth they intend to go to is seven thousand two hundred feet; the depth they *could* go to is nine thousand feet.'

'Either of them sounds an awful lot of feet,' I said.

Phyllis is, in some ways, more precise and practical.

'Seven thousand two hundred feet is just over a mile and a third,' she informed me, 'the pressure will be a little more than a ton and a third.'

'That's my continuity-girl,' I said. 'I don't know where I'd be without you.' I looked at the bathyscope. 'All the same – ' I added doubtfully.

'What?' she asked.

'Well, that chap at the Admiralty, Winters; he was talking in terms of four or five tons pressure – meaning, presumably, four or five miles down.' I turned to the Lieutenant-Commander. 'How deep is it where we're bound for?' I asked him.

'It's an area called the Cayman Trench, between Jamaica and Cuba,' he said. 'Parts of it go below five thousand.'

'But – ' I began, frowning.

'Fathoms, dear,' said Phyllis. 'Thirty thousand feet.'

'Oh,' I said. 'That'll be – er – something like five and a half miles?'

'Yes,' he said.

'Oh,' I said, again.

He returned to his public address manner.

'That,' he told the assembled crowd of us, 'is the present limit of our ability to make direct visual observations. However – ' He paused to make a gesture somewhat in the manner of a conjuror towards a party of A.B.'s, and watched while they pulled the tarpaulin from another, similar, but smaller sphere. ' – here,' he continued, 'we have a new instrument with which we hope to be able to make observations at something like twice the depth attainable by the bathyscope, perhaps even more. It is entirely automatic. In addition to registering pressures, temperature, currents, and so on, and transmitting the readings to the surface, it is equipped with five small television cameras, four of them giving all round horizontal coverage, and one transmitting the view vertically beneath the sphere.'

'This instrument,' continued another voice in good imitation of his own, 'we call the telebath.'

Facetiousness could not put a man like the Commander off his stroke. He continued his lecture. But the instrument had been christened, and the telebath it remained.

The three days after we reached our position were occupied with tests and adjustments of both the instruments. In one test Phyllis and I were allowed to make a dive of three hundred feet or so, cramped up in the bathyscope, 'just to get the feel of it'. We did that, and it gave us no envy of anyone making a deeper dive. Then, with all the gear fully checked, the real descent was announced for the morning of the fourth day.

Soon after sunrise we were clustering round the bathyscope where it rested in its cradle. The two naval technicians, Wiseman and Trant, who were to make the descent, wriggled themselves in through the narrow hole that was the entrance. The warm clothing they would need in the depths was handed in after them, for they could never have squeezed in wearing it. Then followed the packets of food and the vacuum-flasks of hot drinks. They made their final checks, gave their okays. The circular entrance-plug was swung over by the hoist, screwed gradually down into its seating, and bolted fast. The bathyscope was hoisted outboard, and hung there, swinging slightly. One of the men inside switched on his hand television-camera, and we ourselves, as seen from within the instrument, appeared on the screen.

'Okay,' said a voice from the loudspeaker. 'Lower away now.'

The winch began to turn. The bathyscope descended, and the water lapped at it. Presently it had disappeared from sight beneath the surface.

The descent was a long business which I do not propose to describe in detail. Frankly, as seen on the screen in the ship, it was a pretty boring affair to the non-initiate. Life in the sea appears to exist in fairly well-defined levels. In the better inhabited strata the water is full of plankton which behaves like a continuous dust-storm and obscures everything but creatures that approach very closely. At other levels where there is no plankton for food, there are consequently few fish. In addition to the tediousness of very limited views or dark emptiness, continuous attention to a screen that is linked with a slightly swinging and twisting camera has a dizzying effect. Both Phyllis and I spent much of the time during the descent with our eyes shut, relying on the loud-speaking telephone to draw our attention to anything interesting. Occasionally we slipped on deck for a cigarette.

There could scarcely have been a better day for the job. The sun beat fiercely down on decks that were occasionally sluiced with water to cool them off. The ensign hung limp, barely stirring. The sea stretched out flat to meet the dome of the sky which showed only one low bank of cloud, to the north, over Cuba, perhaps. There was scarcely a sound, either, except for the muffled voice of the loudspeaker in the mess, the quiet drone of the winch, and from time to time the voice of a deck-hand calling the tally of fathoms.

The group sitting in the mess scarcely spoke; they left that to the men now far below.

At intervals, the Commander would ask:

'All in order, below there?'

And simultaneously two voices would reply:

'Aye, aye, sir!'

Once a voice inquired:

'Did Beebe have an electrically-heated suit?'

Nobody seemed to know.

'I take my hat off to him if he didn't,' said the voice.

The Commander was keeping a sharp eye on the dials as well as watching the screen.

'Half-mile coming up. Check,' he said.

The voice from below counted:

'Four thirty-eight. .... Four thirty-nine. .... *Now!* Half-mile, sir.'

The winch went on turning. There wasn't much to see. Occasional glimpses of schools of fish hurrying off into the murk. A voice complained:

'Sure as I get the camera to one window a damn great fish comes and looks in at another.'

'Five hundred fathoms. You're passing Beebe now,' said the Commander.

'Bye-bye, Beebe,' said the voice. 'But it goes on looking much the same.'

Presently the same voice said:

'More life around just here. Plenty of squid, large and small. You can probably see 'em. There's something out this way, keeping on the edge of the light. A big thing. I can't quite – might be a giant squid – no! my God! It *can't* be a whale! Not down here!'

'Improbable, but not impossible,' said the Commander.

'Well, in that case – oh, it's sheered off now, anyway. Gosh! We mammals do get around a bit, don't we?'

In due course the moment arrived when the Commander announced:

'Passing Barton now,' and then added with an unexpected change of manner: 'From now on it's all yours, boys. Sure you're quite happy there? If you're not perfectly satisfied you've only to say.'

'That's all right, sir. Everything functioning okay. We'll go on.'

Up on deck the winch droned steadily.

'One mile coming up,' announced the Commander. When that had been checked he asked: 'How are you feeling now?'

'What's the weather like up there?' asked a voice.

'Holding well. Flat calm. No swell.'

The two down below conferred.

'We'll go on, sir. Could wait weeks for conditions like this again.'

'All right – if you're both sure.'

'We are, sir.'

'Very good. About three hundred fathoms more to go, then.'

There was an interval. Then:

'Dead,' remarked the voice from below. 'All black and dead now. Not a thing to be seen. Funny thing the way these levels are quite separate. Ah, now we can begin to see something below. . . . Squids again. . . . Luminous fish. . . . Small shoal, there, see? . . . There's – Gosh! –'

He broke off, and simultaneously a nightmare fishy horror gaped at us from the screen.

'One of nature's careless moments,' he remarked.

He went on talking, and the camera continued to give us glimpses of unbelievable monstrosities, large and small.

Presently the Commander announced:

'Stopping you now. Twelve hundred fathoms.' He picked up the telephone and spoke to the deck. The winch slowed and then ceased to turn.

'That's all, boys,' he said.

'Huh,' said the voice from below, after a pause. 'Well, whatever it was we came here to find, we've not found it.'

The Commander's face was expressionless. Whether he had expected tangible results or not I couldn't tell. I imagined not. In fact, I wondered if any of us there really had. After all, these centres of activity were all Deeps. And from that it would seem to follow that the reason must lie at the bottom. The echogram gave the bottom hereabouts as still three miles or so below where the two men now dangled. . . .

'Hullo, there, bathyscope,' said the Commander. 'We're going to start you up now. Ready?'

'Aye, aye, sir! All set,' said the two voices.

The Commander picked up his telephone.

'Haul away there!'

We could hear the winch start, and slowly gather speed.

'On your way now. All okay?'

'All correct, sir.'

There was an interval without talk for ten minutes or more. Then a voice said:

'There's something out there. Something big – can't see it properly. Keeps just on the fringe of the light. Can't be that whale again – not at this depth. Try to show you.'

The picture on the screen switched and then steadied. We could see the light-rays streaming out through the water, and the brilliant speckles of small organisms caught in the beam. At the very limits there was a suspicion of a faintly lighter patch. It was hard to be sure of it.

'Seems to be circling us. We're spinning a bit, too, I think. I'll try – ah, got a bit better glimpse of it then. It's not the whale, anyway. There, see it now?'

This time we could undoubtedly make out a lighter patch. It was roughly oval, but indistinct, and there was nothing to give it scale.

'H'm,' said the voice from below. 'That's certainly a new one. Could be a fish – or maybe something else kind of turtle-shaped. Monstrous-sized brute, anyway. Circling a bit closer now, but I still can't make out any details. Keeping pace with us.'

Again the camera showed us a glimpse of the thing as it passed one of the bathyscope's ports, but we were little wiser; the definition was too poor for us to be sure of anything about it.

'It's going up now. Rising faster than we are. Getting beyond our angle of view. Ought to be a window in the top of this thing. . . . Lost it now. Gone somewhere up above us. Maybe it'll – '

The voice cut off dead. Simultaneously, there was a brief, vivid flash on the screen, and it, too, went dead. The sound of the winch outside altered as it speeded up.

We sat looking at one another without speaking. Phyllis's hand sought mine, and tightened on it.

The Commander started to stretch his hand towards the telephone, changed his mind, and went out without a word. Presently the winch speeded up still more.

It takes quite a time to reel in more than a mile of heavy cable. The party in the mess dispersed awkwardly. Phyllis and I went up into the bows and sat there without talking much.

After what seemed a very long wait the winch slowed down. By common consent we got up, and moved aft together.

At last, the end came up. We all, I suppose, expected to see the end of the wire-rope unravelled, with the strands splayed-out, brush-like.

They were not. They were melted together. Both the main and the communication cables ended in a blob of fused metal.

We all stared at them, dumbfounded.

In the evening the Captain read the service, and three volleys were fired over the spot . . .

*

The weather held, and the glass was steady. At noon the next day the Commander assembled us in the mess. He looked ill, and very tired. He said, briefly, and unemotionally:

'My orders are to proceed with the investigation, using our automatic instrument. If our arrangements and tests can be completed in time, and provided the weather remains favourable, we shall conduct the operation to-morrow morning, commencing as soon after dawn as possible. I am instructed to lower the instrument to the point of destruction, so there will be no second opportunity for observation.'

The arrangement in the mess the following morning was different from that on the former occasion. We sat facing a bank of five television screens, four for the quadrants about the instrument, and one viewing vertically beneath it. There was also a ciné-camera photographing all five screens simultaneously for the record.

Again we watched the descent through the ocean layers, but this time instead of a commentary we had an astonishing assortment of chirrupings, raspings, and gruntings picked up by externally mounted microphones. The deep sea is, in its lower inhabited strata, it seems, a place of hideous cacophony. It was something of a relief when at about three-quarters of a mile down silence fell, and somebody muttered: 'Huh! Said those mikes'd never take the pressure.'

The display went on. Squids sliding upwards past the cameras, shoals of fish darting nervously away, other fish attracted by curiosity, monstrosities, grotesques, huge monsters dimly seen. On and on. A mile down, a mile and a half, two miles, two and a half. . . . And then, at about that, something came into view which quickened all attention on the screens. A large, uncertain, oval shape at the extreme of visibility that moved from screen to screen as it circled round the descending instrument. For three or four minutes it continued to show on one screen or another, but always tantalizingly ill-defined, and never quite well enough illuminated for one to be quite certain even of its shape. Then, gradually, it drifted towards the upper edges of the screens, and presently it was left behind.

Half a minute later all the screens went blank. . . .

*

Why not praise one's wife? Phyllis can write a thundering good feature script – and this was one of her best. It was too bad that it was not received with the immediate enthusiasm it deserved.

When it was finished, we sent it round to the Admiralty for vetting. A week later we were asked to call. It was Captain Winters who received us. He congratulated Phyllis on the script, as well he might, even if he had not been so taken with her as he so obviously was. Once we were settled in our chairs, however, he shook his head regretfully.

'Nevertheless,' he said, 'I'm afraid I'm going to have to ask you to hold it up for a while.'

Phyllis looked understandably disappointed; she had worked hard on that script. Not just for cash, either. She had tried to make it a tribute to the two men, Wiseman and Trant, who had vanished with the bathyscope. She looked down at her toes.

'I'm sorry,' said the Captain, 'but I did warn your husband that it wouldn't be for immediate release.'

Phyllis looked up at him.

'Why?' she asked.

That was something I was equally anxious to know about. My own recordings of the preparations, of the brief descent we had both made in the bathyscope, and of various aspects that were not on the official tape record of the dive, had been put into cold-storage, too.

'I'll explain what I can. We certainly owe you that,' agreed Captain Winters. He sat down and leant forward, elbows on knees, fingers interlaced between them, and looked at us both in turn.

'The crux of the thing – and of course you will both of you have realized that long ago – is those fused cables,' he said. 'Imagination staggers a bit at the thought of a creature capable of snapping through steel hawsers – all the same, it might just conceivably admit the possibility. When, however, it comes up against the suggestion that there is a creature capable of cutting through them like an oxy-acetylene flame, it recoils. It recoils, and definitely rejects.

'Both of you saw what happened to those cables, and I think you must agree that their condition opens a whole new aspect. A thing like that is not just a hazard of deep-sea diving – and we want to know more about just what kind of a hazard it is before we give a release on it.'

We talked it over for a little time. The Captain was apologetic and understanding, but he had his orders. He assured us that he would make it his business to see that we were notified of release at the earliest possible moment; and with that we had to make do. Phyllis hid her disappointment under her usual philosophic good sense. Before we left, she asked:

'Honestly, Captain Winters – and off the record, if you like – have you any idea what can have done it?'

He shook his head. 'On or off the record, Mrs Watson, I can

think of no explanation that approaches being possible – and, though this is not for publication, I doubt whether anyone else in the Service has an idea, either.'

And so, with the affair left in that unsatisfactory state, we parted.

The prohibition, however, lasted a shorter time than we expected. A week later, just as we were sitting down to dinner, he rang through. Phyllis took the call.

'Oh, hullo, Mrs Watson. I'm glad it's you. I have some good news for you,' Captain Winters' voice said. 'I've just been talking to your EBC people, and giving them the okay, so far as we are concerned, to go ahead with that feature of yours, and the whole story.'

Phyllis thanked him for the news. 'But what's happened?' she added.

'The story's broken, anyway. You'll hear it on the nine o'clock news to-night, and see it in to-morrow's papers. In the circumstances it seemed to me that you ought to be free to take your chance as soon as possible. Their Lordships saw the point – in fact, they would like your feature to go out as soon as possible. They approve of it. So there it is. And the best of luck to you.'

Phyllis thanked him again, and rang off.

'Now what do you suppose can have happened?' she inquired.

We had to wait until nine o'clock to find that out. The notice on the news was scanty, but sufficient from our point of view. It reported simply that an American naval unit conducting research into deep-sea conditions somewhere off the Philippines had suffered the loss of a depth-chamber, with its crew of two men.

Almost immediately afterwards EBC came through on the telephone with a lot of talk about priorities, and altered programme schedules, and available cast.

Audio-assessment told us later that the feature had an excellent reception figure. Coming so soon after the American announcement, we hit the peak of popular interest. Their Lordships were pleased, too. It gave them the opportunity of showing that they did not always have to follow the American lead – though I still think there was no need to make the US a present of the first publicity. Anyway, in view of what has followed, I don't suppose it greatly matters.

In the circumstances, Phyllis rewrote a part of the script, making greater play with the fusing of the cables than before. A flood of correspondence came in, but when all the tentative explanations and suggestions had been winnowed none of us was any wiser than before.

Perhaps it was scarcely to be expected that we should be. Our listeners had not even seen the maps, and at this stage it had not occurred to the general public that there could be any link between the diving catastrophes and the somewhat *démodé* topic of fireballs.

But if, as it seemed, the Royal Navy was disposed simply to sit still for a time and ponder the problem theoretically, the US Navy was not. Deviously we heard that they were preparing to send a second expedition to the same spot where their loss had occurred. We promptly applied to be included, and were refused. How many other people applied, I don't know, but enough for them to allocate a second small craft. We couldn't get a place on that either. All space was reserved for their own correspondents and commentators who would cover for Europe, too.

Well, it was their own show. They were paying for it. All the same, I'm sorry we missed it because, though we did think it likely they would lose their apparatus again, it never crossed our minds that they might lose their ship as well. . . .

About a week after it happened one of the NBC men who had been covering it came over. We more or less shanghaied him for lunch and the personal dope.

'Never saw anything like it – never want to,' he said. 'They were using an automatic instrument pretty much like the one you people lost. The idea was to send that down first, and if it came up again okay, then they'd take another smack at it with a manned depth-chamber – what's more, they had a couple of volunteers for it, too; funny the way you can always find a few guys who seem kind of bored with life on Earth.

'Anyway, that was the project. We lay off a couple of hundred yards or more from the research ship, but we had a cable slung between us to relay the television, so we could watch it on our screens just as well as they could on theirs.

'We did – awhile, but I guess it's one of those subjects you have to have majored in to keep the interest up. The way we saw it, it was more of a test-out. We were aiming to get our real stuff from the depth-chamber dive where there'd be the human angle, even though it'd not go down so far.

'Well, we watched the thing slung overside, then we went into our saloon to look at the screens. I guess what we saw'd likely be what you saw; sometimes it was foggy, sometimes clear, and sometimes there'd be quite a few screwy-looking fish and squids, and whole flocks of things that don't have any names I ever heard of, and, I'd say, don't need 'em, either.

'Over the screens was a lighted panel recording the depth – which was a good idea on account of it all looked like it might be going around on an endless band, anyway. By one mile down all the guys with better-trained consciences had taken them up on deck under the awning, with smokes and cold drinks. By two miles down, I was out there, with them, leaving two or three puritanical characters to cover it and tell us if anything new showed up. After a bit more, one of them quit, too, and joined me.

' "Two and a half miles, and the last half-mile as dark as the Tunnel of Love – and that wouldn't interest even fish a lot, from what they tell me," he said.

'He drew himself a coke and started to move over towards me. Then he stopped short.

' "Christ!" he said. And simultaneously there was some kind of yell from inside the saloon.

'I turned my head and looked the way he was looking – at the research ship.

'A moment before she had been lying there placid, without a visible movement aboard her, and only the sound of the winch coming over the water to tell you she wasn't derelict. And now she was . . .

'Well, I don't know what kind of thunderstorms you folks have over here, but in some places they have a kind where the lightning looks like it's running around all over a building. And that was the way the research ship looked just then. You could hear it crackle, too.

'She can't have looked that way for more than a few seconds, though it seemed a lot longer. Then she blew up. . . .

'I don't know what they had aboard her, but she sure did blow. Every one of us hit the deck in a split second. And then there was spray and scrap coming down all over. When we looked again there wasn't anything there but a lot of water just getting itself smoothed out.

'We didn't have a lot to pick up. A few bits of wood, half a dozen lifebuoys, and three bodies, all badly burnt. We collected what there was, and came home.'

During the longish pause Phyllis poured him another cup of coffee.

'What was it?' she asked.

He shrugged. 'It *could* have been coincidence, but say we rule that out, then I'd guess that if ever lightning were to strike upwards from the sea, that'd be about the way it'd look.'

'I never heard of anything like that,' Phyllis said.

'It certainly isn't on the record,' he agreed. 'But there has to be a first time.'

'Not very satisfactory,' Phyllis commented.

He looked us over.

'Seeing that you two were on that British fishing-party, do I take it you know why we were there?'

'I'd not be surprised,' I told him.

He nodded. 'Well, look,' he said, 'I'm told it isn't possible to persuade a high charge, say a few million volts, to run up an uninsulated hawser in sea-water, so I must accept that; it's not my department. All I say is that *if* it were possible, then

I guess the effect might be quite a bit like what we saw.'

'There'd be insulated cables, too – to the cameras, microphones, thermometers, and things,' Phyllis said.

'Sure. And there was an insulated cable relaying the TV to our ship; but it couldn't carry that charge, and burnt out – which was a darned good thing for us. That would make it look to me like it followed the main hawser – if it didn't so happen that the physics boys won't have it.'

'They've no alternative suggestions?' I asked.

'Oh, sure. Several. Some of them could sound quite convincing – to a fellow who'd not seen it happen.'

'If you are right, this is very queer indeed,' Phyllis said, reflectively.

The NBC man looked at her. 'A nice British back-hand understatement – but it's queer enough, even without me,' he said, modestly. 'However they explain this away, the physics boys are still stumped on those fused cables, because, whatever this may be, those cable severances *couldn't* have been accidental.'

'On the other hand, all that way down, all that pressure . . . ?' Phyllis said.

He shook his head. 'I'm making no guesses. I'd want more data than we've got, even for that. Could be we'll get it before long.'

We looked questioning.

He lowered his voice. 'Seeing you're in this, too, but strictly under your hats, they've got a couple more probes lined up right now. But no publicity this time – the last lot had a nasty taste.'

'Where?' we asked, simultaneously.

'One off the Aleutians, some place. The other in a deep spot in the Guatemala Basin. What're your folks doing?'

'We don't know,' we said, honestly.

He shook his head. 'Always kinda close, your people,' he said, sympathetically.

And close they remained. During the next few weeks we kept our ears uselessly wide open for news of either of the two new investigations, but it was not until the NBC man was passing through London again a month later that we learnt anything. We asked him what had happened. He frowned.

'Off Guatemala they drew blank,' he said. 'The ship south of the Aleutians was transmitting by radio while the dive was in progress. It cut out suddenly. She's reported as lost with all hands.'

*

Official cognizance of these matters remained underground – if that can be considered an acceptable term for their deep-sea investigations. Every now and then we would catch a rumour which showed that the interest had not been dropped, and from time to time a few apparently isolated items could, when put in conjunction, be made to give hints. Our naval contacts preserved an amiable evasiveness, and we found that our opposite numbers across the Atlantic were doing little better with their naval sources. The consoling aspect was that had they been making any progress we should most likely have heard of it, so we took silence to mean that they were stalled.

Public interest in fireballs was down to zero, and few people troubled to send in reports of them any more. I still kept my files going though they were now so unrepresentative that I could not tell how far the apparently low incidence was real.

As far as I knew, the two phenomena had never so far been publicly connected, and presently both were allowed to lapse unexplained, like any silly-season sensation.

In the course of the next three years we ourselves lost interest almost to vanishing point. Other matters occupied us. There was the birth of our son, William – and his death, eighteen months later. To help Phyllis to get over that I wangled myself a travelling-correspondent series, sold up the house, and for a time we roved.

In theory, the appointment was simply mine; in practice, most of the gloss and finish on the scripts which pleased the EBC were Phyllis's, and most of the time when she wasn't dolling up my stuff she was working on scripts of her own. When we came back home, it was with enhanced prestige, a lot of material to work up, and a feeling of being set on a smooth, steady course.

Almost immediately, the Americans lost a cruiser off the Marianas.

The report was scanty, an Agency message, slightly blown up locally; but there was a something about it – just a kind of feeling. When Phyllis read it in the newspaper, it struck her, too. She pulled out the atlas, and considered the Marianas.

'It's pretty deep round three sides of them,' she said.

'That report's not handled quite the regular way. I can't exactly put my finger on it. But the approach is a bit off the line, somehow,' I agreed.

'We'd better try the grape-vine,' Phyllis decided.

We did, without result. It wasn't that our sources were holding out on us; there seemed to be a blackout somewhere. We got no further than the official handout: this cruiser, the *Keweenaw*, had, in fair weather, simply gone down. Twenty survivors had been picked up. There would be an official enquiry.

Possibly there was: I never heard the outcome. The incident was somehow overlayed by the inexplicable sinking of a Russian ship, engaged on some task never specified, to eastward of the Kuriles, that string of islands to the south of Kamchatka. Since it was axiomatic that any Soviet misadventure must be attributable in some way to capitalist jackals or reactionary fascist hyenas, this affair assumed an importance which quite eclipsed the more serious American loss, and the acrimonious innuendoes went on echoing for some time. In the noise of vituperation the mysterious disappearance of the survey-vessel *Utskarpen,* in the Southern Ocean, went almost unnoticed outside her native Norway.

Several others followed, but I no longer have my records to give me the details. It is my impression that quite half a dozen vessels, all seemingly engaged in ocean research in one way or another, had vanished before the Americans suffered again off the Philippines. This time they lost a destroyer, and, with it, their patience.

The ingenuous announcement that since the water about Bikini was too shallow for a contemplated series of deep-water atomic-bomb tests the locale of these experiments would be shifted westwards by a little matter of a thousand miles or so, may possibly have deceived a portion of the general public, but in radio and newspaper circles it touched off a scramble for assignments.

Phyllis and I had better standing now, and we were lucky, too. We flew out there, and a few days later we formed part of the complement of a number of ships lying at a strategic distance from the point where the *Keweenaw* had gone down off the Marianas.

I can't tell you what that specially designed depth-bomb looked like, for we never saw it. All we were allowed to see was a raft supporting a kind of semi-spherical, metal hut which contained the bomb itself, and all we were told was that it was much like one of the more regular types of atomic bomb, but with a massive casing that would resist the pressure at five miles deep, if necessary.

At first light on the day of the test a tug took the raft in tow, and chugged away over the horizon with it. From then on we had to observe by means of unmanned television cameras mounted on floats. In this way we saw the tug cast off the raft, and put on full speed. Then there was an interval while the tug hurried out of harm's way and the raft pursued a calculated drift towards the exact spot where the *Keweenaw* had disappeared. The hiatus lasted for some three hours, with the raft looking motionless on the screens. Then a voice through the loudspeakers told us that the release would take place in approximately thirty minutes. It continued to remind us at intervals until the time was short enough for it to start counting in reverse, slowly and calmly. There was a complete hush as we stared at the screens and listened to the voice:

' – three – two – one – *NOW!*'

On the last word a rocket sprang from the raft, trailing red smoke as it climbed.

'Bomb away!' said the voice.

We waited.

For a long time, as it seemed, everything was intensely still. Around the vision screens no one spoke. Every eye was on one or another of the frames which showed the raft calmly afloat on the blue, sunlit water. There was no sign that anything had occurred there, save the plume of red smoke drifting slowly away. For the eye and the ear there was utter serenity; for the feelings, a sense that the whole world held its breath.

Then it came. The placid surface of the sea suddenly belched into a vast white cloud which spread, and boiled, writhing upwards. A tremor passed through the ship.

We left the screens, and rushed to the ship's side. Already the cloud was above our horizon. It writhed and convolved upon itself in a fashion that was somehow obscene as it climbed monstrously up the sky. Only then did the sound reach us, in a buffeting roar. Much later, amazingly delayed, we saw the dark line which was the first wave of turbulent water rushing towards us.

That night we shared a dinner-table with Mallarby of *The Tidings* and Bennell of *The Senate*. I claim no credit for being included in such illustrious company except in so far as I had had the good sense to marry Phyllis and got her used to having me around before she perceived how widely she could have chosen. This was her show. We have a technique for that. I come off the sidelines just enough to show sociable, but not enough to interfere with her plan of campaign. The rest of the time I watch and admire. It is something like a combination of skilled juggling with expert chess, and her recoveries from an unexpected move are a delight to follow. She seldom loses. This time she had them more or less where she wanted them between the entrée and the joint.

'It's been the reluctance to postulate an intelligence that's been the chief stumbling block,' Mallarby remarked, 'but here, at last, we have a half-admission.'

'I'd still question "intelligence",' Bennell replied. 'The line between instinctive action and intelligent action, particularly as regards self-defence, can be very uncertain – if only because both may often produce the same response.'

'But you can't deny that whatever is the cause of it, it *is* an entirely new factor,' Mallarby said.

At this point I saw Phyllis relax from her efforts to get them going, and settle down to listen.

'I could,' Bennell told him. 'I could say that the factor may have been down there for centuries, but that it remained uninterested in us so long as we did not disturb it by probing into its environment.'

'You could,' agreed Mallarby, 'but if I were you, I wouldn't. Beebe and Barton went down deep, and nothing happened to them. You're disregarding the fused cables, too. There's certainly nothing instinctive there.'

Bennell grinned. 'They're awkward, I admit, but any theory I've heard so far has half a dozen factors quite as troublesome.'

'And the electrification of that American ship? – just static, I suppose?'

'Well – do we know enough of the conditions to be sure that it wasn't?'

Mallarby snorted.

'For heaven's sake! Lulling is for babes and nitwits.'

'Uh-huh. But if the choice lies between that and accepting the Bocker line, I'm inclined to prefer it.'

'I'm no Bocker champion. I doubt whether the thing as presented by him sounds more ludicrous to you than it does to me, but look what we're facing: a lot of explanations that will neither wash singly nor hang together; or Bocker's line. And however we feel about it, he does tie in more factors than anyone else.'

'So, without a doubt, would Jules Verne,' observed Bennell.

The introduction of this Bocker element set me all at sea, and Phyllis, too, though it would have been hard to guess it from the way she said:

'Surely the Bocker line can't be altogether dismissed?' frowning a little as she spoke.

It worked. In a little time we were adequately briefed on the Bocker view, and without either of them guessing that as far as we were concerned he had come into it for the first time.

The name of Alastair Bocker was not, of course, entirely unknown to us: it was that of an eminent geographer, customarily followed by several groups of initials. However, the information on him that Phyllis now prompted forth was something quite new to us. When re-ordered and assembled it amounted to this:

Almost a year earlier Bocker had presented a memorandum to the Admiralty in London. Because he was Bocker it succeeded in getting itself read at some quite important levels although the gist of its argument was as follows:

The fused cables and electrification of certain ships must be regarded as indisputable evidence of intelligence at work in certain deeper parts of the oceans.

Conditions, such as pressure, temperature, perpetual darkness, etc., in those regions made it inconceivable that any intelligent form of life could have evolved there – and this statement he backed with several convincing arguments.

It was to be assumed that no nation was capable of constructing mechanisms that could operate at such depths as indicated by the evidence, nor would they have any purpose in attempting to do so.

But, if the intelligence in the depths were not indigenous, then it must have come from elsewhere. Also, it must be embodied in some form able to withstand a pressure of two tons per square inch, or possibly twice as much. Now, where else on earth could a form find conditions of such pressure wherein to evolve? Clearly, nowhere.

Very well, then if it could not have evolved on earth, it must have evolved somewhere else – say, on a large planet where the pressures were normally very high. If so, how did it cross space and arrive here?

Bocker then recalled attention to the 'fireballs' which had aroused so much speculation a few years ago, and were still occasionally to be seen. None of these had been known to descend on land; none, indeed, had been known to descend anywhere but in areas of very deep water. Moreover, such of them as had been struck by missiles had exploded with such violence as to suggest that they had been retaining a very high degree of pressure.

It was significant, also, that these 'fireball' globes invariably sought the only regions of the earth in which high-pressure conditions compatible with movement were available.

Therefore, Bocker deduced, we were in the process, while almost unaware of it, of undergoing a species of interplanetary invasion. If he were to be asked the source of it, he would point to Jupiter as being most likely to fulfil the conditions of pressure.

His memorandum had concluded with the observation that such an incursion need not necessarily be regarded as hostile. There was such a thing as flight to refuge from conditions that had become intolerable. It seemed to him that the interests of a type of creation which existed at fifteen pounds to the square inch were unlikely to overlap seriously with those of a form which required several tons per square inch. He advocated, therefore, that the greatest efforts should be made to develop some means of making a sympathetic approach to the new dwellers in our depths with the aim of facilitating an exchange of science, using the word in its widest sense.

The views expressed by Their Lordships upon these elucidations and suggestions are not publicly recorded. It is known, however, that no long interval passed before Bocker withdrew his memorandum from their unsympathetic desks, and shortly afterwards presented it for the personal consideration of the Editor of *The Tidings*. Undoubtedly *The Tidings,* in returning it to him, expressed itself with its usual tact. It was only for the benefit of his professional brethren that the Editor remarked:

'This newspaper has managed to exist for more than one hundred years without a comic-strip, and I see no reason to break that tradition now.'

In due course, the memorandum appeared in front of the

Editor of *The Senate*, who glanced at it, called for a synopsis, lifted his eyebrows, and dictated an urbane regret.

Subsequently it occurred upon two other editorial desks of the more cloistered kind, but after that it ceased to circulate, and was known only by word of mouth within a small circle.

'What I have never understood about it,' Phyllis said, with a slight frown and an air of having been familiar with the situation for years, 'is why something like *The Daily Tape* or *The Lens* hasn't run it? Isn't it just their stuff? Or what about the American tabloids?'

'The *Tape* very nearly did,' Mallarby told her. 'Only Bocker said he'd sue them if they mentioned his name – he's after respectable publication, or none at all. So the *Tape* tried to get some other well-known figure to sponsor the idea as if it were his own. Nobody was keen. Bocker got his stuff printed, deposited it, and claimed copyright, so that was off. They dropped it because without some weighty kind of backing it would be just another *Tape* scare, and the circulation figures hadn't justified their last two scares. The *Lens* and the others are in roughly the same jamb. One small American paper did use a chewed-up version, but as it was their third interplanetary danger in four months it didn't register well. The others thought it over and reckoned that it would be too easy to be accused of making cheap capital out of the loss of American lives in the *Keweenaw*, so they threw it out. But it will come. Before long, one or another of them is bound to splash it, with or without Bocker's name and consent – and almost certainly without his main point, which was to try to make some kind of contact. They'll stress just what Bennell, here, stressed just now – the comic-horrific-strip aspect. Make-your-flesh-creep stuff.'

'And what other use *can* you make of a farrago like that?' Bennell inquired.

'Well, you can at least say, as I said before, that he does include more factors than anyone else has – and that anything that includes even most of the factors is, *ipso facto,* bound to be fantastic. We may decry it, but, for all that, until something better turns up, it's the best we have.'

Bennell shook his head.

'You begged the whole thing at the start. Suppose I concede for the moment that there does seem to be intelligence of some kind down there – you've no solid proof that intelligence couldn't evolve at a few tons to the square inch as easily as at fifteen pounds. You've nothing to support you but sheer common sense – the same kind of common sense that was satisfied that heavier-than-air craft could never fly. Prove to me –'

'You've got it wrong. He claims that the intelligence *must* have evolved under high pressure, but that it couldn't do so under the other conditions obtaining in our Deeps. But whatever you concede, and whatever the top naval men may think about Bocker, it is clear enough that they must have been assuming for some time that there *is* something intelligent down there. You don't design and make a special bomb like that all in five minutes, you know. Anyway, whether the Bocker theory is sheer hot air or not, he's lost his main point. This bomb was not the amiable and sympathetic approach that he advocated.'

Mallarby paused, and shook his head.

'I've met Bocker several times. He's a civilized, liberal-minded man – with the usual trouble of liberal-minded men; that they think others are, too. He has an interested, inquiring mind. He has never grasped that the average mind when it encounters something new is scared, and says: "Better smash it, or suppress it, quick." Well, he's just had another demonstration of the average mind at work.'

'But,' Bennell objected, 'if, as you say, it is officially believed that these ship losses have been caused by an intelligence, then there's something to be scared about, and you can't put to-day's affair down as anything stronger than retaliation.'

Mallarby shook his head again.

'My dear Bennell, I not only can, but I do. Suppose, now, that something were to come dangling down to us on a rope out of space; and suppose that that thing was emitting rays on a wavelength that acutely discomforted us, perhaps even caused us physical pain. What should we do? I suggest that the first thing we should do would be to snip the rope and put it out of action. Then we should examine the strange object and find out what we could about it.

'Then suppose that more strange objects began to be reported dangling down from above and causing discomfort to our citizens. We should argue: "This looks like a kind of invasion, or reconnaissance for one. Anyway it is extremely painful to us, so whatever is up there doing it has got to be stopped." And we should forthwith take what steps we could to discourage it. It might be done simply in the spirit of ending a nuisance, or it might be done with some animosity, and regarded as – retaliation. Now, would it be we, or the thing above, that was to blame?

'In the present case, and after to-day's performance the question becomes simply academic. It is difficult to imagine any kind of intelligence that would not resent what we've just done. If this were the only Deep where trouble has occurred, there might well be no intelligence left to resent it – but this *isn't* the only place, as you know; not by any means. So, what form that very natural resentment will take remains for us to see.'

'You think there really will be some kind of response, then?' Phyllis asked.

He shrugged. 'To take up my analogy again: suppose that some violently destructive agency were to descend from space upon one of our cities. What should we do?'

'Well, what *could* we do?' asked Phyllis, reasonably enough.

'We could turn the backroom boys on to it. And if it happened a few times more, we should soon be giving the backroom boys full priorities.'

'You're assuming a lot, Mallarby,' Bennell put in. 'For one thing, an almost parallel state of development. The significance of the word "priority", even, has a semantic dependence on conditions. It could scarcely mean a thing a century ago, and in the eighteenth century you could have howled "priority" until you were blue in the face without creating any technical advance whatever because our modern idea of research wasn't there – nobody would even understand what you were after.'

'True,' agreed Mallarby, 'but after what happened to those ships I'm justified in assuming quite a degree of technology there, I think.'

Phyllis said: 'Is it really too late – for some such approach as Bocker wanted, I mean? There's only been one bomb. If there isn't another they might think it was a natural disaster, an eruption or something.'

Mallarby shook his head.

'It won't be just one bomb. And it was always too late, my dear. Can you imagine us tolerating any form of rival intelligence on earth, no matter how it got here? Why, we can't even tolerate anything but the narrowest differences of views within our own race. No,' he shook his head, 'no, I'm afraid Bocker's idea of fraternization never had the chance of a flea in a furnace.'

*

That was, I think, very likely as true as Mallarby made it sound; but if there ever had been any chance at all it was gone by the time we reached home. Somehow, and apparently overnight, the public had put several twos together at last. The half-hearted attempt to represent the depth-bomb as one of a series of tests had broken down altogether. The vague fatalism with which the loss of the *Keweenaw* and the other ships had been received was succeeded by a burning sense of outrage, a satisfaction that the first step in vengeance had been taken, and a demand for more.

The atmosphere was similar to that at a declaration of war. Yesterday's phlegmatics and sceptics were, all of a sudden, fervid preachers of a crusade against the – well, against whatever it was that had had the insolent temerity to interfere with the freedom of the seas. Agreement on that cardinal point was virtually unanimous, but from that hub speculation radiated in every direction, so that not only fireballs, but every other unexplained phenomenon that had occurred for years was in some way attributed to, or at least connected with, the mystery in the Deeps.

The wave of worldwide excitement struck us when we stopped off for a day at Karachi on our way home, the place was bubbling with tales of sea-serpents and visitations from space, and it was clear that whatever restrictions Bocker might have put on the circulation of his theory, a good many million people had now arrived at a similar explanation by other routes. This gave me the idea of telephoning to the EBC in London to find out if Bocker himself would now unbend enough for an interview.

He did – to the representatives of a few carefully selected organs – but it added little to the script we had already put together on the journey from Karachi to London. His repeated plea for the sympathetic approach was so contrary to the public mood as to be almost unusable.

Once more, however, we had a demonstration that bellicose indignation is not self-sustaining. You just can't have a rousing fight for long with a sandbag, and little happened to animate the situation. The only step for weeks was that the Royal Navy, partly in deference to public feeling, but probably more for reasons of prestige, also sent down a bomb. It went off quite spectacularly, I understand, but the only recorded result was that the shores of the South Sandwich Islands were so littered with dead and decaying fish for weeks afterwards that they stank to heaven.

Then, by degrees, a feeling began to get about that this was not at all the way anyone had expected an interplanetary war to be; so, quite possibly, it was not an interplanetary war after all. From there, of course, it was only a step to deciding that it must be the Russians.

The Russians had all along discouraged, within their dictatorate, any tendency for suspicion to deviate from its proper target of capitalistic warmongers. When whispers of the interplanetary notion did in some way penetrate their curtain, they were countered by the statements that (a) it was all a lie: a verbal smoke screen to cover the preparations of warmongers;

(*b*) that it was true: and the capitalists, true to type, had immediately attacked the unsuspecting strangers with atom bombs; and (*c*) whether it were true or not, the USSR would fight unswervingly for Peace with all the weapons it possessed, except germs.

The swing continued. People were heard to say: 'Huh – that interplanetary stuff? Don't mind telling you that I very nearly fell for it at the time. But, of course, when you start to actually *think* about it – ! Wonder what the Russian game really is? Must've been something pretty big to make 'em use a-bombs on it.' Thus, in quite a short time, the *status quo ante bellum hypotheticum* was restored, and we were back on the familiarly comprehensible basis of international suspicion. The only lasting result was that marine insurance stayed up 1 per cent.

'Things,' Phyllis complained, 'sort of die on us. We looked like being *the* popular authorities on fireballs – in fact, for a week or two we were. Then the interest faded away, and there were fewer of them until now, if anyone sees one, he just regards it as a hallucination that he's not going to be taken in by. We didn't do so badly on that first dive – but you can't go on sustaining interest in just a couple of fused cables. We fell down badly somehow on not hearing of the Bocker business until it was practically stale – and I still don't understand how we missed it. At the bomb-dropping we were simply two of the crowd. When all the excitement boiled up it did look as if we might come into our own – but now that's all fizzled out. Everything's gone quiet again everywhere; it can't be that there's nothing happening.'

'It isn't,' I said. 'If you'd read the papers properly you'd see that two more bombs have gone down in the last week: one in the Cocos-Keeling Basin, and the other in the Prince Edward Deep.'

'I didn't see that.'

'News value practically nil at the moment. You have to read the small print.'

'It doesn't help when they choose outlandish places to send

them down, either. There must be plenty of deep places some-body's heard of.'

'Presumably none of the civilized regions will put up with bombs on their own doorsteps – and who's to blame them? I wouldn't fancy a coastline that's all radio-active water full of dead fish by the million, myself.'

'But it does show that they've not shelved the whole thing – the Navy, I mean.'

'Apparently not.'

'Mightn't it be worth going to Whitehall and seeing your Admiral again?'

'He's a captain,' I told her, but I considered the idea. 'Last time we met it wasn't really I that had the success with him,' I pointed out.

'Oh. Oh, I see,' said Phyllis. 'H'm. Dinner Tuesday?'

'I'll put it to him, from you.'

'I'm sure there must be a name for this kind of thing,' she said. 'The way I have to work! One day you'll find it's misfired and you've cut yourself out.'

'Darling, you know you thoroughly enjoy the art of the little finger. And you'd be furious if I concealed you under a bushel.'

'That's all very well,' she said. 'But I'd just like to feel a little more certain whose little finger we're talking about.'

Captain Winters came to dinner.

'Would you,' asked Phyllis, leaning back on her pillow with her hands behind her head, and studying the ceiling, 'would you call Mildred attractive?'

'Yes, darling,' I replied, promptly.

'Oh,' said Phyllis, 'I thought perhaps so.'

We pondered.

'It looked mutual,' she observed.

'It was *meant* to look – er – absorbed,' I told her.

'Oh, it did,' she assured me.

'Darling, the position is awkward,' I pointed out. 'If I were to tell you that one of your best friends is unattractive –'

'I'm not at all sure that she is one of my best friends. But she's not unattractive.'

'Your own appearance,' I remarked, 'I would describe as rapt. The manner trustful, the eyes a little starry, the smile a little enchanted, the overall effect quite bewitching. You know that, of course, but I thought I'd mention it; it was so well done – unusually well, I thought.'

She shifted slightly.

'The Captain's a very attractive man,' she said.

'Ah, well, then we've had a nice evening with two attractive people, haven't we? And they had to be stopped from attracting one another; channelled, as it were.'

'H'm,' she said.

'Darling, you're not jealous of my poor little histrionic talent?'

'No – it just seemed to have improved, that's all.'

'Sweetie,' I said, 'I am almost constantly treated to the spectacle of a variety of men wrestling with the pangs of temptation, and I feel great sympathy for them.'

She let the nearer hand stray from behind her head.

'I don't want them,' she said . . .

'Darling,' I remarked, somewhat later, 'I begin to wonder if we ought not to see more of Mildred.'

'M'm,' she said, doubtfully, 'but the Captain, too.'

'Which reminds me, if you aren't too sleepy – what did the Captain have to say?'

'Oh, lots of nice things. Irish blood there, I think.'

'But, passing from the really important, to matters of mere worldwide interest – ?' I suggested, patiently.

'He wouldn't let go of much, but what he did say wasn't encouraging. Some of it was rather horrid.'

'Tell me.'

'Well, the main situation doesn't seem to have altered a lot on the surface, but they're getting increasingly worried about what's happening below. The general flap and scare worried the authorities. It unsettled people, and they were uneasy lest what was just an excitement and a thrill might turn into a panic.

From the way he spoke I think there must have been quite a bit of manoeuvring behind the way it has all calmed down.

'And he didn't actually *say* that investigation has made no progress either, but what he did say implied it. For instance, echo soundings don't help. You can tell where the bottom is, but that tells you nothing about what may be *on* the bottom there. The shallower, secondary echoes may be off large creatures, shoals of fish, or anything, but there's no means of being sure what they *are* off. Some of them seem to be static, but no one's sure about that.

'Depth microphones don't help much. At some levels there's practically nothing, at others there's just a meaningless pandemonium of fish-noises, like we heard from that telebath thing. And they daren't let them down really deep on a steel cable because of what happened to that research-ship and some of the others. They've tried with a cable which was a non-conductor, but the mike leads burnt out at about a thousand fathoms. They sent down a television camera adapted for infra-red instead of visible rays, on the theory that it might be less provocative, and insulated the gear from all the rest of the ship. That was a good thing because at about eight hundred fathoms up came a charge that jumped fuses and melted half their instruments.

'He says that atomic bombs are out, for the moment at any rate. You can only use them in isolated places, and even then the radio-activity spreads widely. They kill an awful lot of fish quite uselessly, and make a lot more radio-active. The fisheries experts on both sides of the Atlantic have been raising hell, and saying that it's because of the bombings that some shoals have been failing to turn up in the proper places at the proper times. They've been blaming the bombs for upsetting the ecology, whatever that is, and affecting the migratory habits. But a few of them are saying that the data aren't sufficient to be absolutely sure that it is the bombs that have done it, but something certainly has, and it may have serious effects on food supplies. And so, as nobody seems to be quite clear what the bombs were expected to do, and all they do do is to kill and bewilder lots of fish at great expense, they've become unpopular just now.'

'Most of that we already know,' I remarked, 'but when it's on parade it certainly makes a fine upstanding body of negatives.'

'Well, here's one you didn't know. Two of those bombs they've sent down haven't gone off.'

'Oh,' I said, 'and what do we infer from that?'

'I don't know. But it has them worried, very worried. You see, the way they are set to operate is by the pressure at a given depth; simple and pretty accurate.'

'Meaning that they never reached the right pressure-zone? Must have got hung up somewhere on the way down?'

Phyllis nodded. 'That alone would take a bit of explaining, but what worries them still more is that there is a secondary setting, quite independent, just in case it happens to land on a submarine mountain, or something. It works with a time-switch – only with these two it hasn't.'

'Ah,' I said, 'perfectly simple, my dear Watson – the water got in and stopped the clock,' I told her.

'It's your name that's very suitably Watson – I'm only labelled that way for the duration,' Phyllis said, coldly. 'Anyway, there's nothing perfectly simple about it; and it's made them extremely anxious.'

'Understandably, too. I'd not feel too happy myself if I'd mislaid a couple of live atom bombs,' I admitted. 'What else?'

'Three cable-repair ships have unaccountably disappeared. One of them was cut off in the middle of a radio message. She was known to be grappling for a defective cable at the time.'

'When was this?'

'One about six months ago, one about three weeks ago, and one last week.'

'They might not be anything to do with it.'

'They *might* not – but everyone's pretty sure they are.'

'No survivors to tell what happened?'

'None.'

Presently I asked:

'Anything more?'

'Let me see. Oh, yes. They are developing some kind of

guided depth-missile which will be high-explosive, not atomic. But it hasn't been tested yet.'

I turned to look at her admiringly. 'That's the stuff, darling. The real Mata Hari touch. Have you got the drawings?'

'You goof. It's only because they don't want people unsettled that it's not been published in the newspapers – that, and the fact that the newspapers agree. The last hullabaloo sent the sales-graphs dipping everywhere, and the advertisers didn't like it. There's no need for ordinary security measures. No-body's going to dangle a telephone into the Mindanao Trench and ask if anybody down there would like to buy some interesting information.'

'I suppose not,' I admitted.

'Even the Services use common sense sometimes,' she said pointedly, and then added, on a second thought: 'Though there are probably several things he didn't tell me.'

'Probably,' I agreed again.

'The most important thing is that he is going to give me an introduction to Dr Matet, the oceanographer.'

I sat up. 'But, darling, the Oceanographical Society has more or less threatened to excommunicate anybody who deals with us after that last script – it's part of their anti-Bocker line.'

'Well, Dr Matet happens to be a friend of the Captain's. He's seen his fireball-incidence maps, and he's a half-convert. Any-way, we're not convinced Bockerites, are we?'

'What we think we are isn't necessarily what other people think we are. Still, if he's willing – When can we see him?'

'*I* hope to see him in a few days' time, darling.'

'Don't you think I should –'

'No. But it's sweet of you not to trust me still.'

'But –'

'No. And now it's time we went to sleep,' she said, firmly.

*

The beginning of Phyllis's interview was, she reported, almost standard:

'*EBC*?' said Doctor Matet, raising eyebrows like miniature doormats. 'I thought Captain Winters said *BBC*.'

He was a man with a large frame sparingly covered, which gave his head the appearance of properly belonging to a still larger frame. His tanned forehead was high, and well polished back to the crown. This dome was hedged about with wiry grey hair which stuck out in tufts over each ear. His bright eyes peered at one past a pronouncedly Roman nose. His large, responsive mouth surmounted a slightly cleft chin. As if all this dominating apparatus were slightly too heavy for him, he stooped. He gave one, Phyllis said, a feeling of being over-hung.

She sighed inwardly, and started on the routine justification of the English Broadcasting Company's existence, with the assurances that sponsorship did not necessarily connote venality, venenosity, or even vapidity. He found this an interesting point of view. Phyllis recited examples of illustrious EBC occasions and persons, and worked him round gradually until he had reached the position of considering us nice enough people striving manfully to overcome the disadvantages of being considered a slightly second class oracle. Then, after making it quite clear that any material he might supply was strictly anonymous in origin, he opened up a bit.

The trouble from Phyllis's point of view was that he did it on a pretty academic level, full of strange words and instances which she had to interpret as best she could. The gist of what he had to tell her, however, seemed to be this:

A year ago there had begun to be reports of discolorations in certain ocean currents. The first observation of the kind had been made in the Kuro Siwo current in the North Pacific – an unusual muddiness flowing north-east, becoming less discernible as it gradually widened out along the West Wind Drift until it was no longer perceptible by the naked eye.

'Samples were taken and sent for examination, of course, and what do you think the discoloration turned out to be?' said Dr Matet.

Phyllis looked properly expectant. He told her:

'Mainly radiolarian ooze, but with an appreciable percentage of diatomaceous ooze.'

'How very remarkable!' Phyllis said, safely. 'Now what on earth could produce a result like that?'

'Ah,' said Dr Matet, 'that is the question. A disturbance on a quite remarkable scale – even in samples taken on the other side of the ocean, off the coast of California, there was still quite a heavy impregnation of both these oozes.'

'That's astonishing, isn't it?' said Phyllis. 'The effects – ?'

'One cannot hope to foresee more than the most obvious effects. Some changes in fish migrations are already becoming noticeable, and a certain increase in sea vegetation along the course, as one would expect. Naturally, with the water diatomaceously richer – '

He went on for some time, with Phyllis trying not to look too much as if she were grasping straws behind him. At last he said: 'This, obviously, is of immense interest and the greatest importance, but naturally the most interesting question to us is why it should happen at all, and is continuing to happen. What, in fact, can have occurred that could be responsible for sending this sediment from the greatest depths to the surface in such amazing quantities?'

Phyllis felt that it was time she made a contribution.

'Well, there was that atomic bomb off the Marianas. I should think that would have made quite a stir down below,' she said.

Dr Matet regarded her severely. 'That bomb was dropped *after* the phenomenon had been observed, and in any case it is highly doubtful whether the results of a disturbance there would have been concentrated into the Kuro Siwo.'

'Oh,' said Phyllis.

'It is, as you know, an actively volcanic area,' Dr Matet launched off again, 'so that one's natural inclination would be to attribute the disturbance to the opening of some new vent, or vents, on the sea-bottom. The seismograph records, however, give no support to that view. No major seismic shock has been registered – '

Phyllis went on listening patiently while he demolished earthquakes as a possible cause.

'And yet,' she remarked at the end of it, 'something not only was, but still is, going on down there?'

'Something is,' he agreed, looking at her. Then, with a sudden descent to the vernacular, he added: 'But, to be honest with you, Lord knows what it is.'

He went on. Phyllis learned that, since then, similarly unexplained somethings had been throwing up deep-sea sediments into the Monsoon Drifts, off Guatemala; and also across the other side of the isthmus into the Mosquito Current. A thickening of the waters in equatorial mid-Atlantic had been observed, and the most recent report was of ooze appearing in the West Australian Current. There were also several minor irregularities of the same kind. Phyllis did her best to list them for possible reference, but just before she left she managed to put in a question on the aspect which seemed to her most interesting and important.

'Tell me this, Dr Matet,' she asked. 'Do you think it is serious – I mean, is it a thing that worries you?'

He smiled at her. 'It doesn't keep me awake at night, if that's what you mean. No, our worry about it, if you can call it that, is that we don't like having to admit that we are utterly baffled in our own bailiwick. As for its effect – well, I should think that might be beneficial. There is a great deal of nutritious ooze lying wasted on the sea-bottom. The more of it that comes up, the more the plankton will thrive; and the more the plankton thrives, the more the fish will thrive; consequently the price of fish ought to go down, which will be very nice for those who like fish – of which I am not one. No, what troubles me is that I feel I ought to be able to answer a simple "why?" on the matter – after all, I am supposed to have been an expert for a number of years now. . . . '

*

'Too much geography,' said Phyllis, 'and too much oceanography, and too much bathyography: too much of all the ographies, and lucky to escape ichthyology.'

'Tell me,' I said.

She did, with notes. 'And,' she concluded, 'I'd like to see even Mrs Hawkes scribe a script out of that lot.'

'H'm,' I said.

'There's no h'm about it. Some kind of ographer might give a talk on it to highbrows and low listening figures, but even if he were intelligible, where'd it get anybody?'

'That,' I remarked, 'is the key question each time. But little by little the bits do accumulate. This is another bit. You didn't really expect to come back with the stuff for a whole script, anyway. He didn't suggest how this might link up with the rest of it?'

'No. I said it was sort of funny how everything seemed to be happening down in the most inaccessible parts of the ocean lately, and a few things like that, but he didn't rise. Very cautious. I think he was rather wishing he had not agreed to see me, so he stuck to verifiable facts. Eminently non-wheedlable – at first meeting, anyhow. He admitted he doesn't know, but he is not going to make any guesses that might send his reputation the way Bocker's has gone. What it amounts to is that he'd like it to be volcanic, but it can't be because of the evidence, and it's not likely that it is due to an explosion, or series of explosions, of any kind because it keeps on coming up in a more or less steady flow which suggests that the force at work is both immense and continuous. Now you have a shot at it.'

'Look,' I said. 'Bocker must have got to know about this as soon as anyone did. He ought to have some views on it, and it might be worth trying to find out what they are. That select Press-Conference of his that we went to was almost an introduction.'

'He went very coy after that,' she said, doubtfully. 'Not surprising, really. Still, we weren't among the ones who panned him publicly – in fact, we were very objective.'

'Toss you which of us rings him up,' I offered.

'I'll do it,' she said.

'I suppose it's being a victim of the charm myself that stops me being jealous of the supreme self-confidence it inspires,' I said. 'Okay. Go ahead.'

So I leant back comfortably in my chair, and listened to her going through the opening ceremony of making it clear that she was the EBC, *not* the BBC.

I will say for Bocker that having proposed his mouthful of a theory and then sold it to himself, he had not ratted on the deal when he found it unpopular. At the same time he had no great desire to be involved in a further round of controversy when he would be pelted with cheap cracks and drowned in the noise from empty vessels. He made that quite clear when we met. He looked at us earnestly, his head a little on one side, a lock of his grey hair hanging slightly forward, his hands clasped together. He nodded thoughtfully, and then said:

'You want a theory from me because nothing you can think of will explain this phenomenon. Very well, you shall have one. I don't suppose you'll accept it, but I do ask you if you use it at all to use it anonymously. When people come round to my view again, I shall be ready, but I prefer not to be thought of as keeping my name before the public by letting out sensational driblets - is that quite clear?'

We nodded.

'What we are trying to do,' Phyllis explained, 'is to fit a lot of bits and pieces into a puzzle. If you can show us where one of them should go, we're very grateful. If you would rather not have the credit for it, well, that is your own affair, and we'll respect it.'

'Exactly. Well, you already know my theory of the origin of the deep-water intelligences, so we'll not go into that now. We'll deal with their present state, and I deduce that to be this: having settled into the environment best suited to them, these creatures' next thought would be to develop that environment in accordance with their ideas of what constitutes a convenient, orderly, and, eventually, civilized condition. They are, you see, in the position of - well, no, they are *actually* pioneers, colonists. Once they have safely arrived they set about improving and exploiting their new territory. What we have been seeing are the results of their having started work on the job.'

'By doing what?' I asked.

He shrugged his shoulders. 'How can we possibly tell? But judging by the way we have received them, one would imagine that their primary concern would be to provide themselves with some form of defence against us. For this they would presumably require metals. I suggest to you, therefore, that somewhere down in the Mindanao Deep, and also somewhere in the Deep in the south-east of the Cocos-Keeling Basin, you would, if you could go there, find mining operations now in progress.'

I glimpsed the reason for his demand for anonymity.

'Er – but the working of metals in such conditions – ?' I said.

'How can we guess what technology they may have developed? We ourselves have plenty of techniques for doing things which would at first thought appear impossible in an atmospheric pressure of fifteen pounds per square inch; there are also a number of unlikely things we can do under water.'

'But, with a pressure of tons, and in continual darkness, and –' but Phyllis cut across me with that decisiveness which warns me to shut up and not argue.

'Dr Bocker,' she said, 'you named two particular Deeps then; why was that?'

He turned from me to her.

'Because that seems to me the only reasonable explanation where those two are concerned. It may be, as Mr Holmes once remarked to your husband's illustrious namesake, "a capital mistake to theorize before one has data," but it is mental suicide to funk the data one has. I know of nothing, and can imagine nothing, that could produce the effect we have here except some exceedingly powerful machine for continuous ejection.'

'But,' I said, a little firmly, for I get rather tired of being dogged by the ghost of Mr Holmes, 'if it is mining as you suggest, then why is the discoloration due to ooze, and not grit?'

'Well, firstly there would be a great deal of ooze to be shifted before one could get at the rock, immense deposits, most likely; and secondly, the density of the ooze is little more than that of the water, whereas the grit, being heavy, would begin to settle long before it got anywhere near the surface, however fine it might be.'

Before I could pursue that, Phyllis cut me off again:

'What about the other places, Doctor. Why mention just those two?'

'I don't say that the others don't also signify mining, but I suspect, from their locations, that they may have another purpose.'

'Which is – ?' prompted Phyllis, looking at him, all girlish expectation.

'Communications, I think. You see, for instance, close to, though far below, the area where discoloration begins to occur in the equatorial Atlantic lies the Romanche Trench. It is a gorge through the submerged mountains of the Atlantic Ridge. Now, when one considers the fact that it forms the only deep link between the eastern and western Atlantic Basins, it seems more than just a coincidence that signs of activity should show up there. In fact, it strongly suggests to me that something down below is not satisfied with the natural state of that Trench. It is quite likely that it is blocked here and there by falls of rock. It may be that in some parts it is narrow and awkward; almost certainly, if there were a prospect of using it, it would be an advantage to clear it of ooze deposits down to a solid bottom. I don't *know*, of course, but the fact that something is un-doubtedly taking place in that strategic Trench leaves me with little doubt that whatever is down there is concerned to improve its methods of getting about in the depths – just as we have improved our ways of getting about on the surface.'

There was a silence while we took in that one, and its implications. Phyllis rallied first.

'Er – and the other two main places – the Caribbean one, and the one west of Guatemala?' she asked.

Dr Bocker offered us cigarettes, and lit one himself.

'Well, now,' he remarked, leaning back in his chair, 'doesn't it strike you as probable that for a creature of the depths a tunnel connecting the Deeps on either side of the isthmus would offer advantages almost identical with those that we ourselves obtain from the existence of the Panama Canal?'

*

People may say what they like about Bocker, but they can never truthfully claim that the scope of his ideas is mean or niggling. What is more, nobody has ever actually *proved* him wrong. His chief trouble was that he usually provided such large, indigestible slabs that they stuck in all gullets – even mine, and I would class myself as a fairly wide-gulleted type. That, however, was a subsequent reflection. At the climax of the interview I was chiefly occupied with trying to convince myself that he really meant what he had said, and finding nothing but my own resistance to suggest that he did not.

Before we left, he gave us one more thing to think about, too. He said:

'Since you are following this along, you've probably heard of two atomic bombs that failed to go off?'

We told him we had.

'And have you heard that there was an unsponsored atomic explosion yesterday?'

'No. Was it one of them?' Phyllis asked.

'I should very much hope so – because I should hate to think it could be any other,' he replied. 'But the odd thing is that though one was lost off the Aleutians, and the other in the process of trying to give the Mindanao Deep another shake up, the explosion took place not so far off Guam – a good twelve hundred miles from Mindanao.'

*

'I wish,' said Phyllis, 'that I had been kinder and tried to pay more attention to dear Miss Popple who used to try to teach me geography, poor thing. Every day the world gets fuller of places I never heard of.'

'That's perfectly in order,' I told her. 'Haven't you noticed that the places mentioned in military communiqués are scarcely ever to be found on the maps? The geographers never heard of them, either.'

'Well, it says here that over sixty people were drowned when a tsunami struck Roast Beef Island. Where's Roast Beef Island? And what's a tsunami?'

'I don't know where Roast Beef Island is, though I can offer you two Plum Pudding Islands. But tsunami is Japanese for an earthquake-wave.'

She regarded me.

'You needn't look so smug, dear. It's only half marks. The thing is, would it be anything to do with us?'

'Us?'

'Well, with those things down there, I mean.'

'Not unless it was a phoney tsunami.'

'How euphonious! "Phoney tsunami!" ' She went on crooning; 'Euphony – euphony – phoney – tsunami' to herself for a bit until she ended suddenly: 'How would we know?'

'Look, I'm trying to think. Know what?'

'Whether it's phoney or not, of course.'

'Well, you could ring up your learned pal, Dr Matet. Oceanographers have meters and things to tell them what kind of wave's what, and where it comes from.'

'Do they really. How?'

'How would I know how? They just do. He'd be sure to have heard if there were anything funny about it.'

'All right,' she said, and went off.

Presently she came back.

'It's okay,' she reported, disappointedly. 'There was, I quote: "a minor seismic disturbance in the neighbourhood of St Ambrose Island, longitude something, latitude something else." Anyway, off Chile. And Roast Beef Island is another name for Esperanzia Island.'

'Where's Esperanzia Island?' I inquired.

'I don't know,' she said, happily.

She sat down and picked up the paper. 'Everything seems to have gone very quiet lately,' she said.

'I hadn't noticed it. I might, if you would try to do some work, too,' I replied.

A few minutes' silence ensued. Then she said:

'Captain Winters rang up yesterday. Did you know there hasn't been a single fireball reported for over two months?'

Evidently this was one of those mornings. I put my pen into its holder, and took out a cigarette.

'I didn't, but it's not very surprising; they've been rare for quite a time now. Had he any comments?'

'Oh, no. He just sort of mentioned it.'

'I suppose the Bocker view would be that the first phase of colonization has been completed: the pioneers have established themselves, and the settlement is now on its own to sink or swim.'

'Predominantly, sink,' said Phyllis.

'Anybody who happened to overhear the home twitterings of EBC's clever feature-script writer could blackmail us for years,' I told her.

It passed her by.

'I've been thinking about what Mallarby said,' she remarked, 'and I don't see why people couldn't make up their minds to leave those things down there alone. I mean, if there is one part of the world that can be of no conceivable use to us, a part we can't even reach, and it happens to suit them, then why not let them have it?'

'That's reasonable – superficially, at any rate,' I agreed, 'but Mallarby's point was, and I agree with that, that it's a matter of instinct, not reason. The instinct of self-protection is opposed to the very idea of an alien intelligence – and not without pretty good cause. It's difficult to imagine any kind of intelligence, except a sheer abstraction, that wouldn't be concerned to modify its environment for its own betterment. But it is very unlikely that the ideas of betterment held by two different types would be identical – so unlikely that it suggests a hypothesis that, given two intelligent species with differing requirements on one planet, it is inevitable that, sooner or later, one will exterminate the other.'

Phyllis thought it over.

'That has a pretty grim, Darwinian sound, Mike,' she remarked.

' "Grim" isn't an objective word, darling. It's simply the way things usually work. If one species lived in salt water, and the other in fresh, you would, in the course of time, inevitably reach a situation where the interests of the races demanded that one should freshen the sea while the other was doing its damnedest to salt the lakes and rivers. It looks to me as if that is bound to apply unless the needs are identical – and if the needs *are* identical, then they are *not* a different species.'

'You mean, you're in favour of going on sending down atom bombs, and that kind of thing?' she said.

'Darling, if I happen to mention that, as a process, autumn follows summer, it does not follow that I am all for getting a ladder and pulling the leaves off the trees.'

'I don't see why you should want to.'

'I don't.'

'You mean, you're *not* in favour of sending down atom bombs? By the way you were talking before, I thought –'

'Look, let's drop atom bombs for the moment – no, damn it, I mean, let's leave them out of it. The thing is that once we had developed intelligence *we* weren't satisfied with the world as we found it; so, are the things down there likely to be satisfied with it as *they* find it? Such evidence as we have suggests that they are not – they don't like being bombed by us, for instance. Then the real point is, how long will it be before the efforts to change it for the convenience of both parties come into serious opposition?'

'Well, since you've asked me, I should say you have answered your own question: it happened when we prodded them with the first atom bomb. That's what I'm complaining about.'

'Scarcely a matter for *complaint*, darling, and anyway, it's too late. We must have gone down then on their environment-improvement list with a high priority, even if we hadn't before. There was a certain ominousness in the speed with which they took up the defensive – as if they might have expected something of the kind and prepared for it. What really remains to be seen is whether the natural obstacles that now separate us will defeat their abilities – as they almost defeat ours – and, if they do not, then how we can meet them when they come.'

'Then, on the whole, you *are* in favour of dropping bombs?' suggested Phyllis.

'For goodness sake! Let's get this thing straight. Darling, I and the Royal Navy are *not* in favour of dropping atom bombs: we think it poisons too much water, for problematical results. But I, and, I hope, the Royal Navy, too, are prepared to take up arms against this sea of troubles, as and when it may appear necessary and effective. In this I have no doubt that others will join us. The weapons to be chosen will be dictated largely by the time, place, and nature of the need.'

Phyllis sat with her head propped on her left hand, her eyes unseeingly on the newspaper.

'You said, "inevitable". Do you really think that?' she asked, after a time.

'Yes. Even if only part of what Bocker thinks is right. We can't *both* inherit the Earth.'

'When, do you think?'

I shrugged my shoulders. 'When you think of the difficulties that both lots must overcome to get at the other effectively, it looks as if it might be a long time coming to a head – a generation or two, perhaps, or a century or two. I don't see how anybody could hope to get nearer than a wild guess.'

Phyllis picked up a pencil, and watched her fingers abstractedly as they twiddled it. Presently she became quite still, staring rigidly at nothing. I knew the symptoms, and forbore to interrupt. After a time she said:

'How would this be? Start with sounds of a tearing wind and an angry sea. Perhaps a lifeboat putting out, with the men's words blown away as they speak. Then fade out all but the natural sounds of wind and sea. Then – how would you contrive the effect of sinking under the water? Keep the water-sounds, and diminish the wind? Then give the water-sounds a slower rhythm, diminishing, too, gradually. Voice counts: " – three fathoms – four fathoms – full fathom five – and down – down – down – " There's only a slow, indefinite surge to suggest water movement now. As it gets fainter you begin to hear the chirruping fish, then the squawking ones, and the others until there's fish pandemonium, which gradually diminishes to a final chirrup. Then – I'm not sure whether it ought to be the voice telling the fathoms, or whether a mysterious silence would be more effective – but next, deep grunts, some snarls, and galumphing noises. Voice intones about Leviathan and the monsters of the deep, and repeats " – down – down – down – " Occasional, indefinable sounds until absolute silence, out of which Voice says:

' "The deep-sea bottom! The uttermost part of the Earth! It is dark; it has always been dark; it will always be dark until the seas dry up and the arid Earth spins on her endless way, with life a tale that has long been told and finished.

' "But now, that is far away in the future, as far away in time as it will take the sun to scorch up the five miles of water above our heads; and it is dark.

' "It is cold, too, as cold as any glacier; and quiet ... and still ... It has been still for aeons ...

' "We have brought down light with us from the world far above, and we switch it on. We see a wide floor flanked by gigantic rocky cliffs. But it is not a solid floor. If we were to try to step on it we should sink through many feet of ooze before it became solid enough to support us.

' "All the time, in the beam of our lights we can see motes endlessly descending and descending to make the great bed of ooze.

' "It is an eerie place, an awful place, death's own place; for the floor, the rock shelves, everything but the perpendicular faces of the cliffs, is drifted deep with the mortal remains of untold billion millions of minute creatures. 'Nothing,' you would say, 'absolutely nothing could live here. This is beyond the reach of life: the nethermost pit.'

' "But – " and then some stuff about the improbable places you do find life, leading up to: " – is this, the most secret womb in the world, not barren, after all?" Er, well, words to that effect, anyway. And then, giving the Bocker line a complete miss: 'Is a new form of life – and not only of life, but of intelligent life – about to emerge from these depths, from this slime, and struggle up through the miles of water to the sunlight, perhaps to challenge the supremacy of man himself? Millions of years ago our own ancestors crawled from the sea on to the land – " Then sprinkle in some bits which support the possibility. Then *you* can follow on with a piece about the inevitable animosity, and I can take the line that should the two forms of intelligence be complementary they may be able to solve all the riddles of the universe between them. What about something along those lines?'

I considered. 'Well, to be frank, darling, I don't quite see the over-all form, and conclusion.'

'I'm seeing it rather as one of those "Whither – ?" things, only not highbrow. You know, ending on a question.'

'As well it may. If I may say so, Voice doesn't seem to have quite made up his mind whether he is a florid moralist, or a metaphorical guide. But I think I see the mood you're after – the picture of a new kind of life emerging from the mysteries of a sort of super Celtic-twilight – that kind of thing?'

'Well, allowing for the fact that I shouldn't express it at all like that – roughly, yes, I suppose.'

'Well, Phyl, you'd have an awful handful there, because, honestly, I don't think this thing can be made to lend itself to a romantic treatment. Why not wait until we get a few more facts to add to it, and then try again along more documentary lines? They're always your real hits, you know.'

She thought it over. 'You're probably right, Mike. But I'd like to get in first with that angle, so I hope we don't have to wait too long for the extra facts.'

'I, on the other hand, would prefer that we should never have them at all. I should be a lot happier if I were to hear that the things down there had simply drowned themselves, but I'm prepared to be disappointed.'

And I thought I was. Nobody, however, was really prepared for the next day's news.

Phase Two

WE made an early start that morning. The car, ready loaded, had stood out all night, and we were away a few minutes after five, with the intention of putting as much of southern England behind us as we could before the roads got busy. It was two hundred and sixty-eight point eight (when it wasn't point seven or point nine) miles to the door of the cottage that Phyllis had bought with a small legacy from her Aunt Helen.

I had rather favoured the idea of a cottage a mere fifty miles or so away from London, but it was Phyllis's aunt who was to be commemorated with what was now Phyllis's money, so we became the proprietors of Rose Cottage, Penllyn, Nr Constantine, Cornwall, Telephone Number: Navasgan 333. It was a grey-stone, five-roomed cottage set on a south-easterly sloping. heathery hillside, with its almost eavesless roof clamped down tight on it in the true Cornish manner. Straight before us we looked across the Helford River, and on towards the Lizard where, by night, we could see the flashing of the lighthouse. To the left was a view of the coast stretching raggedly away on the other side of Falmouth Bay, and if we walked a hundred yards ahead, and so out of the lee of the hillside which protected us from the south-westerly gales, we could look across Mount's Bay, towards the Scilly Isles, and the open Atlantic beyond. Falmouth, 7 miles; Helston, 9; elevation 332 feet above sea-level; several, though not all, mod. con. When you did reach it you decided that it was worth travelling two hundred and sixty-eight point eight (or nine) miles, after all.

We used it in a migratory fashion. When we had enough commissions and ideas on hand to keep us going for a time we would withdraw there to drive our pens and bash our typewriters in pleasant, undistracting seclusion for a few weeks. Then we would return to London for a while, market our wares, cement relations, and angle for commissions until we felt the call to go down there again with another accumulated batch of work – or we might, perhaps, simply declare a holiday.

That morning, I made pretty good time. It was still only half past eight when I removed Phyllis's head from my shoulder and woke her up to announce: 'Yeovil, and breakfast, darling.' I left her trying to pull herself together to order breakfast intelligibly while I went to get some newspapers. By the time I returned she was functioning better, and had already started on the cereal. I handed over her paper, and looked at mine. The main headline in both was given to a shipping disaster. That this should be so when the ship concerned was Japanese suggested that there was little news from elsewhere.

I glanced at the 'story' below the picture of the ship. From a welter of human interest I unearthed the fact that the Japanese liner, *Yatsushiro,* bound from Nagasaki to Amboina, in the Moluccas, had sunk. Out of some seven hundred people on board, only five survivors had been found.

Now, in common with most of my fellow-countrymen, though independently of foundation, I have the feeling that in the Occident we construct, but in the Orient they contrapt. Thus the news of an oriental bridge collapsing, train leaving the rails, or, as in the present case, ship sinking, never impinges with quite the novelty its western counterpart would arouse, and the sense of concern is consequently less acute. I do not defend this phenomenon; I regard it as reprehensible. Nevertheless, it is so, and in consequence I turned the page with my sense of tragedy somewhat qualified by non-surprise. Before I could settle down to the leader, however, Phyllis interrupted with an exclamation. I looked across. Her paper carried no picture of the vessel; instead, it printed a small sketch-map of the area, and she was intently studying the spot marked 'X'.

'What is it?' I asked.

She put her finger on the map. 'Speaking from memory, and always supposing that the cross was made by somebody with a conscience,' she said, 'doesn't that put the scene of this sinking pretty near our old friend the Mindanao Trench?'

I looked at the map, trying to recall the configuration of the ocean floor around there.

'It can't be far off,' I agreed.

I turned back to my own paper, and read the account there more carefully. 'Women,' apparently, 'screamed when – ,' 'Women in night-attire ran from their cabins,' 'Women, wide-eyed with terror, clutched their children – ,' 'Women' this and 'Women' that when 'death struck silently at the sleeping liner.' When one had swept all this woman jargon and the London Office's repertoire of phrases suitable for trouble at sea aside, the skeleton of a very bare Agency message was revealed – so bare that for a moment I wondered why two large newspapers had decided to splash it instead of giving it just a couple of inches. Then I perceived the real mystery angle which lay submerged among all the phoney dramatics. It was that the *Yatsu-shiro* had, without warning, and for no known reason, suddenly gone down like a stone.

I got hold of a copy of this Agency message later, and I found its starkness a great deal more alarming and dramatic than this business of dashing about in 'night-attire'. Nor had there been much time for that kind of thing, for, after giving particulars of the time, place, etc., the message concluded laconically: 'Fair weather, no (no) collision, no (no) explosion, cause unknown. Foundered less one (one) minute alarm. Owners state quote impossible unquote.'

So there can have been very few shrieks that night. Those unfortunate Japanese women – and men – had time to wake, and then, perhaps, a little time to wonder, bemused with sleep, and then the water came to choke them: there were no shrieks, just a few bubbles as they sank down, down, down in their nineteen-thousand-ton steel coffin.

When I had read what there was I looked up. Phyllis was regarding me, chin on hands, across the breakfast table. Neither of us spoke for a moment. Then she said:

'It says here: " – in one of the deepest parts of the Pacific Ocean." Do you think this can be *it*, Mike – so soon?'

I hesitated. 'It's difficult to tell. So much of this stuff's obviously synthetic. . . . If it actually was only one minute. . . . No, I suspend judgement, Phyl. We'll see *The Times* to-morrow and find out what really happened – if anyone knows.'

We drove on, making poorer time on the busier roads, stopped to lunch at the usual little hotel on Dartmoor, and finally arrived in the late afternoon – two hundred and sixty-eight point seven, this time. We were sleepy and hungry again, and though I did remember, when I telephoned London, to ask for cuttings on the sinking to be sent, the fate of the *Yatsushiro* on the other side of the world seemed as remote from the concerns of a small grey Cornish cottage as the loss of the *Titanic*.

The Times noticed the affair the next day in a cautious manner which gave an impression of the staff pursing their lips and staying their hands rather than mislead their readers in any way. Not so, however, the reports in the first batch of cuttings which arrived on the afternoon of the following day. We put the stack between us, and drew from it. Facts were evidently still meagre, but there was plenty of comment. My first read:

'Mystery still shrouds the fate of the ill-starred Japanese liner, *Yatsushiro,* which plunged to her doom bringing sudden death to all but five of her seven hundred passengers, including women and children, on Monday night off the southern islands of the Philippine group. No mystery of the sea since the still unsolved riddle of the *Marie Celeste* has presented more baffling queries . . .'

The next one read:

'It seems likely that the fate of the *Yatsushiro* may well take a place in the long list of unsolved mysteries of the sea. Nothing quite so unaccountable has occurred since the schooner, *Marie Celeste,* was discovered adrift with . . .'

And the next:

'Statements made by the five Japanese sailors, the only survivors of the *Yatsushiro* disaster, serve only to deepen the mystery surrounding the ship's fate. Why did she sink? How could she sink so swiftly? Answers to these questions may never be forthcoming, any more than they were to the questions posed by the mystery of the *Marie Celeste* which have eluded solution . . .'

And the next:

'Even in these modern times of radio, etc., the sea can still produce mysteries to defeat us. The loss of the liner, *Yatsushiro,* presents puzzles as baffling as any in the annals of navigation, and to all appearance no more likely to be satisfactorily explained than were the problems aroused by the famous *Marie Celeste,* which, it will be recalled . . .'

I reached for another.

'It says here,' Phyllis broke in, looking at the cutting in her hand, with a slight frown: ' "The tragic loss of the *Yatsushiro* bids fair to rank high among the unsolved problems of the high seas. It is, in its way, only a little less baffling than the still unanswered questions posed by the famous *Marie Celeste* . . . " '

'Yes, darling,' I agreed.

And the one before said: ' "A mystery even deeper than that surrounding the celebrated *Marie Celeste* veils the fate of the vanished *Yatsushiro* . . . " Wasn't the whole point about the *Marie Celeste* that she *didn't* sink?'

'Roughly – yes, darling.'

'Well, then what is all this about her for?'

'It is what is known as an "angle", darling. It means in translation, that nobody has the ghost of an idea why the *Yatsushiro* sank. Consequently she has been classified as a Mystery-of-the Sea. This gives her a natural affinity with other Mysteries-of-the-Sea, and the *Marie Celeste* was the only specific M-of-the-S that anyone could call to mind in the white heat of composition. In other words, they are completely stumped.'

'It's not worth looking through the rest, then?'

'Scarcely. But we'd better. I'd like to know if anybody is speculating – and if not, why not? We can't be the only people who are putting two and two together. So just keep an eye out for guesses.'

She nodded, and we went on working through the pile, learning more about the *Marie Celeste* than we did about the *Yatsushiro*. There was only one check. Phyllis gave a 'Ha' of discovery.

'This one's different,' she said. 'Listen! "The full story behind the sinking of the Japanese vessel. *Yatsushiro,* is not likely to be revealed. This luxury liner, lavishly decorated and furnished, was built in Japan, with capital emanating largely from Wall Street, at a time when the gap between uncontrolled wage-levels and the rising cost of living for the Japanese worker –" Oh, I see.'

'What do they work round to?' I asked.

She skimmed the rest. 'I don't think they do. There's just a kind of all-through suggestion that it was too contaminated by capital to keep afloat.'

'Well, that's the only theory out of this lot,' I said. 'All got a strong dose of not-before-the-children this time. And not altogether surprising, seeing the hell the advertisers raised over the last global panic they pulled. But they're going to have to do better than this skulking behind the *Marie Celeste;* you can't just proclaim a thing a Mystery-of-the-Sea and stop all theories for long. For one thing, the more intelligent weeklies haven't such sensitive advertisers. Somehow I can't see *Tribune* or the –'

Phyllis cut me off:

'Mike, this isn't a game, you know. After all, a big ship *has* gone down, and seven hundred poor people have been drowned. That is a terrible thing. I dreamt last night that I was shut up in one of those little cabins when the water came bursting in.'

'Yesterday –' I began, and then stopped. I had been about to say that yesterday Phyllis had poured a kettle of boiling water down a crack in order to kill a lot more than seven hundred ants, but thought better of it. 'Yesterday,' I amended, 'a lot of people were killed in road accidents, a lot will be to-day.'

'I don't see what that has to do with it,' she said.

She was right. It was not a very good amendment – but neither had it been the right moment to postulate the existence of a menace that might think no more of us than we of ants.

'As a race,' I said, 'we have allowed ourselves to become accustomed to the idea that the proper way to die is in bed. at a ripe age. It is a delusion. The normal end for all creatures comes suddenly. The –'

But that wasn't the right thing to say at that time, either. She withdrew, using those short, brisk, hard-on-the-heel steps.

I was sorry. I was worried, too, but it takes me differently.

I was evidently not alone in thinking that a solution would have to be provided. The next day, it was. Almost every newspaper explained it, and on Friday the weeklies elaborated it. It could be compressed into two words – metal-fatigue.

Certain new alloys recently developed in Japanese laboratories had, it seemed, been used, for the first time on any considerable scale, in the construction of the *Yatsushiro*. Metallurgical experts conceded it as not impossible that some, or one, of these alloys might, if the ship's engines were to produce vibrations of a certain critical periodicity, become fatigued, and therefore brittle. A fracture of one member so affected would throw on others a sudden strain which, in their weakened state, they might be unable to take. Thus, the collapse of susceptible members might be rapidly successive and conducive to speedy disintegration of the whole. Or, one might put it that the whole ship was ready to fall apart at the drop of a hat.

This could not, at the moment, be positively established as the sole cause of the disaster since detailed examination of the structure was at present precluded by circumstances. Or, again, five or six miles of water.

It had been decided, however, that all work on the *Yatsushiro's* sister-ship, now on the stocks, would be suspended pending the application of exhaustive tests regarding the crystalline structure of the alloys intended for use in her construction.

'Ah! The blinding light of science,' I said after reading several closely similar versions in different papers. 'A bit hard on that shipyard, and not, perhaps, very consoling to the relatives, but a pretty piece of work, all the same. So reassuring for all the rest of us. Observe the nicer points: not just general metal-fatigue, nor even weld-fatigue, which might alarm people about welded ships in general; no, just the fatigue of an unspecified alloy or two used in *one Japanese* ship. No other ship is likely to suffer from this deciduous complaint: no need for the seafaring public to feel the least concern lest any other ship should get a touch of this ague and shake itself to bits. And the sea ... ? Nothing to do with it. The sea is as safe as ever it was.'

'But it *could* be so, couldn't it?' said Phyllis.

'That's the beauty of it. It had to be something that *could* be – if only just. And I think they'll very likely get away with it. The general public will take it, and the technical men won't stand to gain anything by contesting it – in public, anyway.'

'I'd *like* to believe it,' said Phyllis. 'I think I even might, if I hadn't given myself to a cynic – and, of course, if the thing hadn't happened to happen just where it did.'

I pondered.

'I imagine,' I said, 'that marine insurance rates will be pegged at the moment, to preserve confidence – but we ought to keep an eye on the prices of shipping shares.'

Phyllis got up and went to the window. From where she stood, at the side of it, she had a view of the blue water stretching to the horizon.

'Mike,' she said, 'I'm sorry about yesterday. The thing – this ship going down like that – suddenly got me. Until now this has been a sort of guessing game, a puzzle. Losing the bathyscope with poor Wiseman and Trant was bad, and so was losing the naval ships. But this – well, it suddenly seemed to put it into a different category – a big liner full of ordinary, harmless men, women, and children peacefully asleep, to be wiped out in a few seconds in the middle of the night! It's somehow a different *class* of thing altogether. Do you see what I mean ? Naval people are always taking risks doing their jobs – but these people on a liner hadn't anything to do with it. It made me feel that those things down there had been a working hypothesis that I had hardly believed in, and now, all at once, they had become horribly real. I don't like it, Mike. I suddenly started to feel afraid. I don't quite know why.'

I went over and put an arm round her.

'I know what you mean,' I said. 'I think it is part of it – the thing is not to let it get us down.'

She turned her head. 'Part of what?' she asked, puzzled.

'Part of the process we are going through – the instinctive reaction. The idea of an alien intelligence here *is* intolerable to us, we *must* hate and fear it. We can't help it – even our own kind of intelligence when it goes a bit off the rails in drunks and crazies alarms us not very rationally.'

'You mean I'd not be feeling quite the same way about it if I knew that it had been done by – well, the Chinese, or somebody?'

'Do you think you would?'

'I – I'm not sure.'

'Well, for myself, I'd say I'd be roaring with indignation. Knowing that it was somebody hitting well below the belt, I'd at least have a glimmering of who, how, and why, to give me focus. As it is, I've only the haziest impressions of the who, no idea about the how, and a feeling about the why that makes me go cold inside, if you really want to know.'

She pressed her hand on mine.

'I'm glad to know that, Mike. I was feeling pretty lonely yesterday.'

'My protective coloration isn't intended to deceive you, my sweet. It is intended to deceive me.'

She thought.

'I must remember that,' she said, with an air of extensive implication that I am not sure I have fully understood yet.

*

One of the grubs in the raspberry at Rose Cottage was that our guests almost invariably arrived in the middle of the night, having (*a*) over-estimated the average speed they would maintain, (*b*) spent longer over dinner on the way than they had intended, (*c*) developed in the course of the last few miles a compulsion towards bacon and eggs.

Harold and Tuny were no exception. Two-ten a.m. on Saturday was the time when I heard their car draw up. I went out into the moonlight and found Harold pulling things out of the boot, while Tuny who had not been there before looked about her with a doubtful expression which cleared somewhat as she recognized me.

'Oh, it *is* the right place,' she said. 'I was just telling Harold it couldn't be because – '

'I'm sorry,' I apologized, 'we shall really have to grow some. Everybody expects it of us – except the natives.'

'I've explained,' said Harold, 'but she won't have it.'

'All you kept on saying was that in Cornwall rose doesn't mean rose.'

'It doesn't,' I told her, 'it means "heath".'

'Well, then I don't see why you don't call it Heath Cottage, to make it plainer.'

'Let's go inside,' I suggested, laying hold of a case.

Wondering why one's friends chose to marry the people they did is unprofitable, but recurrent. One could so often have done so much better for them. For instance, I could think of three girls who would have been better for Harold, in their different ways; one would have pushed him, another would have looked after him, the third would have amused him. It is true that they were none of them quite as decorative as Tuny, but that's not – well, it's something like the difference between the room you live in and the one at the Ideal Home Exhibition. However, there it was, and, as Phyllis said, a girl who makes good with a name like Petunia must at least have something her parents didn't have.

The bacon and eggs made their appearance. Tuny admired the plates, which were part of a set that we had found in Milan, and presently she and Phyllis were well away. After a while I asked Harold how the metal-fatigue theory was going down. He held a public-relations job with a large engineering firm, so he'd be likely to know. He looked at me, and gave a quick glance at Tuny who was still chatting china.

'It's not pleasing our people a lot,' he said, briefly, and then switched over to telling me of some minor noise that his car had developed on the way down.

Untraceable noises in other people's cars tend to bore: this one was so mysterious in its habits that I suggested that we put it down to metal-fatigue, and leave it at that until the morning, at least. Across the table, Tuny caught the phrase. She gave a – well, there used to be something called a 'tinkling laugh'; this was probably it.

'Metal-fatigue!' she repeated, and tinkled again.

Harold said hurriedly: 'We were talking about the funny noise the car was making, dear.' Tuny paid him no attention.

'Metal-fatigue!' she repeated.

Since there is nothing intrinsically funny in metal-fatigue, we judged that her amusement was the kind that invites inquiry. In our lack of response we were not being wilfully unkind, merely contra-suggestible; besides, it was ten minutes to three a.m. Harold pushed back his chair.

'It's been a pretty long run,' he said, 'I think –' But Tuny was not to be stalled.

'Oh, my dears,' she said, 'you don't mean to say that people down here really believe all that stuff about metal-fatigue?'

I caught Phyllis's surprised eye. I was somewhat taken aback myself. Earlier I had been saying that it was well done, and that the general public would believe it because they would prefer to believe it. Now here was Tuny confuting me almost at once. I glanced at Harold who was looking at his plate. He would not, I decided, be the one who had enlightened Tuny. She belonged irretrievably to the class of woman who believes from the church-door that, having let her bring it off, her man must be a mental weakling, and that any views he may put forward should be treated accordingly.

'Why not?' asked Phyllis. 'There's nothing very new about the idea of metal-fatigue.'

'Of course not,' Tuny agreed, 'that's where they are being clever in putting this out. I mean, it's the kind of thing lots of quite sensible people will fall for,' she added kindly. 'But in this case it's all quite phoney, of course.'

I was about to speak when a look from Phyllis quenched me. It was the kind of look I sometimes get when she is doing her stuff.

'But it's practically official. It's in all the papers,' she said.

'Oh, my dear, surely you don't believe *official* statements any more,' said Tuny, indulgently. 'Of course they had to make *some* kind of statement, or else do something about it. And it being only a Japanese steamer made a difference. But it's pretty much like Munich over again.'

'Oh, come, I'd not go as far as that,' said Phyllis in mild expostulation, while I was still wondering how on earth we had arrived at Munich.

'Near enough,' Tuny told her, 'if they can do it once and have the whole thing explained away for them, they'll just be encouraged to do it again, and go on doing it. The only proper way of dealing with it is to take a firm stand. It's simply no good appeasing and dodging. We ought to have called their bluff months and months ago.'

'Bluff?' repeated Phyllis, raising her eyebrows.

'All this story about things in the sea, and those balloon things, and all that silly stuff about Martians, and so on.'

'Martians?' Phyllis said, bemusedly.

'Well, Neptunians – it's the same sort of thing. The rubbish that that Bocker man put about. I can't think why he wasn't arrested long ago. I happen to know from somebody who used to know him that he joined the Party when he first went up to the University, and of course he's been working for them ever since. He didn't *invent* it, I don't mean that. No, the whole thing was thought up in Moscow, and they just *used* him to put it across because he was influential. And he did it very well – that story about the things in the sea was all over the world, and a whole lot of people believed it for a bit, but of course he's quite done for now. That doesn't matter to them, they do that to people. He was just wanted to lay a foundation, you see.'

We had begun to see.

'But the Russians tried to explode the idea. They said at the time it was just a smokescreen to cover the preparations of warmongers,' I pointed out.

'That,' said Tuny, 'wasn't even subtle. It's their regular technique to get in the first accusation against someone else of what they are doing themselves.'

'You mean that the whole thing has been engineered by them right from the beginning?' asked Phyllis.

'But of course,' Tuny told her. 'Quite a long time ago now they had their first try with the flying-saucers, but that didn't come off because most people didn't believe in them, and nobody was really scared. So this time they improved it. First they sent out the red balloons to puzzle people. Then there was all this business about the bottom of the sea that Bocker helped to spread, and to make that more convincing they cut cables, and even sank a few ships –'

'Er – what with?' I inquired.

'With these new midget submarines of theirs, of course; the same kind that they used on this Japanese ship. And now they'll just be able to go on sinking ships because once people have seen through this metal-fatigue business they'll just say it's being done by the Bocker things in the sea. As long as people believe that, there'll be no popular backing for reprisals.'

'So the metal-fatigue idea was just put about to keep people quiet?' Phyllis asked.

'Exactly,' Tuny agreed. 'The Government doesn't want to admit that it's the Russians, because then there would be a demand that they should take action, and they can't afford to do that with all the Red influence there is. But if they officially pretend to think it's these Bocker things, well, then they'd have to pretend, too, that they were doing something about that, *and* that'd make them look pretty silly later when it is all exploded. So this is their way out, and as it's only a Japanese ship it's all right – for the moment. But it won't last long. We can't afford to have the Russians getting away with this kind of thing. People are starting to demand a strong line, and no more appeasement.'

'People – ?' I put in.

'People in Kensington – and some other places,' Tuny explained.

Phyllis looked thoughtful as she collected the plates.

'It's shocking how out of touch one gets in a little place like this,' she said, with a slightly apologetic air, and for all the world as if she had been immured in Rose Cottage for several years.

Harold choked a little, and coughed. Then he yawned largely.

'More fresh air than I'm used to,' he explained, and helped to break the party up by carrying out the plates.

In the course of the week-end we learnt more about Russian intentions, though their reasons for sinking a harmless passenger-liner never emerged very clearly. The Sunday papers all had articles, informative in different degrees, on metal-fatigue, and Tuny had a nice day reading them with the smile of a cognoscenta.

Whatever might be the opinion in Kensington, and the lesser Kensingtons of other towns, it was clear that the official theory was being well received in Cornwall. The public bar of *The Pick* in Penllyn had its own expert on the crystalline structure of metals, with several tales to tell of mysterious collapses of mine machinery which could be attributed to nothing but brittleness induced by prolonged vibration. All old miners, he said, had known this by instinct, long before the scientists got at it. And also, since matters of the sea are of perennial interest to all Cornishmen, heads were knowledgeably shaken over the behaviour of certain Liberty-ships.

Harold looked a little worried as we left there to walk back to the cottage.

'I can see a busy time ahead,' he said, gloomily. 'Months of writing stuff to prove that none of our products can possibly suffer from metal-fatigue.'

'What's it matter? They'll have to use your products,' I said.

'Yes, but all our competitors will be saying how *their* goods aren't affected by it, so it'll look bad if we don't do the same. I'll have to put in for an extra allocation,' he grumbled. 'If only the damned ship had turned turtle nobody would have been greatly surprised, seeing its nationality, and there'd have been no need for all this. What's more,' he added, 'there's such a lot of trouble for so little result. A good many million people may be lapping it up, but it isn't going home in the places that matter. How much of that is due to Tuny's friends with their usual universal political solvent, and how much to other causes, I wouldn't know, but the fact remains that the number of passage-cancellations has risen well above average, and the number of extra airline bookings about balances it. Also, do you happen to have noticed the shipping shares?'

I said that I had.

'Well, that isn't good. It wouldn't be Tuny's friends selling just now. It points to a number of people who aren't satisfied with the metal-fatigue *or* the red-menace explanations.'

'Well, are you?' I asked.

'No, of course not, but that isn't the point. I'm not the kind of fellow who can make a difference to the price of shipping shares. The chaps who can are influential: if they start a scare, people start cancelling orders, and trade bogs down. It doesn't matter a hoot whether there *are* things at the bottom of the sea or not. What does matter is if people swing back to *thinking* there are – if they do, we'll have a worse trade recession than last time.' He paused. Then he added: 'And you people haven't helped a lot, either.'

'We've not been doing world-trade a lot of harm lately,' I told him. 'We've not had the chance. I don't say we haven't got a few scripts up our sleeves against the day when truth shall be more important than world-trade, but for the last few months now not a word about those things down there has gone out from any of our transmitters; the sponsors don't like it – '

'Good for them,' interrupted Harold.

' – any more than the advertisers liked mention of Hitler when we were on the brink of World War II,' I concluded.

'Implying – just what?' asked Harold.

'Well, roughly, that if you do happen to have any money in shipping, I should take it out, and put it into aircraft.'

Harold gave a disapproving grunt.

'I know you and Phyl have been specializing in this thing and following it along. What you've learnt seems to have convinced you – but have you any solution?'

I shook my head.

'Well, then, what good do you think you'll do to anybody by

simply broadcasting: "Woe! Woe!"? All that happened in that
scare after the first atomic depth-bomb was that a lot of people
were worried, trade fell off, and everyone suffered, to no purpose. And then it took a lot of work to get them all soothed
down again. If there *is* anything in it, then let them worry when
they *have* to, but leave them in peace till then.'

'If – !' I repeated. 'What do *you* suppose sank that ship,
Harold? When did any good come of burying your head in the
sand?'

'It's safer for my neck than sticking it out,' said Harold,
rather pleased with himself.

I found that Phyllis, when I recounted the gist of the con
versation to her later, took a not dissimilar view.

'If we had come across a single practicable suggestion for
countering the things it would have been worth campaigning
for it, but we haven't,' she said. 'All my life I have been surrounded by things I'd rather not know too much about, so I
have come to feel that truth made naked without purpose is
really a wanton. It – I say, that was rather good, wasn't it?
Where did I put my notebook?'

Tuny and Harold duly departed, and we settled again to our
tasks – Phyllis to the search for something which had not
already been said about Beckford of Fonthill. I, to the less
literary occupation of framing a series on royal love-matches,
to be entitled provisionally either, The Heart of Kings, or,
Cupid Wears a Crown.

A pleasant month followed. The outer world intruded little.
Phyllis finished the Beckford script, and two more, and picked
up the threads of the novel that never seemed to get finished.
I went steadily ahead with the task of straining the royal love-
lives free from any political contaminations, and writing an
article or two in between, to clear the air a bit. On days that we
thought were too good to be wasted we went down to the coast
and bathed, or hired a sailing dinghy. The newspapers forgot
about the *Yatsushiro*. Local parlance had adopted the term
metal-fatigue as a useful cover for various misfortunes, and the

terms china-fatigue and glass-fatigue were becoming current conveniences. The deep-sea, and all our speculations concerning it, seemed very far away.

Then, on a Wednesday night, the nine o'clock bulletin announced that the *Queen Anne* had been lost at sea . . .

The report was very brief. Simply the fact, followed by: 'No details are available as yet, but it is feared that the list of the missing may prove to be very heavy indeed.' There was silence for fifteen seconds, then the announcer's voice resumed: 'The *Queen Anne*, the current holder of the Transatlantic record, was a vessel of ninety thousand tons displacement. She was built – '

I leant forward, and switched off. We sat looking at one another. Tears came into Phyllis's eyes. The tip of her tongue appeared, wetting her lips.

'The *Queen Anne!* Oh, God!' she said.

She searched for a handkerchief.

'Oh, Mike. That lovely ship!'

I crossed to sit beside her, and put my arm round her. For the moment she was seeing simply the ship as we had last seen her, putting out from Southampton. A creation that had been somewhere between a work of art and a living thing, shining and beautiful in the sunlight, moving serenely out towards the high seas, leaving a flock of little tugs bobbing behind. But I knew enough of her to realize that in a few minutes she would be on board, dining in the fabulous restaurant, or dancing in the ballroom, or up on one of the decks, watching it happen, feeling what they must have felt there. I put my other arm round her, and held her closer.

I am thankful that such imagination as I, myself, have is more prosaic, and seated further from the heart.

Half an hour later the telephone rang. I answered it, and recognized the voice with some surprise.

'Oh, hullo, Freddy. What is it?' I asked, for nine-thirty in the evening was not a time that one expected to be called by the EBC's Director of Talks & Features.

'Good. 'Fraid you might be out. You've heard the news?'

'Yes.'

'Well, we want something from you on this deep-sea menace of yours, and we want it quick. Half-hour length.'

'But, look here, the last thing I was told was to lay off any hint – '

'This has altered all that. It's a *must*, Mike. You don't want to be too sensational, but you *do* want to be convincing. Make 'em really believe there is something down there.'

'Look here, Freddy, if this is some kind of leg-pull – '

'It isn't. It's an urgent commission.'

'That's all very well, but for over a year now I've been regarded as the dumb coot who can't let go of an exploded crackpot theory. Now you suddenly ring me at about the time when a fellow might have made a fool bet at a party, and say – '

'Hell, I'm not at a party. I'm at the office, and likely to be here all night.'

'You'd better explain,' I told him.

'It's like this. There's a rumour running wild here that the Russians did it. Somebody launched that one off within a few minutes of the news coming through on the tape. Why the hell anybody'd think they would want to start anything that way, heaven knows, but you know how it is when people are emotionally worked up; they'll swallow anything for a bit. My own guess is that it is the let's-have-a-showdown-now school of thought seizing the opportunity, the damn fools. Anyway, it's got to be stopped. If it isn't, there might be enough pressure worked up to force the Government out, or make it send an ultimatum, or something. So stopped it's damned well going to be. Metal-fatigue isn't good enough this time, so the line is to be your deep-sea menace. To-morrow's papers are using it, the Admiralty is willing to play, we've got several big scientific names already, the BBC's next bulletin, and ours, will have good strong hints in order to start the ball rolling, the big American networks have started already, and some of their evening editions are coming on the streets with it. So if you want to put in your own pennyworth towards stopping the atom bombs falling, get cracking right away.'

'Okay. A half-hour feature. What angle?'

'It's to be a topical-special. Serious, but not blood-curdling. Not too technical. Intelligent man-in-the-street stuff. Above all, *convincing*. I suggest the line: Here is a menace more serious and more quickly developed than we had expected. A blow that has found us as unprepared as the Americans were at Pearl Harbour, but men of science are mobilizing already to give us the means to hit back, et cetera. Cautious but confident optimism. Okay?'

'I'll try – though I don't know what the optimism is to be founded on.'

'Never mind about that; just express it. Your primary job is to help fix the thing in their minds as a fact, so that it keeps out this anti-Russian nonsense. Once that is well established we can find ways to keep it going.'

'You think you'll need to?' I asked.

'What do you mean?'

'Well, after the *Yatsu,* and now this, it looks to me as if the things may have gone over to the offensive, and these won't be the only ones to suffer.'

'I'd not know about that. The thing is, will you get down to this right away? When you're through, ring us, and we'll have a recorder fixed ready for you. You'll give us a free hand to fiddle it around as necessary? The BBC are sure to have something along pretty similar lines.'

'Okay, Freddy. You shall have it,' I agreed, and hung up.

'Darling,' I said, 'work for us.'

'Oh, not to-night, Mike. I couldn't . . .'

'All right,' I said 'but it's work for me.' I handed on what Freddy Whittier had just told me. 'It looks,' I went on, 'as if the best way would be to decide the thesis and the style and approach, and then rake together the bits out of old scripts that will suit it. The devil of it is that most of the scripts and all the data are in London.'

'We can remember enough. It doesn't have to be intellectual – in fact, it mustn't,' Phyllis said. She thought for some moments. 'We've got all that organized scoffing to break down,' she added.

91

'If the papers really do their stuff to-morrow morning it ought to be cracked a bit. Our job is pressing home what they will have started.'

'But we need a line. The first thing people are going to ask is: "If this thing is so serious, why has nothing been done, and why have we been hoodwinked?" Well, why?'

I considered.

'I don't think that need be too difficult. Viz: the sober, sensible people of the West would have reacted wisely, and no doubt will; but the more emotional and excitable peoples elsewhere have less predictable reactions. It was therefore decided as a matter of policy that the Service Chiefs and scientists who have been studying the trouble should preserve discretion in the hope that it might be scotched before it became serious enough to cause public alarm. How's that?'

'Um – yes. As good as we're likely to get,' she agreed.

'Then we can use Freddy's unpreparedness angle as a challenge – the brains of the world getting together and turning the full force of modern science and technique on to the job of avenging the loss, and preventing any more. A duty to those who have been lost, and a crusade to make the seas safe.'

'That's what it *is*, Mike,' Phyllis said, quietly, and with a reproving note.

'Of course it is, darling. Why do you so often think that I say what I say by accident?'

'Well, you start off as if truth is going to be the first casualty, as usual, and then end up like that. It's kind of bewildering.'

'Never mind, my Sweet. I intend to write it the right way. Now, you run up to bed, and I'll get on with it.'

'To bed? What on earth – ?'

'Well, you said you couldn't – '

'Don't be absurd, darling. Do you think I'm going to let you loose on this on your own? Now, which of us had the atlas last . . . ?'

It was eleven o'clock the next morning when I made my mazy way into the kitchen and subconsciously got together coffee and toast and boiled eggs, and fumbled back upstairs with them.

It had been after five that morning when I had finished dictating our combined work in the recording machine in London, by which time we had both been too tired to know whether it was good or bad, or to care.

Phyllis lit a cigarette to accompany the second cup of coffee.

'I think,' she suggested, 'that we had better go into Falmouth this morning.'

So to Falmouth we went, and, in the course of duty, visited four of the most popular bars in that port.

Freddy Whittier had not exaggerated the need for swift action. The rumour of Russian responsibility for the loss of the *Queen Anne* was tentatively about already; noticeably stronger among the double-scotches than among the pints of beer. There could have been little doubt that it would have swept the field but for the unanimity with which the morning papers had laid responsibility on the things down below. In the circumstances, their solidarity succeeded in producing an impression that the anti-Russian talk must be an entirely local product sponsored by a few well-known local diehards and fire-eaters.

That did not mean, however, that the deep-sea menace was fully accepted. Too many people could recall their first uncritical alarm, followed by their swing to derision, to be able to make the new *volte-face* all at once. But the serious views in the morning's leaders had got as far as damping the derision and causing many to wonder whether there might not have been something in it after all. It looked to me as if, assuming that we had a fair sample, the first objective had been reached: the danger of a concerted popular demand for war on the wrong enemy had been averted. Undoing the effects of a year or more's propaganda, and establishing the reality of an enemy that could not even be described, were matters for steady perseverance.

'To-morrow,' said Phyllis, knocking back the fourth gin-and-lime occasioned by our researches, 'I think we ought to go back to London. You must have quite enough of those morganatic marriages in the bag to be going on with, and there'll probably be quite a lot of work for us to do on this business.'

It was only in expressing the idea that she had forestalled me. The next morning we made our customary early start.

When we arrived at the flat, and switched on the radio, we were just in time to hear of the sinkings of the aircraft-carrier *Meritorious,* and the liner *Carib Princess.*

*

The *Meritorious,* it will be recalled, went down in mid-Atlantic, eight hundred miles south-west of the Cape Verde Islands: the *Carib Princess* not more than twenty miles from Santiago de Cuba: both sank in a matter of two or three minutes, and from each very few survived. It is difficult to say whether the British were the more shocked by the loss of a brand-new naval unit, or the Americans by their loss of one of their best-found cruising liners with her load of wealth and beauty: both had already been somewhat stunned by the *Queen Anne,* for in the great Atlantic racers there was community of pride. Now, the language of resentment differed, but both showed the characteristics of a man who has been punched in the back in a crowd, and is looking round, both fists clenched, for someone to hit.

The American reaction appeared more extreme for, in spite of the violent nervousness of the Russians existing there, a great many found the idea of the deep-sea menace easier to accept than did the British, and a clamour for drastic, decisive action swelled up, giving a lead to a similar clamour at home.

In a pub off Oxford Street I happened across the whole thing condensed. A medium-built man who might have been a salesman in one of the large stores was putting his views to a few acquaintances.

'All right,' he said, 'say for the sake of argument they're right, say there *are* these whatsits at the bottom of the sea: then what I want to know is why we're not getting after 'em right away? What do we pay for a navy for? And we've got atom bombs, haven't we? Well, why don't we go out to bomb 'em to hell before they get up to more trouble? Sitting down here and letting 'em think they can do as they like isn't going to help.

Show 'em, is what I say, show 'em quick, and show 'em proper. Oh, thanks; mine's a light ale.'

Somebody raised the question of poisoning the ocean.

'Well, damn it, the sea's big enough. It'll get over it. Anyway, you could use H.E., too,' he suggested.

Somebody else agreed that the size of the sea was a point: indeed, there was an awful lot of it for games of blind man's buff. The first man wouldn't have that.

'They said the Deeps,' he pointed out. 'They've kept on talking about the Deeps. Then, for God's sake why don't they get cracking right away, and sock the Deeps good and hard. They do know where *they* are, anyway. Who bought this one? Here's luck.'

'I'll tell you why, chum,' said his neighbour, '*if* you want to know. It's because the whole thing's a lot of bloody eyewash, that's why. Things in the frickin' Deeps, for crysake! Horsemarines, Dan Dare, and bloody Martians! Look, tell me this: we lose ships, the Yanks lose ships, the Japs lose ships – but do the Russians lose ships? Do they hell – and I'd like to know why not.'

Somebody suggested that it might be because the Russians hadn't many ships, anyway.

Somebody else remembered that away back at the time when the *Keweenaw* was lost the Russians *had* lost a ship, and not quietly, either.

'Ah,' said the complainant, 'but where are the independent witnesses? That's just the kind of camouflage you could expect from them.'

The feeling of the meeting, however, was not with him. But neither was it altogether with the first speaker. A third man seemed to talk for most of them when he said:

'You got to plan for it, like for anything else, I s'pose; but I must say – well, thanks, old man, just one for the road – I must say it'd make you feel easier to know somebody was really *doing* something about it.'

Probably it was in deference to similar views, more vigorously expressed, that the Americans decided to make the gesture of depth-bombing the Cayman Trench close to the point where the *Carib Princess* had vanished – they can scarcely have expected any decisive result from the random bombing of a Deep some fifty miles wide and four hundred miles long.

The occasion was well publicized on both sides of the Atlantic. American citizens were proud that their forces were taking the lead in reprisals: British citizens, though vocal in their dissatisfaction at being left standing at the post when the recent loss of two great ships should have given them the greater incentive to swift action, decided to applaud the occasion loudly, as a gesture of reproof to their own leaders. The flotilla of ten vessels commissioned for the task was reported as carrying a number of H.E. bombs specially designed for great depth, as well as two atomic bombs. It put out from Chesapeake Bay amid an acclamation which entirely drowned the voice of Cuba plaintively protesting at the prospect of atomic bombs on her doorstep.

None of those who heard the broadcast put out from one of the vessels as the task-force neared the chosen area will ever forget the sequel. The voice of the announcer when it suddenly broke off from his description of the scene to say sharply: 'Something seems to be – my God! She's blown up!' and then the boom of the explosion. The announcer gabbling incoherently, then a second boom. A clatter, a sound of confusion and voices, a clanging of bells. Then the announcer's voice again; breath short, sounding unsteady, talking fast:

'That explosion you heard – the first one – was the destroyer, *Cavort*. She has entirely disappeared. Second explosion was the frigate, *Redwood*. She has disappeared, too. The *Redwood* was carrying one of our two atomic bombs. It's gone down with her. It is constructed to operate by pressure at five miles depth. . . .

'The other eight ships of the flotilla are dispersing at full-speed to get away from the danger area. We shall have a few minutes to get clear. I don't know how long. Nobody here can tell me. A few minutes, we think. Every ship in sight is using every ounce of power to get away from the area before the bomb goes off. The deck is shuddering under us. We're going flat out. . . . Everyone's looking back at the place where the *Redwood* went down. . . . Hey, doesn't anybody here know how long it'll take that thing to sink five miles . . . ? Hell, *somebody must* know. . . . We're pulling away, pulling away for all we're worth. . . . All the other ships, too. All getting the hell out of it, fast as we can make it. . . . Anybody know what the area of the main spout's reckoned to be . . . ? For crysake! Doesn't anybody know any damn thing around here . . . ? We're pulling off now, pulling of. . . . Maybe we *will* make it. . . . Wish I knew how long . . . ? Maybe. . . . Maybe. . . . Faster, now, faster, for heaven's sake. . . . Pull the guts out of her, what's it matter? . . . Hell, slog her to bits. . . . Cram her along . . .

'Five minutes now since the *Redwood* sank. . . . How far'll she be down in five minutes . . . ? For God's sake, somebody: *How long does that damn thing take to sink . . . ?*

'Still going . . . Still keeping going . . . Still beating it for all we're worth. . . . Surely to heaven we must be beyond the main spout area by now. . . . Must have a chance now. . . . We're keeping it up. . . . Still going. . . . Still going flat out. . . . Everybody looking astern. . . . Everybody watching and waiting for it. . . . And we're still going. . . . How can a thing be sinking all this time . . . ? But thank God it is. . . . Over seven minutes now. . . . Nothing yet. . . . Still going. . . . And the other ships, with great white wakes behind them. . . . Still going. . . . Maybe it's a dud. . . . Or maybe the bottom isn't five miles around here. . . . Why can't somebody tell us how long it *ought* to take . . . ? Must be getting clear of the worst now. . . . Some of the other ships are just black dots on white spots now. . . . Still going. . . . We're still hammering away. . . . Must have a chance now. . . . I guess we've really got a chance now. . . . Everybody still staring aft. . . . Oh, God! The whole sea's –'

And there it cut off.

But he survived, that radio announcer. His ship and five others out of the flotilla of ten came through, a bit radio-active, but otherwise unharmed. And I understand that the first thing that happened to him when he reported back to his office after treatment was a reprimand for the use of over-colloquial language which had given offence to a number of listeners by its neglect of the Third Commandment.

*

That was the day on which argument stopped, and propaganda became unnecessary. Two of the four ships lost in the Cayman Trench disaster had succumbed to the bomb, but the end of the other two had occurred in a glare of publicity that routed the sceptics and the cautious alike. At last it was established beyond doubt that there was something – and a highly dangerous something, too – down there in the Deeps.

Such was the wave of alarmed conviction spreading swiftly round the world that even the Russians sufficiently overcame their national reticence to admit that they had lost one large freighter and one unspecified naval vessel, both, again, off the Kuriles, and one more survey craft off eastern Kamchatka. In consequence of this, they were, they said, willing to co-operate with other powers in putting down this menace to the cause of world Peace.

The following day the British Government proposed that an International Naval Conference should meet in London to make a preliminary survey of the problem. A disposition among some of those invited to quibble about the locale was quenched by the unsympathetically urgent mood of the public. The Conference assembled in Westminster within three days of the announcement, and, as far as England was concerned, none too soon. In those three days cancellations of sea-passages had been wholesale, overwhelmed air-line companies had been forced to apply priority schedules, the Government had clamped down fast on the sales of oils of all kinds, and was rushing out a rationing system for essential services, the bottom had dropped out of the shipping market, the price of many foodstuffs had doubled, and all kinds of tobacco had vanished under the counters.

On the day before the Conference opened Phyllis and I had met for lunch.

'You ought to see Oxford Street,' she said. 'Talk about panic-buying! Cottons particularly. Every hopeless line is selling out at double prices, and they're scratching one another's eyes out for things they wouldn't have been seen dead in last week. Every decent piece of stuff has disappeared, presumably into store for later on. It's a better picnic than any of the Sales.'

'From what they tell me of the City,' I told her, 'it's about as good there. Sounds as if you could get control of a shipping-line for a few bob, but you couldn't buy a single share in anything to do with aircraft for a fortune. Steel's all over the place; rubbers are, too; plastics are soaring; distilleries are down; about the only thing that's holding its own seems to be breweries.'

'I saw a man and a woman loading two sacks of coffee-beans into a Rolls, in Piccadilly. And there were – ' She broke off suddenly as though what I had been saying had just registered. 'You *did* get rid of Aunt Mary's shares in those Jamaican Plantations?' she inquired, with the expression that she applies to the monthly housekeeping accounts.

'Some time ago,' I reassured her. 'The proceeds went, oddly enough, into aero-engines, and plastics.'

She gave an approving nod, rather as if the instructions had been hers. Then another thought occurred to her:

'What about the Press Tickets for to-morrow?' she asked.

'There aren't any for the Conference proper,' I told her. 'There will be a statement afterwards.'

She stared at me. *Aren't any?* For heaven's sake! What do they think they're doing?'

I shrugged. 'Force of habit, I imagine. They are planning a campaign. When you plan a campaign, you tell the Press as much as it is good for it to know, later on.'

'Well, of all the – '

'I know, darling, but you can't expect a Service to change its spots overnight.'

'It's absolutely silly. More like Russia every day. Where's the telephone in this place?'

'Darling, this is an *International Conference*. You can't just go –'

'Of course I can. It's sheer nonsense!'

'Well, whatever VIP you have in mind will be out at lunch now,' I pointed out.

That checked her for a moment. She brooded. 'I never heard of such rubbish. How do they expect us to do our job?' she muttered, and brooded some more.

When Phyllis said 'our job' the words did not connote exactly what they would have implied a few days before. The job had somehow changed quality under our feet. The task of persuading the public of the reality of the unseen, indescribable menace had turned suddenly into one of keeping up morale in the face of a menace which everyone now accepted to the point of panic. EBC ran a feature called News-Parade in which we appeared to have assumed, as far as we understood the position, the roles of Special Oceanic Correspondents, without being quite sure how it had occurred. In point of fact, Phyllis had never been on the EBC staff, and I had technically left it when I ceased, officially, to have an office there some two years before; nobody, however, seemed to be aware of this except the Accounts Department which now paid by the piece instead of by the month. We had been briefed together on this change to a morale-sustaining angle by a director who was clearly under the impression that we were a part of his staff. The whole situation was anomalous, but not unrewarding. All the same, there was not going to be much freshness of treatment in our assignment if we could get no nearer to the sources than official handouts. Phyllis was still brooding about it when I left her to go back to the office I officially didn't have in EBC.

She rang me up there about five.

'Darling,' she said, 'you have invited Dr Matet to dine with you at your club at seven-thirty to-morrow evening. I shall be there, too. I explained how it was, and he quite agreed that it was a lot of nonsense. I tried to get Captain Winters to come as well, as he's a friend of his – he thought it was a lot of nonsense, too, but he said the Service was the Service, and he'd better not come, so I'm having lunch with him to-morrow. You don't mind?'

'I don't quite see why the Service should be less the Service *tête-à-tête*,' I told her, 'but I appreciate the Matet move. So, darling, you may pat yourself on the back because this town must now be full of assorted ographers that he's not set eyes on for years.'

'He'll be seeing plenty of them by day,' Phyllis said, modestly.

This time there was no need for Phyllis to coax Dr Matet. He started off like a man with a mission, over sherries in the bar.

'The Service makes its own rules, of course,' he said, 'but no pledges were required from the rest of us, so I choose to regard myself as at liberty to discuss the proceedings – I think it's a duty to let people know all the main facts. You've heard the official pronouncement, of course?'

We had. It amounted to little more than advice to all shipping to keep clear of the major Deeps when possible, until further notice. One imagined that many masters would already have taken this decision for themselves, but now they would at least have official advice to quote in any argument with their owners.

'Not very specific,' I told him. 'One of our draughtsmen for television has produced a work of bathymetric – or do I mean hydrographic? – art showing areas over twenty thousand feet. Very pleased with it, he was, but last seen tearing his hair because someone had told him that it's not technically a Deep unless it's over twenty-five thousand.'

'For present purposes the danger area is being reckoned as anything over four thousand,' said Dr Matet.

'*What?*' I exclaimed, wildly.

'Fathoms,' added Dr Matet.

'Twenty-four thousand feet, darling. You multiply by six,' said Phyllis, kindly. She ignored my thanks, and went on to Dr Matet:

'And what depth did you advise as marking the danger area, Doctor?'

'How do you know I did not advise four thousand fathoms, Mrs Watson?'

'Use of the passive, Doctor Matet – "is being reckoned,"' Phyllis told him, smiling sweetly.

'And there are people who claim that French is the subtle language,' he said. 'Well, I'll admit that I recommended that three thousand five hundred should be regarded as the safe maximum, but the shipping interests were all for keeping the extra distances involved as low as possible.'

'Isn't this supposed to be a *Naval* Conference?' Phyllis asked.

'Oh, they have the real say on strategy, of course, but this was in the first general session. And, anyway, the Navies agreed. You see, the more sea they declare unsafe, the worse it is for their prestige.'

'Oh, dear. Oh, dear. Is it going to be one of *those* Conferences?' said Phyllis.

'Less so than most, I hope,' Dr Matet replied.

We went in to dinner. Phyllis prattled lightly through the soup, and then steered gracefully back to the topic.

'The first time I came to see you was about that ooze that was coming up into currents – and you were dreadfully careful. What did you really think then?'

He smiled. 'The same as I think now – that if you get yourself made a kind of mental outlaw, you also make your purposes very much harder to attain. Poor old Bocker – though everybody's had to come round to accepting the second part of his contention now, yet he's still out beyond the Pale. I could not afford to say it, but I believed then that he was right about the mining. One could think of nothing else that would account for it, so, as the genius of Baker Street once remarked to your husband's namesake – '

I headed him off: 'But you didn't want to join Bocker in the wilderness.'

'I did not. Nor have I been by any means the only one. Bocker's miscarriage warned us all to allow full gestation. Incidentally, I suppose you know that there have been further discolorations of currents, and that those first discoloured have returned to normal?'

'Yes, Captain Winters told me. What do you think would cause that?' Phyllis asked, just as one might who had not immediately rung up Bocker the moment she heard it, to demand an explanation.

'Well, pursuing the mining theory, one would suggest that all the loose sediment near the scene of operations would gradually be washed away. Imagine sticking the end of a suction-pipe into sand. At first you'd get sand coming through it, and you'd create a funnel-shaped depression. After a while you'd reach rock, but there'd still be some sand trickling down the sides of your depression, and having to be sucked clear. In time, however, your depression would be of such a shape that very little sand – which, of course, represents the sedimental ooze – would trickle down, and you would be able to work on the cleared rock-face without disturbing the surrounding sand, or ooze, at all.

'But, of course, on the sea-bed the scale of such an operation would be immense, and a colossal quantity of ooze would have to be shifted before you could get to a rock-face that would remain clear. It would certainly be better to mine horizontally where possible. Once work on the rock itself had begun, the detritus would be too heavy to rise more than a few hundred feet before it began to settle, so the surface-water would no longer be discoloured.'

No one observing Phyllis's rapt attention would have suspected that she had already made use of this theory in a script.

'I see. You make it easy to understand, Doctor. Then the various discolorations will have enabled you to locate quite closely where this mining is going on?'

'With reasonable accuracy, I think,' he agreed. 'And so, of course. those spots become priority targets – in fact, to be honest, the only closely-localized targets, so far.'

'There'll be an attack on them, then? Soon?' Phyllis asked.

He shook his head. 'Not my side of things, but I imagine that any delay will be due simply to technical reasons. How much of the sea can we afford to poison with atomic weapons? Are we to risk ships on the task? Or how long will it take to construct a depth-bomb light enough for air transport? The others have been exceedingly heavy, you know. There must be quite a number of points of that kind.'

'And that is all we can do as a counter-attack?' said Phyllis.

'All that I have heard of,' Dr Matet told her, cautiously. 'The emphasis at the moment is naturally defensive, and on securing safety for ships. There again, that's not my department at all: I can only give you what I have picked up.' And he went on to do so.

It was generally agreed, it seemed, that ships were liable to two forms of attack (three forms if one included electrification, but this had occurred only to ships using cables at considerable depths for grappling or other purposes, and could be disregarded as far as the rest were concerned). Neither of these weapons was explosive: the explosions suffered by some of the ships were almost certainly due to their own boilers blowing up when the stokeholds were flooded, for there had been no similar explosions with the motor-vessels that had been lost.

One of the weapons appeared to be vibratory and capable of setting up sympathetic vibrations of such intensity in the attacked craft that she literally shook herself to pieces in a minute or two. The other was less obscure in its nature, but even more puzzling in its capacity. It was undoubtedly some contrivance which attacked the hull below the waterline. There were several obvious ways in which a device could be made to do this: what was less comprehensible was its method of assault, since the rapidity with which its victims sank, the fact that the air trapped in the hull blew the decks upwards, and various other effects, all tended to suggest some instrument that was capable, not simply of holing a ship, but of something that must be very like slicing the bottom clean off her.

Even before the Conference had begun Bocker had suggested that these devices might be found to form strategic barrages, or minefields, about certain deep areas, and might very well be regarded as perimeter defences. There would, he pointed out, be no great difficulty in constructing a mechanism to lurk inertly at any predetermined depth, and become active only on the approach of a ship – that, indeed, had been the principle of both the acoustic and magnetic mines. But on the means by which it could be made to slice through the hull of a ship with, apparently, the efficiency of a wire through cheese, even Bocker had no suggestions to make.

No one had disagreed with this, in general, but neither had anyone as yet been able to amplify it. The suddenness and success of the attacks, the small numbers of the survivors and the loose quality of their accounts gave very little data.

'To my mind,' said Dr Matet, 'the important thing at the moment is to get across to the public that the danger is not incomprehensible, and so stop this silly panicking – for which we may blame the Stock Exchanges more than any other persons or institutions. The attack comes from an utterly unexpected direction, it is true, but, like any other, it can and will be met, and the sooner people can be made to realize that it is simply a matter of finding a counter to a new kind of weapon, the sooner they'll cool off. I gather your job is to cool them off, so that is why I decided to tell you all this. In a few days I imagine there will be quite full and frank reports from the various Committees that are now being set up – once they have been brought to realize that here, at least, is one war in which there are no enemy spies listening.' And on that note we parted.

Phyllis and I did our best during the next few days to play our part in putting across the idea of firm hands steady on the wheel, and of the backroom boys who had produced radar, asdic, and other marvels nodding confidently, and saying in effect: 'Sure. Just give us a few days to think, and we'll knock together something that will settle this lot!' There was a satisfactory feeling that confidence was gradually being restored.

Perhaps the main stabilizing factor, however, emerged from a difference of opinion on one of the Technical Committees.

General agreement had been reached that a torpedo-like weapon designed to give submerged escort to a vessel could profitably be developed to counter the assumed mine-form of attack. The motion was accordingly put that all should pool information likely to help in the development of such a weapon.

The Russian delegation demurred. Remote control of missiles, they pointed out, was, of course, a Russian invention in any case; moreover, Russian scientists, zealous in the fight for Peace, had already developed such control to a degree greatly in advance of that achieved by the capitalist-ridden science of the West. It could scarcely be expected of the Soviets that they should make a present of their discoveries to warmongers.

The Western spokesman replied that, while respecting the intensity of the fight for Peace and the fervour with which it was being carried on in every department of Soviet science, except, of course, the biological, the West would remind the Soviets that this was a conference of peoples faced by a common danger and resolved to meet it by co-operation.

The Russian leader responded frankly that he doubted whether, if the West had happened to possess a means of controlling a submerged missile by radio, such as had been invented by Russian engineers working under the inspiration of the world's greatest scientist, the late Josef Stalin, they would care to share such knowledge with the Soviet people.

The Western spokesman assured the Soviet representative that since the West had called the Conference for the purpose of co-operation, it felt in duty bound to state that it had indeed perfected such a means of control as the Soviet delegate had mentioned.

Following a hurried consultation, the Russian delegate announced that *if* he believed such a claim to be true, he would also know that it could only have come about through theft of the work of Soviet scientists by capitalist hirelings. And, since neither a lying claim nor the admission of successful espionage showed that disinterest in national advantage which the Conference had professed, his delegation was left with no alternative but to withdraw.

This action, with its reassuring ring of normality, exerted a valuable tranquillizing influence.

Concerning the less easily comprehensible vibratory weapon, it was announced that experiments with damping devices and counter-vibration fields had been begun, and were already showing hopeful results. The Conference appointed a Research and Co-ordination Committee to work in conjunction with Unesco, another for Naval Co-ordination, a Standing Committee for Action, several lesser Committees, and adjourned itself, *pro tem.*

Amid the widespread satisfaction and resuscitating confidence, the voice of Bocker, dissenting, rose almost alone: It was late, he proclaimed, but it still might not be too late for some kind of pacific approach to be made to the sources of the disturbance. They had already been shown to possess a technology equal to, if not superior to, our own. In an alarmingly short time they had been able not only to establish themselves, but to produce the means of taking effective action for their self-defence. In the face of such a beginning one was justified in regarding their powers with respect, and, for his part, with apprehension.

The very differences of environment that they required made it seem unlikely that human interests and those of these xenobathetic intelligences need seriously overlap. Before it should be altogether too late, the very greatest efforts should be made to establish communication with them in order to promote a state of compromise which would allow both parties to live peacefully in their separate spheres.

Very likely this was a sensible suggestion – though whether the attempt would ever have produced the desired result is a different matter. In circumstances where there was no will whatever to compromise, however, the only evidence that his appeal had been noticed at all was that the word, 'xenobathetic', and a derived noun, 'xenobath', began to be used in print.

'More honoured in the dictionary than in the observance,' remarked Bocker, with some bitterness. 'If it is Greek words they are interested in, there are others – Cassandra, for instance.'

The decision to avoid crossing the greater Deeps proved

wise. For several weeks not a ship was reported lost. The markets settled down, confidence became convalescent, and the passenger lists began to fill up again, though slowly. Delays and higher freight-rates were continuing effects, nevertheless there presently arose a disposition to feel that the long-suffering public had once again been stampeded by sensationalism, and the advertising departments of all journals threatened falling revenues unless a note of sprightly plerophory were maintained.

Meanwhile, the brains moiled in the backrooms, and after some four months the Admiralty were able to announce that when certain naval craft had been equipped with the new counter-devices a test would be held over the series of Deeps south of Cape Race, in the neighbourhood where the *Queen Anne* had been lost.

It is possible that the omission of the Press from the test-party was due to a lukewarm enthusiasm in demanding its rights. Certainly no representative of my acquaintance was genuinely burning to be included – or, it may have been that the authorities were disinclined to take greater risks than necessary. Whatever the cause, there was no correspondent further forward than the reserve ships. For first-hand accounts we had to depend on a somewhat inexpert running commentary, and the descriptions given later by the personnel of the test vessels.

Phyllis got herself an introduction to a young Lieutenant Royde, and worked on him. When he came back, we took him out to dinner, gave him some drinks, and listened.

'It turned out to be a piece of cake,' he assured us. 'Though, mind you, most of us were feeling pretty windy about it beforehand, and didn't mind admitting it.

'We all sailed together, and then hove-to some fifty miles short of the Deeps, and our party got its stuff all set up.

'The anti-vibration gadget is a bit wearing at first. In fact, anti- isn't quite the word I'd use because it sets up a constant hum which you can half-feel, half hear; but you get used to it after a time.

'The other gimmick is a tin fish that you sling overboard – a dolphin, they're calling it. It promptly makes away forward, and then settles down to travel about two hundred feet ahead of the ship at about five fathoms. It's under control, of course, but when it spots anything it flashes a signal on a screen, and goes for it automatically. What its spotting range is, *how* it spots, and just why it doesn't lash about and go for the parent ship isn't my pigeon. You'll have to ask the boffins if you want to know about that – but, in the rough, that's the way it works.

'Well, when it was all fixed, and the boffins had finished tearing round and testing everything in sight, we set off with the whole ship buzzing like a beehive and the dolphin leading the way, and none of us feeling too good in our bellies – anyway, I wasn't. Everybody wore jackets, and orders were for all personnel who hadn't duty below to keep on deck, just in case.

'For about three hours nothing happened, and the sea looked just like any other sea. Then, while we were wondering whether the whole thing was going to turn out phoney, a voice from the hailer said:

' "Number One dolphin away! Make ready Number Two dolphin!"

'The dolphin party had just time to get Number Two swung out when Number One got home. And did it get home! By the record, it contacted whatever it was after at around thirty-five fathoms. When it blew, what we saw was several acres of sea going up in the air off the port bow. We raised a bit of a cheer. The hailer came through with:

' "Lower away there Number Two dolphin. Stand by Number Three dolphin."

'Dolphin Number Two went down in her sling, and ran away forward, and they hitched Number Three's sling ready.

'There was a boffin standing by me, looking pretty pleased with himself. He said:

' "Well, whatever it was, there was some pressure there. A dolphin going up on its own has about a quarter the punch of that."

'We kept steady on the same course, all looking out like hawks now, though there wasn't anything to be seen. After about five minutes the hailer said:

' "Dolphin away! Make ready Number Three dolphin!"

'It didn't take so long this time before another lot of sea went up with a woomph, and Number Three dolphin was lowered away.

'After that nothing happened for quite a while. Then the pitch of the humming that we'd got so used to that we didn't notice it began to change so that we *did* notice it. The boffin beside me gave a grunt and whipped back like a streak into a kind of float-off instrument-room they had rigged up on deck. You could feel a sort of trembling in the deck, and the humming kept on changing pitch, and everybody gave a hitch to his life-jacket, and got ready for something to happen.

'The thing that did happen was that Number Three dolphin way ahead of us blew up. It was a far smaller blow than the others had been, and they reckon it was just the vibrations that set her off. She certainly didn't go for anything. The hailer started to order out Number Four dolphin, and in the middle of that an excited boffin bounced out of the instrument-room and ordered the depth-charge-thrower to work. It lobbed off a couple of spherical containers which just sank. We kept on waiting for a couple of bangs until we realized that they weren't going to come. And that was roughly that.

'After a bit the humming settled down to what it had been before, and there was a noise of uproarious boffins slapping one another on the back in the instrument-room.

'We altered course to the north. About an hour later Number Four dolphin went up with a thundering good wham. The boffins, all of them pretty tight by this time, tumbled out on deck to cheer and sing *Steamboat Bill,* and that was about the end of it. We still had Number Five dolphin running serenely ahead of us when we reckoned we were clear of the area.'

A nice lad, Lieutenant Royde, but not, perhaps, a source of technical information. However, it was eye-witness stuff we were after. We knew in a general way how the 'dolphins' worked, and we had heard that the spheres launched by the mine-thrower were intended to home on the source of the vibrations, and were capable of reaching far greater depths than the dolphins. Even if it had been explained to us exactly how they did it we should probably not have understood.

The effects of the successful tests were immediate. There was an overwhelming demand for the defensive gear, and shipping shares began to rally. Freights, however, remained high. There was the cost of the gear to be covered, consumption of dolphins to be offset, and it would take some time before all cargo vessels could be equipped and revert to their normal courses. Meanwhile, the price of everything went up.

Progress in equipment was such, however, that six months later it was possible for London and Washington to speak optimistically. The Prime Minister announced to the House:

'The Battle of the Deeps has been won. Our ships, which we had to divert, are able once more to ply upon their usual courses.

'But we have seen before, and we must remember, that to win a battle is not of necessity to win a war. These menaces that have for a time played the highwayman upon our vital sea-lanes and caused us such grievous losses, these menaces still remain. And, as long as they remain, they are a potential danger.

'We cannot afford, therefore, any slackening of effort in combating them. We must use all our capacities and our wits to find out more, everything we can, about this peril that is lurking beneath our seas. For still, and in spite of the fact that we have won this battle, we know virtually nothing of it, save that it exists. No one – no one can describe these creatures – if creatures they are; no one, so far as we know, has ever seen them. To us, here in the sunlight, these creatures of the darkness and the depths, are still, anonymously and amorphously, "those things down there".

'When we know more about them, their nature, their strength, and, most importantly, their weaknesses: when, in fact, we have a full view of what we are about, then we shall be able to launch our attack upon this pestilence so that, with its utter destruction, our ships and our seamen shall be free to sail upon the high seas of the world facing only such perils as their gallant fathers faced before them.'

But, a month later, a dozen ships of various sizes were sunk in a week, four of them while attempting to rescue survivors of earlier disasters. The few men who were brought safely back could tell little, but from their accounts it appeared that the dolphins had operated successfully; the other gear for some reason had failed to prevent the ships shaking to pieces under their feet.

Official advice once more recommended that the neighbourhoods of all the greater Deeps should be avoided pending further investigations.

Hard on that, but with a significance that was not immediately recognized, came the news first from Saphira, and then from April Island.

Saphira, a Brazilian island in the Atlantic, lies a little south of the Equator and some four hundred miles south-east of the larger island of Fernando de Noronha. In that isolated spot a population of a hundred or so lived in primitive conditions, largely on its own produce, content to get along in its own way, and little interested in the rest of the world. It is said that the original settlers were a small party who, arriving on account of a shipwreck some time in the eighteenth century, remained perforce. By the time they were discovered they had settled to the island life and already become interestingly inbred. In due course, and without knowing or caring much about it, they had ceased to be Portuguese and become technically Brazilian citizens, and a token connexion with their foster-mother country was maintained by a ship which called at roughly six-monthly intervals to do a litle barter.

Normally, the visiting ship had only to sound its siren, and the Saphirans would come hurrying out of their cottages down to the minute quay where their few fishing boats lay, to form a reception committee which included almost the entire population. On this occasion, however, the hoot of the siren echoed emptily back and forth in the little bay, and set the sea-birds wheeling in flocks, but no Saphiran appeared at the cottage doors. The ship hooted again, but still there was no sign of anyone making for the quay. There was no response whatever, save from the sea-birds.

The coast of Saphira slopes steeply. The ship was able to approach to within a cable's length of the shore, but there was nobody to be seen – nor, still more ominously, was there any trace of smoke from the cottages' chimneys.

A boat was lowered and a party, with the mate in charge, rowed ashore. They made fast to a ringbolt and climbed the stone steps up to the little quay. They stood there in a bunch, listening and wondering. There was not a sound to be heard but the cry of the sea-birds and the lapping of the water.

'Must've made off, the lot of 'em. Their boats's gone,' said one of the sailors, uneasily.

'Huh,' said the mate. He took a deep breath, and gave a mighty hail, as though he had greater faith in his own lungs than in the ship's siren.

They listened for an answer, but none came, save the sound of the mate's voice echoing faintly back to them across the bay.

'Huh,' said the mate again. 'Better take a look.'

The uneasiness which had come over the party kept them together. They followed him in a bunch as he strode towards the nearest of the small, stone-built cottages. The door was standing half-open. He pushed it back.

'Phew!' he said.

Several putrid fish decomposing on a dish accounted for the smell. Otherwise the place was tidy and, by Saphiran standards, reasonably clean. There were no signs of disorder or hasty packing-up. In the inner room the beds were made up, ready to be slept in. The occupant might have been gone only a matter of a few hours, but for the fish and the lack of warmth in the turf-fire ashes.

In the second and third cottages there was the same air of unpremeditated absence. In the fourth they found a dead baby in its cradle in the inner room. The party returned to the ship, puzzled and subdued.

The situation was reported by radio to Rio. Rio in its reply suggested a thorough search of the island. The crew started on the task with reluctance and a tendency to keep in close groups, but, as nothing fearsome revealed itself, gradually gained confidence.

On the second day of their three-day search they discovered a party of four women and six children in two caves on a hillside. All had been dead for some weeks, apparently from starvation. By the end of the third day they were satisfied that if there were any living person left, he must be deliberately in hiding. It was only then, on comparing notes, that they realized also that there could not be more than a dozen sheep and two or three dozen goats left out of the island's normal flocks of some hundreds.

They buried the bodies they had found, radioed a full report to Rio, and then put to sea again, leaving Saphira, with its few surviving animals, to the sea-birds.

In due course the news came through from the agencies and won an inch or two of space here and there. Two newspapers bestowed on Saphira the nickname of *Marie Celeste* Island, but failed at the time to inquire further into the matter.

The April Island affair was set in quite a different key, and might have continued undiscovered for some time but for the coincidence of official interest in the place.

The interest stemmed from the existence of a group of Javanese malcontents variously described as smugglers, terrorists, communists, patriots, fanatics, gangsters, or merely rebels who, whatever their true affiliations, operated upon a troublesome scale. In due course the Indonesian police had tracked them down and destroyed their headquarters, with which loss went much of the prestige which had enabled them to dominate and extort support from several square miles of territory. In the dispersal which resulted, most of the rank and file following melted swiftly away into more conventional occupations: but, for two dozen moving spirits with varying prices on their heads, disappearance was less easy.

In difficult terrain and with small forces at their disposal the Indonesian authorities did not pursue them, but awaited the arrival of the informer who, sooner or later, would be tempted by easy money. In the course of a few months several informers applied; none, however, collected the rewards, for on each occasion the government party arrived only to find that the outlaws had moved on. After several such expeditions, informing fell off. No more was heard of the trouble-makers, who seemed to have vanished for good.

About a year after the dispersal, a trading-steamer put in to Jakarta carrying a native who had an interesting tale to tell the authorities there. He came, it appeared, from April Island which lies south of the Sunda Strait, and at no great distance from the British possession of Christmas Island. According to him, April Island had been pursuing its normal and not very arduous life in its immemorial manner until some six months previously when a party of eighteen men had arrived in a small motor-vessel. They had immediately introduced themselves as the new administration of the island, taken charge of the only small radio transmitter, posted up new laws and regulations, ordered that houses should be built for them, and helped themselves to wives. After the salutary shooting of a few persons who raised objections, a régime of a severely feudal type set in and was, so far as the informant knew, still in operation. Possible trouble with infrequently visiting ships was forestalled by coralling a number of the inhabitants under the muzzles of rifles as hostages. This, since the invaders' trigger-fingers were well known to work with very slight provocation, had been effective, and the vessels had left again without suspecting that anything was amiss.

The informant himself had succeeded in hiding a canoe and getting away by night. He had been trying to reach the mainland in order to question the authenticity of this unpopular form of administration when he had been picked up by the steamer.

A few questions and his descriptions of the invaders satisfied the Jakarta authorities that they were once more on the track of their malcontents, and a small gunboat, flying the flag of the Indonesian Republic, was commissioned to deal with them.

In order to minimize the risk of a number of innocent people dying by the hostage technique the approach to April Island was made by night. Under starlight the gunboat stole stealthily into a little-used bay which was masked from the main village by a headland. There, a well-armed party, accompanied by the informant who was to act as their guide, was put ashore with the task of taking the village by surprise. The gunboat then drew off, moved a little way along the coast, and lay in lurk behind the point of the headland until the landing party should summon her to come in and dominate the situation.

Three-quarters of an hour had been the length of time estimated for the party's crossing of the isthmus, and then perhaps another ten or fifteen minutes for its disposal of itself about the village. It was, therefore, with concern that after only forty minutes had passed the men aboard the gunboat heard the first burst of automatic fire, succeeded presently by several more.

With the element of surprise lost, the Commander ordered full speed ahead, but even as the boat surged forward the sound of firing was drowned by a dull, reverberating boom. The crew of the gunboat looked at one another with raised eyebrows: the landing-party had carried no higher forms of lethalness than automatic rifles and grenades. There was a pause, then the automatic rifles started hammering again. This time, it continued longer in intermittent bursts until it was ended again by a similar boom.

The gunboat rounded the headland. In the dim light it was impossible to make out anything that was going on in the village two miles away. For the moment all there was dark. Then a twinkling broke out, and another, and the sound of firing reached them again. The gunboat, continuing at full speed, switched on her searchlight. The village and the trees behind it sprang into sudden miniature existence. No figures were visible among the houses. The only sign of activity was some froth and commotion in the water, a few yards out from the edge. Some claimed afterwards to have seen a dark, humped shape showing above the water a little to the right of it.

As close inshore as she dared go the gunboat put her engines astern, and hove-to in a flurry. The searchlight played back and forth over the huts and their surroundings. Everything lit by the beam had hard lines, and seemed endowed with a curious glistening quality. The man on the Oerlikons followed the beam, his fingers ready on the triggers. The light made a few more slow sweeps and then stopped. It was trained on several sub-machine-guns lying on the sand, close to the water's edge.

A stentorian voice from the hailer called the landing-party from cover. Nothing stirred. The searchlight roved again, prying between the huts, among the trees. Nothing moved there. The patch of light slid back across the beach and steadied upon the abandoned arms. The silence seemed to deepen.

The Commander refused to allow landing until daylight. The gunboat dropped anchor. She rode there for the rest of the night, her searchlight making the village look like a stage-set upon which at any moment the actors might appear, but never did.

When there was full daylight the First Officer, with a party of five armed men, rowed cautiously ashore under cover from the ship's Oerlikons. They landed close to the abandoned arms, and picked them up to examine them. All the weapons were covered with a thin slime. The men put them in the boat, and then washed their hands clean of the stuff.

The beach was scored in four places by broad furrows leading from the water's edge towards the huts. They were something over eight feet wide, and curved in section. The depth in the middle was five or six inches; the sand at the edges was banked up a trifle above the level of the surrounding beach. Some such track, the First Officer thought, might have been left if a large boiler had been dragged across the foreshore. Examining them more closely he decided from the lie of the sand that though one of the tracks led towards the water, the other three undoubtedly emerged from it. It was a discovery which caused him to look at the village with increased wariness. As he did so, he became aware that the scene which had glistened oddly in the searchlight was still glistening oddly. He regarded it curiously for some minutes without learning more. Then he shrugged. He tucked the butt of his sub-machine-gun comfortably under his right arm, and slowly, with his eyes flicking right and left for the least trace of movement, he led his party up the beach.

The village was formed of a semi-circle of huts of various sizes fringing upon an open space, and as they drew closer the reason for the glistening look became plain. The ground, the huts themselves, and the surrounding trees, too, all had a thin coating of the slime which had been on the guns.

The party kept steadily, slowly on until they reached the centre of the open space. There they paused, bunched together, facing outwards, examining each foot of cover closely. There was no sound, no movement but a few fronds stirring gently in the morning breeze. The men began to breathe more evenly.

The First Officer removed his gaze from the huts, and examined the ground about them. It was littered with a wide scatter of small metal fragments, most of them curved, all of them shiny with the slime. He turned one over curiously with the toe of his boot, but it told him nothing. He looked about them again, and decided on the largest hut.

'We'll search that,' he said.

The whole front of its glistened stickily. He pushed the un-fastened door open with his foot, and led the way inside. There was little disturbance; only a couple of overturned stools suggested a hurried exit. No one, alive or dead, remained in the place.

They came out again. The First Officer glanced at the next hut, then he paused, and looked at it more closely. He went round to examine the side of the hut they had already entered. The wall there was quite dry and clear of slime. He considered the surroundings again.

'It looks,' he said, 'as if everything had been sprayed with this muck by something in the middle of the clearing.'

A more detailed examination supported the idea, but took them little further.

'But how?' the officer asked, meditatively. 'Also what? And why?'

'Something came out of the sea,' said one of his men, looking back uneasily towards the water.

'Some things – three of them,' the First Officer corrected him. They returned to the middle of the open semi-circle. It was clear that the place was deserted, and there did not seem to be much more to be learned there at present.

'Collect a few of these bits of metal – they may mean something to somebody,' the officer instructed.

He himself went across to one of the huts, found an empty bottle, scraped some of the slime into it, and corked it up.

'This stuff's beginning to stink now the sun's getting at it,' he said, on his return. 'We might as well clear out. There's nothing we can do here.'

Back on board, he suggested that a photographer should take pictures of the furrows on the beach, and showed the Commander his trophies, now washed clean of the slime.

'Queer stuff,' he said, holding a piece of the thick, dull metal. 'A shower of it around.' He tapped it with a knuckle. 'Sounds like lead; weighs like feathers. Cast, by the look of it. Ever seen anything like that, sir?'

The Commander shook his head. He observed that the world seemed to be full of strange alloys these days.

Presently the photographer came rowing back from the beach. The Commander decided:

'We'll give 'em a few blasts on the siren. If nobody shows up in half an hour we'd better make a landing some other place and find a local inhabitant who can tell us what the hell goes on.'

A couple of hours later the gunboat cautiously nosed her way into a bay on the north-east coast of April Island. A similar though smaller village stood there in a clearing, close to the water's edge. The similarity was uncomfortably emphasized by an absence of life as well as by a beach displaying four broad furrows to the water's edge.

Closer investigation, however, showed some differences: of these furrows, two had been made by some objects ascending the beach; the other two by, apparently, the same objects *de-*

scending it. There was no trace of the slime either in or about the deserted village.

The Commander frowned over his charts. He indicated another bay.

'All right. We'll try there, then,' he said.

This time there were no furrows to be seen on the beach, though the village was just as thoroughly deserted. Again the gunboat's siren gave a forlorn, unheeded wail. They examined the scene through glasses, then the First Officer, scanning the neighbourhood more widely, gave an exclamation.

'There's a fellow up on that hill there, sir. Waving a shirt, or something.'

The Commander turned his own glasses that way.

'Two or three others, a bit to the left of him, too.'

The gunboat gave a couple of hoots, and moved closer inshore. The boat was lowered.

'Stand off a bit till they come,' the Commander directed. 'Find out whether there's been an epidemic of some kind before you try to make contact.'

He watched from his bridge. In due course a party of natives, eight or nine strong, appeared from the trees a couple of hundred yards east of the village, and hailed the boat. It moved in their direction. Some shouting and counter-shouting between the two parties ensued, then the boat went in and grounded on the beach. The First Officer beckoned the natives with his arm, but they hung back in the fringe of the trees. Eventually the First Officer jumped ashore and walked across the strand to talk to them. An animated discussion took place. Clearly an invitation to some of them to visit the gunboat was being declined with vigour. Presently the First Officer descended the beach alone, and the landing-party headed back.

'What's the trouble there?' the Commander inquired as the boat came alongside.

The First Officer looked up.

'They won't come, sir.'

'What's the matter with them?'

'They're okay themselves, sir, but they say the sea isn't safe.'

'They can see it's safe enough for us. What do they mean?'

'They say several of the shore villages have been attacked, and they think theirs may be at any moment.'

'Attacked! What by?'

'Er – perhaps if you'd come and talk to them yourself, sir – ?'

'I sent a boat so that they could come to me – that ought to be good enough for them.'

'I'm afraid thev'll not come, short of force, sir.'

The Commander frowned. '*That* scared are they? What's been doing this attacking?'

The First Officer moistened his lips; his eyes avoided his commander's.

'They – er, they say – whales. sir.'

The Commander stared at him.

'They say – *what?*' he demanded.

The First Officer looked unhappy.

'Er – I know, sir But that's what they keep on *saying*. Er – whales, and er – giant jelly-fish. I really think that if you'd speak to them yourself, sir – ?'

*

The news about April Island did not exactly 'break' in the accepted sense. A curious going-on on an atoll which could not even be found in most atlases had, on the face of it, little news value, and the odd line or two which recorded the matter was allowed to slip past. Possibly it would not have attracted attention or been remembered until much later, if at all, but for the chance that an American journalist who happened to be in Jakarta discovered the story for himself, took a speculative trip to April Island, and wrote the affair up for a weekly magazine.

A pressman, reading it, recalled the Saphira incident, linked the two, and splashed a new peril across a Sunday newspaper. It happened that this preceded by one day the most sensational communiqué yet issued by the Standing Committee for Action, with the result that the Deeps had the big headlines once more. Moreover the term 'Deeps' was more comprehensive than formerly, for it was announced that shipping losses in the last month had been so heavy, and the areas in which they had occurred so much more extensive that, pending the development of a more efficient means of defence, all vessels were strongly advised to avoid crossing deep water and keep, as far as was practicable, to the areas of the Continental Shelves.

It was obvious that the Committee would not have dealt such a blow to recovering confidence in shipping without the gravest reasons. Nevertheless, the answering outburst of indignation from the shipping interests accused it of everything from sheer alarmism to a vested interest in air-lines. To follow such advice, they protested, would mean routing transatlantic liners into Iceland and Greenland waters, creeping coastwise down the Bay of Biscay and the West African coast, etc. Transpacific commerce would become impossible, and Australia and New Zealand, isolated. It showed a shocking and lamentable lack of a sense of responsibility that the Committee should be allowed to advise, in this way, and without full consultation with all interested parties, these panic-inspired measures which would, if heeded, bring the maritime commerce of the world virtually to a stop. Advice which could never be implemented should never have been given.

The Committee hedged slightly under the attack. It had not ordered, it said. It had simply suggested that wherever possible vessels should attempt to avoid crossing any extensive stretch of water where the depth was greater than two thousand fathoms and thus avoid exposing itself to danger unnecessarily.

This, retorted the shipowners, curtly, was virtually putting the same thing in different words; and their case, though not their cause, was upheld by the publication in almost every newspaper of sketch-maps showing hurried and somewhat varied impressions of the two-thousand fathom line.

Before the Committee was able to re-express itself in still different words the Italian liner, *Sabina,* and the German liner, *Vorpommern,* disappeared on the same day – the one in mid-Atlantic, the other in the South Atlantic – and reply became superfluous.

The news of the latest sinking was announced on the 8 a.m.

news bulletin on a Saturday. The Sunday papers took full advantage of their opportunity. At least six of them slashed at official incompetence with almost eighteenth-century gusto, and set the pitch for the Dailies. *The Times* screwed down rebukes to make the juice run out. The *Guardian*'s approach was similar in intention, but more like an advancing set of circular-saws in manner. The *News-Chronicle*'s was not unlike, though with the teeth set slightly wider apart. The *Express* turned its hammer from the forging of imperial links to flailing those whose ineptitudes were now weakening them. The *Mail* denounced the failure to rule the seas as supreme treachery, and demanded the impeachment of the saboteurs, omissive and commissive. The *Herald* told the housewife that the price of food would rise. The *Worker,* after pointing out that in a properly ordered society such tragedies would have been impossible since luxury liners would not exist and therefore could not be sunk, rounded upon owners who drove seamen into danger in unprotected ships at inadequate wages.

On the Wednesday I rang up Phyllis.

It used to come upon her periodically when we had had a longer spell than usual in London that she could not stand the works of civilization any longer without a break for refresh-ment. If it happened that I were free, I was allowed along, too; if not, she withdrew to commune with nature on her own. As a rule, she returned spiritually refurbished in the course of a week or so. This time, however, the communion had already been going on for almost a fortnight, and there was still no sign of the postcard which customarily preceded her return by a short head, when it did not come on the following day.

The telephone down in Rose Cottage rang forlornly for some time. I was on the point of giving up when she answered it.

'Hullo, darling!' said her voice.

'I might have been the butcher, or the income-tax,' I reproved her.

'They'd have given up more quickly. Sorry I was so long answering. I was busy outside.'

'Digging the garden?' I asked, hopefully.

'No, as a matter of fact. I was bricklaying.'

'This line's not good. It sounded like bricklaying.'

'It was, darling.'

'Oh,' I said. 'Bricklaying.'

'It's very fascinating when you get into it. Did you know there are all kinds of bonds and things; Flemish Bond, and English Bond, and so on? And you have things called "headers" and other things called – '

'What is this, darling? A tool-shed, or something?'

'No. Just a wall, like Balbus and Mr Churchill. I read somewhere that in moments of stress Mr Churchill used to find that it gave him tranquillity, and I thought that anything that could tranquillize Mr Churchill was probably worth following up.'

'Well, I hope it has cured the stress.'

'Oh, it has. It's very soothing. I love the way when you put the brick down the mortar squudges out at the sides and you – '

'Darling, the minutes are ticking up. I rang you up to say that you are wanted here.'

'That's sweet of you, darling. But leaving a job half – '

'It's not me – I mean – it is me, but not only. The EBC wants a word with us.'

'What about?'

'I don't really know. They're being cagey, but insistent.'

'Oh. When do they want to see us?'

'Freddy suggested dinner on Friday. Can you manage that?' There was a pause.

'Yes. I think I'll be able to finish. All right. I'll be on that train that gets into Paddington about six.'

'Good. I'll meet it. There is the other reason, too, Phyl.'

'It being?'

'The running sand, darling. The unturned coverlet. The tarnished thimble. The dull, unflavoured drops from life's clepsydra. The – '

'Mike, you've been rehearsing.'

'What else had I to do?'

'Couldn't you have taken Mildred out to dinner?'

'I tried that. And she does begin to grow on one as one sees more of her. It's surprising, really. All the same – '

'Mike, I happen to know that Mildred has been in Scotland for the last three weeks.'

'Oh, did you say Mildred? I thought – '

'Come off it, darling. See you Friday.'

'I shall hold my breath until then,' I assured her.

We were only twenty minutes late, but Freddy Whittier might have been desiccating for some hours from the urgency with which we were swept into the bar. He disappeared into the mob round the counter with a nicely-controlled violence and presently emerged with a selection of double and single sherries on a tray.

'Doubles first,' he said.

Soon his mind broadened out of the single track. He looked more himself, and noticed things. He even noticed Phyllis's hands; the abraded knuckles on the right, the large piece of plaster on the left. He frowned and seemed about to speak, but thought better of it. I observed him covertly examining my face and then my hands.

'My wife,' I explained, 'has been down in the country. The start of the bricklaying season, you know.'

He looked relieved rather than interested.

'Nothing wrong with the old team spirit?' he inquired with a casual air.

We shook our heads.

'Good,' he said, 'because I've got a job for you two.'

He went on to expound. It seemed that one of EBC's favourite sponsors had put a proposition to them. This sponsor had apparently been feeling for some time that a description, some photographs, and definite evidence of the nature of the Deeps creatures was well overdue.

'A man of perception,' I said. 'For the last five or six years – '

'Shut up, Mike,' said my dear wife, briefly.

'Things,' Freddy went on, 'have in his opinion now reached a pass where he might as well spend some of his money while it still has value, and might even bring in some valuable information. At the same time, he doesn't see why he shouldn't get some benefit out of the information if it is forthcoming. So he proposes to fit out and send out an expedition to find out what it can – and of course the whole thing will be tied up with exclusive rights and so on. By the way, this is highly confidential: we don't want the BBC to get on to it first.'

'Look, Freddy,' I said. 'For several years now everybody has been trying to get on to it, let alone the BBC. What the – ?'

'Expedition where to?' asked Phyllis, practically.

'That,' said Freddy, 'was naturally our first question. But he doesn't know. The whole decision on a location is in Bocker's hands.'

'Bocker!' I exclaimed. 'Is he becoming un-untouchable, or something?'

'His stock has recovered quite a bit,' Freddy admitted. 'And, as this fellow, the sponsor, said: If you leave out all the outer-space nonsense, the rest of Bocker's pronouncements have had a pretty high score – higher than anyone else's, anyway. So he went to Bocker, and said: "Look here. These things that came up on Saphira and April Island; where do you think they are most likely to appear next – or, at any rate, soon?" Bocker wouldn't tell him, of course. But they walked; and the upshot was that the sponsor will subsidize an expedition led by Bocker to a region to be selected by Bocker. What is more, Bocker also selects the personnel. And part of the selection, the EBC's blessing and your approval, could be you two.'

'He was always my favourite ographer,' said Phyllis. 'When do we start?'

'Wait a minute,' I put in. 'Once upon a time an ocean voyage used to be recommended for the health. Recently, however, so far from being healthy – '

'Air,' said Freddy. 'Exclusively air. People have doubtless got a lot of personal information about the things the other way, but we would prefer you to be in a position to bring it back.'

'Such thoughtfulness is greatly appreciated,' I assured him.

'Good. Well, go and talk it over with Bocker to-morrow,

and then come round to my office and we'll go into contracts
and all the rest of it.'

Phyllis wore an abstracted air at intervals during the evening.
When we got home I said:

'If you'd rather not take this up –'

'Nonsense. Of course we're going,' she said. 'But do you
think "subsidize" means we can get suitable clothes and things
on expenses?'

*

'Even,' I said, surveying the scene, 'even a diet of lotuses can
pall.'

'I like idleness – in the sun,' said Phyllis.

I reflected. 'I think it is more than that, more than just "like".
I mean,' I suggested, 'twentieth-century woman appears to
regard sunlight as a kind of cosmetic effulgence with a light
aphrodisiac content – which makes it a funny thing that none
of her female ancestors are recorded as seeing it the same way.
Men, of course, just go on sweating in it from century to
century.'

'Yes,' said Phyllis.

'You can't answer a whole observation like that with simply
"yes",' I pointed out.

'I have reached a comfortable stage of enervation where I
can say "yes" to practically anything. It is a well-known effect
of the tropics, often underlined by Mr Maugham.'

'Darling, Mr Maugham depends very largely on the wrong
people saying "yes", even outside the tropics. It is not so much
a matter of temperature as his system of triangulation, in which
he is second only to Euclid, another best-seller, by the way,
makes one wonder whether a trinitarian approach to litera-
ture –'

'Mike, you're rambling – that's probably the heat, too. Let's
just contemplate idly, shall we?'

So we resumed the occupation which had been the leading
eature of the last few weeks.

From where we sat at an umbrellaed table in front of the

mysteriously named Grand Hotel Britannia y la Justicia it was possible to direct this contemplation on tranquillity or activity. Tranquillity was on the right. Intensely blue water glittered for miles until it was ruled off by a hard, straight horizon line. The shore, running round like a bow, ended in a palm-tufted headland which trembled mirage-wise in the heat. A backcloth which must have looked just the same when it formed a part of the Spanish Main.

To the left was a display of life as conducted in the capital, and only town, of the island of Escondida.

The island's name derived, presumably, from erratic seamanship in the past which had caused ships to arrive mistakenly at one of the Caymans, but through all the vicissitudes of those parts it had managed to retain it, and much of its Spanishness, too. The houses looked Spanish, the temperament had a Spanish quality, in the language there was more Spanish than English, and, from where we were sitting at the corner of the open space known indifferently as the Plaza or the Square, the church at the far end with the bright market-stalls in front of it looked positively picture-book Spanish. The population, however, was somewhat less so, and ranged from sunburnt-white to coal-black. Only a bright-red British pillar-box prepared one for the surprise of learning that the place was called Smithtown – and even that took on romance when one learnt also that the Smith commemorated had been a pirate in a prosperous way.

Behind us, and therefore behind the hotel, one of the two mountains which make Escondida climbed steeply, emerging far above as a naked peak with a scarf of greenery about its shoulders. Between the mountain's foot and the sea stretched a tapering rocky shelf, with the town clustered on its wider end.

And there, also, had clustered for five weeks the Bocker Expedition.

Bocker had contrived a probability-system all his own. Eventually his eliminations had given him a list of ten islands as likely to be attacked, and the fact that four of them were in the Caribbean area settled our course.

That was about as far as he cared to go simply on paper, and it landed us all at Kingston, Jamaica. There we stayed a week in company with Ted Jarvey, the cameraman; Leslie Bray, the recordist; and Muriel Flynn, one of the technical assistants; while Bocker himself and his two male assistants flew about in an armed coastal-patrol aircraft put at his disposal by the authorities, and considered the rival attractions of Grand Cayman, Little Cayman, Cayman Brac, and Escondida. The reasoning which led to their final choice of Escondida was no doubt very nice, so that it seemed a pity that two days after the aircraft had finished ferrying us and our gear to Smithtown it should have been a large village on Grand Cayman which suffered the first visitation in those parts.

But if we were disappointed, we were also impressed. It was clear that Bocker really had been doing something more than a high-class eeny-meany-miny-mo, and had brought off a very near miss.

The plane took four of us over there as soon as we had the news. Unfortunately we learnt little. There were grooves on the beach, but they had been greatly trampled by the time we arrived. Out of two hundred and fifty villagers about a score had got away by fast running. The rest had simply vanished. The whole affair had taken place in darkness, so that no one had seen much. Each survivor felt an obligation to give any inquirer his money's worth, and the whole thing was almost folklore already.

Bocker announced that we should stay where we were. Nothing would be gained by dashing hither and thither; we should be just as likely to miss the occasion as to find it. Even more likely, for Escondida in addition to its other qualities had the virtue of being a one-town island so that when an attack did come (and he was sure that sooner or later it would) Smithtown must almost certainly be the objective.

We hoped he knew what he was doing, but in the next two weeks we doubted it. The radio brought reports of a dozen raids – all, save one small affair in the Azores, were in the Pacific. We began to have a depressed feeling that we were in the wrong hemisphere.

When I say 'we', I must admit I mean chiefly me. The others continued to analyse the reports and go stolidly ahead with their preparations. One point was that there was no record of an assault taking place by day; lights, therefore, would be necessary. Once the town council had been convinced that it would cost them nothing we were all impressed into the business of fixing improvised floods on trees, posts, and the corners of buildings all over Smithtown, though with greater proliferation towards the waterside, all of which, in the interests of Ted's cameras, had to be wired back to a switchboard in his hotel room.

The inhabitants assumed that a fiesta of some kind was in preparation; the council considered it a harmless form of lunacy but were pleased to be paid for the extra current we consumed, most of us were growing more cynical, until the affair at Gallows Island which, though Gallows was in the Bahamas, put the wind up the whole Caribbean, nevertheless.

Port Anne, the chief town on Gallows, and three large coastal villages there were raided the same night. About half the population of Port Anne, and a much higher proportion from the villages disappeared entirely. Those who survived had either shut themselves in their houses or run away, but this time there were plenty of people who agreed that they had seen things like tanks – like military tanks, they said, but larger – emerge from the water and come sliding up the beaches. Owing to the darkness, the confusion, and the speed with which most of the informants had either made off or hidden themselves, there were only imaginative reports of what these tanks from the sea had then done. The only verifiable fact was that from the four points of attack more than a thousand people in all had vanished during the night.

All around there was a prompt change of heart. Every islander in every island shed his indifference and sense of security, and was immediately convinced that his own home would be the next scene of assault. Ancient, uncertain weapons were dug out of cupboards, and cleaned up. Patrols were organized, and for the first night or two of their existence went on duty with a fine swagger. Talks on an inter-island flying defence system were proposed.

When, however, the next week went by without trace of further trouble anywhere in the area, enthusiasm waned. Indeed, for that week there was a pause in sub-sea activity all over. The only report of a raid came from the Kuriles, for some Slavonic reason, undated, and therefore assumed to have spent some time under microscope examination from every security angle.

By the tenth day after the alarm Escondida's natural spirit of mañana had fully reasserted itself. By night and siesta it slept soundly; the rest of the time it drowsed, and we with it. It was difficult to believe that we shouldn't go on like that for years, so we were settling down to it, some of us. Muriel explored happily among the island flora; Johnny Tallton, the pilot, who was constantly standing-by, did most of it in a café where a charming señorita was teaching him the patois; Leslie had also gone native to the extent of acquiring a guitar which we could now hear tinkling through the open window above us; Phyllis and I occasionally told one another about the scripts we might write if we had the energy; only Bocker and his two closest assistants, Bill Weyman and Alfred Haig, retained an air of purpose. If the sponsor could have seen us he might well have felt dubious about his money's worth.

While we still contemplated idly, Leslie's voice up above started on its repertoire with *O Sole Mio*. The other part of the repertoire, *La Paloma*, would undoubtedly follow. I groaned, and sipped at my gin-sling.

'I think,' said Phyllis, 'that while we are here we really ought to dig up – oh, dear – !'

Out of the street leading to the waterfront came a din with which the mere human voice could not compete. Presently a very small, coffee-coloured boy almost eclipsed by a very large hat emerged leading a yoke of rhythmically swaying oxen. Behind them a steel-shod mountain sledge clattered, squealed, and rasped on the cobbles. When it had descended, loaded with bananas, we had thought it noisy; now that it was unladen the row was fiendish. One could only wait while the oxen made their unhurried way across the Plaza. Presently it became possible to hear Leslie again, now dealing with *La Paloma*.

'I think,' Phyllis began once more, 'that we ought to find out what we can about this Smith while we are here. I mean, he might turn out to be a kind of illegitimate Hornblower, or we might be able to turn him into one. How much do you know about square-rigged ships?'

'Me? Why should I know anything about square-rigged ships?'

'Well, nearly all men seem to feel it incumbent upon them to appear to know something about ships, so I thought – ' She broke off. *La Paloma* had just finished with a triumphant chord, and the guitar pranced off on an entirely different rhythm. Leslie's voice rose:

> *Oh, I'm burning my brains in the backroom,*
> *Almost setting my cortex alight*
> *To find a new thing to go crack-boom!*
> *And blow up a xenobathite.*
>
> *Oh, I've pondered the nuclear thermals*
> *And every conceivable ray.*
> *I've mugged up on technical journals,*
> *And now I'm just starting to pray.*
>
> *What I'd like is the germ of the know-how*
> *To live at five tons per square inch,*
> *Then to bash at the bathies below now*
> *Would verge on the fringe of a cinch.*
>
> *I've scouted above ultra-violet,*
> *I've burrowed around infra-red,*
> *And the –*

'Poor Leslie,' I said. 'You see what happens in a climate like this, Phyl. We are being warned. Backroom – crackboom! –

For heaven's sake! Softening sets in without the victim being aware of it. We must give Bocker a time limit – a week from now to produce his phenomena. If not, he'll have had it, as far as we are concerned. Any longer, and real deterioration will get us. We, too, shall start composing songs in outdated rhythms. Our moral fibres will rot so that we shall find ourselves going around doing dreadful things like rhyming "thermals" with "journals". What do you say, one week's grace?'

'Well –' Phyllis began, doubtfully.

A step sounded behind us as Leslie came out of the hotel door.

'Hullo, you two,' he said, cheerfully. 'Time for a quick one before el almuerzo? Hear the new song? A smasher, isn't it? Phyllis called it "The Boffin's Lament", but I suggest "The Lay of the Baffled Boffin!" Three gin-slings? Okay.' And he departed to fetch them.

Phyllis was studying the view.

'So?' I remarked grimly. 'Well, I said a week, and I'll stand by it - though it'll very likely be fatal.'

Which was truer than I knew.

Less than a week nearly was fatal.

*

'Darling, stop worrying that moon now, and come to bed.'

'No soul – that's the trouble. I often wonder why I married you.'

'It's by no means impossible to have too much soul. Look at Laurence Hope.'

'Pig! I hate you!'

'Darling, it's late. Nearly one o'clock.'

'On Escondida, life laughs at clocksmiths.'

'Wasted, darling. You mislaid your notebook this afternoon. Remember?'

'Oh, I *do* hate you. Sweet, sweet Diana, take me from this man!'

I got up and joined her at the window.

'See?' she said. ' "A ship, an isle, a sickle moon ..." So fragile, so eternal. ... Isn't it lovely?'

We gazed out, across the empty Plaza, past the sleeping houses, over the silvered sea.

'I want it. It's one of the things I'm putting away to remember,' she said.

Faintly from behind the opposite houses, down by the waterfront, came the tinkling of a guitar.

'El amor tonto – y dulce,' she sighed. 'Why don't you see and hear what I see and hear, Mike? You don't, you know.'

'Mightn't it be a little dull for us if I did – both of us crying upon Diana, for instance? I have my own gods.'

She turned to look at me. 'I suppose you have. But they are rather obscure ones, aren't they?'

'You think so? I don't find them difficult. I'll quote Flecker back to you. "And some to Mecca turn to pray, and I toward thy bed, Yasmin." '

'Oh!' she said. 'Oh, Mike!'

And then, suddenly, the distant player dropped his guitar, with a clang.

Down by the waterfront a voice called out, unintelligible, but alarming. Then other voices. A woman screamed. We turned to look at the houses that screened the little harbour.

'Listen!' said Phyllis. 'Mike, do you think – ?'

She broke off at the sound of a couple of shots.

'It must be! Mike, they must be coming!'

There was an increasing hubbub in the distance. In the Square itself windows were opening, people calling questions from one to another. A man ran out of a door, round the corner, and disappeared down the short street that led to the water. There was more shouting now, more screaming, too. Among it the crack of three or four more shots. I turned from the window and thumped on the wall which separated us from the next room.

'Hey, Ted!' I shouted. 'Turn up your lights! Down by the waterfront, man. Lights!'

I heard his faint okay. He must have been out of bed already, for almost as I turned back to the window the lights began to go on in batches.

There was nothing unusual to be seen except a dozen or more men pelting across the Square towards the harbour.

Quite abruptly the noise which had been rising in crescendo was cut off. Ted's door slammed. His boots thudded along the corridor past our room. Beyond the houses the yelling and screaming broke out again, louder than before, as if it had gained force from being briefly dammed.

'I must – ' I began, and then stopped when I found that Phyllis was no longer beside me.

I looked across the room, and saw her in the act of locking the door. I went over.

'I must go down there. I must see what's – '

'No!' she said.

She turned and planted her back firmly against the door. She looked rather like a severe angel barring a road, except that angels are assumed to wear respectable cotton night-dresses, not nylon.

'But, Phyl – it's the job. It's what we're here for.'

'I don't care. We wait a bit.'

She stood without moving, severe angel expression now modified by that of mutinous small girl. I held out my hand.

'Phyl. Please give me that key.'

'No!' she said, and flung it across the room, through the window. It clattered on the cobbles outside. I gazed after it in astonishment. That was not at all the kind of thing one associated with Phyllis. All over the now floodlit Square people were now hurriedly converging towards the street on the opposite side. I turned back.

'Phyl. Please get away from that door.'

She shook her head.

'Don't be a fool, Mike. You've got a job to do.'

'That's just what I – '

'No, it isn't. Don't you see? The only reports we've had at all were from the people who *didn't* rush to find out what was happening. The ones who either hid, or ran away.'

I was angry with her, but not too angry for the sense of that to reach me and make me pause. She followed up: 'It's what Freddy said – the point of our coming at all is that we should be able to go back and tell them about it.'

'That's all very well, but –'

'No! Look there.' She nodded towards the window.

People were still converging upon the street that led to the waterside; but they were no longer going into it. A solid crowd was piling up at the entrance. Then, while I still looked, the previous scene started to go into reverse. The crowd backed, and began to break up at its edges. More men and women came out of the street, thrusting it back until it was dispersing all over the Square.

I went closer to the window to watch. Phyllis left the door and came and stood beside me. Presently we spotted Ted, turret-lensed ciné-camera in hand, hurrying back.

'What is it?' I called down.

'God knows. Can't get through. There's a panic up the street there. They all say it's coming this way, whatever it is. If it does, I'll get a shot from my window. Can't work this thing in that mob.' He glanced back, and then disappeared into the hotel doorway below us.

People were still pouring into the Square, and breaking into a run when they reached a point where there was room to run. There had been no further sound of shooting, but from time to time there would be another outbreak of shouts and screams somewhere at the hidden far end of the short street.

Among those headed back to the hotel came Dr Bocker himself, and the pilot, Johnny Tallton. Bocker stopped below, and shouted up. Heads popped out of various windows. He looked them over.

'Where's Alfred?' he asked.

No one seemed to know.

'If anyone sees him, call him inside,' Bocker instructed. 'The rest of you stay where you are. Observe what you can, but don't expose yourselves till we know more about it. Ted, keep all your lights on. Leslie –'

'Just on my way with the portable recorder, Doc,' said Leslie's voice.

'No, you're not. Sling the mike outside the window if you like, but keep under cover yourself. And that goes for everyone, for the present.'

'But, Doc, what is it? What's –'

'We don't know. So we keep inside until we find out why it makes people scream. Where the hell's Miss Flynn? Oh, you're there. Right. Keep watching, Miss Flynn.'

He turned to Johnny, and exchanged a few inaudible words with him. Johnny nodded, and made off round the back of the hotel. Bocker himself looked across the Square again, and then came in, shutting the door behind him.

Running, or at least hurrying, figures were still scattering over the Square in all directions, but no more were emerging from the street. Those who had reached the far side turned back to look, hovering close to doorways or alleys into which they could jump swiftly if necessary. Half a dozen men with guns or rifles laid themselves down on the cobbles, their weapons all aimed at the mouth of the street. Everything was much quieter now. Except for a few sounds of sobbing, a tense, expectant silence held the whole scene. And then, in the background, one became aware of a grinding, scraping noise; not loud, but continuous.

The door of a small house close to the church opened. The priest, in a long black robe, stepped out. A number of people nearby ran towards him, and then knelt round him. He stretched out both arms as though to encompass and guard them all.

The noise from the narrow street sounded like the heavy dragging of metal upon stone.

Three or four rifles fired suddenly, almost together. Our angle of view still stopped us from seeing what they fired at, but they let go a number of rounds each. Then the men jumped to their feet and ran further back, almost to the inland side of the Square. There they turned round, and reloaded.

From the street came a noise of cracking timbers and falling bricks and glass.

Then we had our first sight of a 'sea-tank'. A curve of dull, grey metal sliding into the Square, carrying away the lower corner of a housefront as it came.

Shots cracked at it from half a dozen different directions. The bullets splattered or thudded against it without effect. Slowly, heavily, with an air of inexorability, it came on, grinding and scraping across the cobbles. It was inclining slightly to its right, away from us and towards the church, carrying away more of the corner house, unaffected by the plaster, bricks, and beams that fell on it and slithered down its sides.

More shots smacked against it or ricochetted away whining, but it kept steadily on, thrusting itself into the Square at something under three miles an hour, massively undeflectible. Soon we were able to see the whole of it.

Imagine an elongated egg which has been halved down its length and set flat side to the ground, with the pointed end foremost. Consider this egg to be between thirty and thirty-five feet long, of a drab, lustreless leaden colour, and you will have a fair picture of the 'sea-tank' as we saw it pushing into the Square.

There was no way of seeing how it was propelled; there may have been rollers beneath, but it seemed, and sounded, simply to grate forward on its metal belly with plenty of noise, but none of machinery. It did not jerk to turn, as a tank does, but neither did it sheer like a car. It simply moved to the right on a diagonal, still pointing forwards. Close behind it followed another, exactly similar contrivance which slanted its way to the left, in our direction, wrecking the housefront on the nearer corner of the street as it came. A third kept straight ahead into the middle of the Square, and then stopped.

At the far end, the crowd that had knelt about the priest scrambled to its feet, and fled. The priest himself stood his ground. He barred the thing's way. His right hand held a cross extended against it, his left was raised, fingers spread, and palm outward, to halt it. The thing moved on, neither faster nor slower, as if he had not been there. Its curved flank pushed him aside a little as it came. Then it, too, stopped.

A few seconds later the one up our end of the Square reached what was apparently its appointed position and also stopped.

'Troops will establish themselves at first objective in extended order,' I said to Phyllis, as we regarded the three evenly spaced out in the Square. 'This isn't haphazard. Now what?'

For almost half a minute it did not appear to be now anything. There was a little more sporadic shooting, some of it from windows which, all round the Square, were full of people hanging out to see what went on. None of it had any effect on the targets, and there was some danger from ricochets.

'Look!' said Phyllis suddenly. 'This one's bulging.'

She was pointing at the nearest. The previously smooth fore-and-aft sweep of its top was now disfigured at the highest point by a small, dome-like excrescence. It was lighter-coloured than the metal beneath; a kind of off-white, semi-opaque substance which glittered viscously under the floods. It grew as one watched it.

'They're all doing it,' she added.

There was a single shot. The excrescence quivered, but went on swelling. It was growing faster now. It was no longer dome-shaped, but spherical, attached to the metal by a neck, inflating like a balloon, and swaying slightly as it distended.

'It's going to pop. I'm sure it is,' Phyllis said, apprehensively.

'There's another coming further down its back,' I said. 'Two more, look.'

The first excrescence did not pop. It was already some two foot six in diameter and still swelling fast.

'It *must* pop soon,' she muttered.

But still it did not. It kept on expanding until it must have been all of five feet in diameter. Then it stopped growing. It looked like a huge, repulsive bladder. A tremor and a shake passed through it. It shuddered jellywise, became detached, and wobbled into the air with the uncertainty of an overblown bubble.

In a lurching, amoebic way it ascended for ten feet or so. There it vacillated, steadying into a more stable sphere. Then, suddenly, something happened to it. It did not exactly explode. Nor was there any sound. Rather, it seemed to split open, as if it had been burst into instantaneous bloom by a vast number of white cilia which rayed out in all directions.

The instinctive reaction was to jump back from the window away from it. We did.

Four or five of the cilia, like long white whiplashes, flicked in through the window, and dropped to the floor. Almost as they touched it they began to contract and withdraw. Phyllis gave a sharp cry. I looked round at her. Not all of the long cilia had fallen on the floor. One of them had flipped the last six inches of its length on to her right forearm. It was already contracting, pulling her arm towards the window. She pulled back. With her other hand she tried to pick the thing off, but her fingers stuck to it as soon as they touched it.

'Mike!' she cried. 'Mike!'

The thing was tugging hard, looking tight as a bow-string. She had already been dragged a couple of steps towards the window before I could get after her in a kind of diving tackle. The force of my jump carried her across to the other side of the room. It did not break the thing's hold, but it did move it over so that it no longer had a direct pull through the window, and was forced to drag round a sharp corner. And drag it did. Lying on the floor now, I got the crook of my knee round a bed-leg for better purchase, and hung on for all I was worth. To move Phyllis then it would have had to drag me and the bedstead, too. For a moment I thought it might. Then Phyllis screamed, and suddenly there was no more tension.

I rolled her to one side, out of line of anything else that might come in through the window. She was in a faint. A patch of skin six inches long had been torn clean away from her right forearm, and more had gone from the fingers of her left hand. The exposed flesh was just beginning to bleed.

Outside in the Square there was a pandemonium of shouting and screaming. I risked putting my head round the side of the window. The thing that had burst was no longer in the air. It was now a round body no more than a couple of feet in diameter surrounded by a radiation of cilia. It was drawing these back into itself with whatever they had caught, and the tension was keeping it a little off the ground. Some of the people it was pulling in were shouting and struggling, others were like inert bundles of clothes.

I saw poor Muriel Flynn among them. She was lying on her back, dragged across the cobbles by a tentacle caught in her red hair. She had been badly hurt by the fall when she was pulled out of her window, and was crying out with terror, too. Leslie dragged almost alongside her, but it looked as if the fall had mercifully broken his neck.

Over on the far side I saw a man rush forward and try to pull a screaming woman away, but when he touched the cilium that held her his hand became fastened to it, too, and they were dragged along together.

As the circle contracted, the white cilia came closer to one another. The struggling people inevitably touched more of them and became more helplessly enmeshed than before. They struggled like flies on a fly-paper. There was a relentless deliberation about it which made it seem horribly as though one watched through the eye of a slow-motion camera.

Then I noticed that another of the misshapen bubbles had wobbled into the air, and drew back hurriedly before it should burst.

Three more cilia whipped in through the window, lay for a moment like white cords on the floor, and then began to draw back. When they had vanished across the sill I leaned over to look out of the window again. In several places about the Square there were converging knots of people struggling helplessly. The first and nearest had contracted until its victims were bound together into a tight ball out of which a few arms and legs still flailed wildly. Then, as I watched, the whole compact mass tilted over and began to roll away across the Square towards the street by which the sea-tanks had come.

The machines, or whatever the things were, still lay where they had stopped, looking like huge grey slugs, each engaged in producing several of its disgusting bubbles at different stages.

I dodged back as another was cast off, but this time nothing happened to find our window. I risked leaning out for a moment to pull the casement windows shut, and got them closed just in time. Three or four more lashes smacked against the glass with such force that one of the panes was cracked.

Then I was able to attend to Phyllis. I lifted her on to the bed, and tore a strip off the sheet to bind up her arm.

Outside, the screaming and shouting and uproar was still going on, and among it the sound of a few shots.

When I had bandaged the arm I looked out again. Half a dozen objects, looking now like tight round bales, were rolling over and over on their way to the street that led to the waterfront. I turned back again and tore another strip off the sheet to put round Phyllis's left hand.

While I was doing it I heard a different sound above the hubbub outside. I dropped the cotton strip, and ran back to the window in time to get a glimpse of a plane coming in low. The cannon in the wings started to twinkle, and I threw myself back, out of harm's way. There was a dull woomph! of an explosion. Simultaneously the windows blew in, the light went out, bits of something whizzed past, and something else splattered all over the room.

I picked myself up. The outdoor lights down our end of the Square had gone out, too, so that it was difficult to make out much there, but up the other end I could see that one of the sea-tanks had begun to move. It was sliding back by the way it had come. Then I heard the sound of the aircraft returning, and went down on the floor again.

There was another woomph! but this time we did not catch the force of it, though there was a clatter of things falling outside.

'Mike ?' said a voice from the bed, a frightened voice.

'It's all right, darling. I'm here,' I told her.

The moon was still bright, and I was able to see better now.

'What's happened?' she asked.

'They've gone. Johnny got them with the plane – at least, I suppose it was Johnny,' I said. 'It's all right now.'

'Mike, my arms do hurt.'

'I'll get a doctor as soon as I can, darling.'

'What was it? It had got me, Mike. If you hadn't held on –'

'It's all over now, darling.'

'I –' She broke off at the sound of the plane coming back once more. We listened. The cannon were firing again, but this time there was no explosion.

'Mike, there's something sticky – is it blood? You're not hurt?'

'No, darling. I don't know what it is, it's all over everything.'

'You're shaking, Mike.'

'Sorry. I can't help it. Oh, Phyl, darling Phyl . . . So nearly . . . If you'd seen them – Muriel and the rest . . . It might have been . . .'

'There, there,' she said, as if I were aged about six. 'Don't cry, Micky. It's over now.' She moved. 'Oh, Mike, my arm does hurt.'

'Lie still, darling. I'll get that doctor,' I told her.

I went for the locked door with a chair, and relieved my feelings on it quite a lot.

*

It was a subdued remnant of the expedition that foregathered the following morning – Bocker, Ted Jarvey, and ourselves. Johnny had taken off earlier with the films and recordings, including an eye-witness account I had added later, and was on his way to Kingston with them.

Phyllis's right arm and left hand were swathed in bandages. She looked pale, but had resisted all persuasions to stay in bed. Bocker's eyes had entirely lost their customary twinkle. His wayward lock of grey hair hung forward over a face which looked more lined and older than it had on the previous evening. He limped a little, and put some of his weight on a stick. Ted and I were unscathed. He looked questioningly at Bocker.

'If you can manage it, sir,' he said. 'I think our first move ought to be to get out of this stink.'

'By all means,' Bocker agreed. 'A few twinges are nothing compared with this. The sooner, the better,' he added, and got up to lead the way to windward.

The cobbles of the Square, the litter of metal fragments that lay about it, the houses all round, the church, everything in sight glistened with a coating of slime, and there was more of it that one did not see, splashed into almost every room that fronted on the Square. The previous night it had been simply a strongly fishy, salty smell, but with the warmth of the sun at work upon it it had begun to give off an odour that was already fetid and rapidly becoming miasmic. Even a hundred yards made a great deal of difference, another hundred, and we were clear of it, among the palms which fringed the beach on the opposite side of the town from the harbour. Seldom had I known the freshness of a light breeze to smell so good.

Bocker sat down, and leant his back against a tree. The rest of us disposed ourselves and waited for him to speak first. For a long time he did not. He sat motionless, looking blindly out to sea. Then he sighed.

'Alfred,' he said, 'Bill, Muriel, Leslie. I brought you all here. I have shown very little imagination and consideration for your safety, I'm afraid.'

Phyllis leaned forward.

'You mustn't think like that, Dr Bocker. None of us *had* to come, you know. You offered us the *chance* to come, and we took it. If – if the same thing had happened to me I don't think Michael would have felt that you were to blame, would you, Mike?'

'No,' I said. I knew perfectly well whom I should have blamed – for ever, and without reprieve.

'And I shouldn't, and I'm sure the others would feel the same way,' she added, putting her uninjured right hand on his sleeve.

He looked down at it, blinking a little. He closed his eyes for a moment. Then he opened them, and laid his hand on hers. His gaze strayed beyond her wrist to the bandages above.

'You're very good to me, my dear,' he said.

He patted the hand, and then sat straight, pulling himself together. Presently, in a different tone:

'We have some results,' he said. 'Not, perhaps, as conclusive as we had hoped, but some tangible evidence at least. Thanks to Ted the people at home will now be able to see what we are up against, and thanks to him, too, we have the first specimen.'

'Specimen?' repeated Phyllis. 'What of?'

'A bit of one of those tentacle things,' Ted told her.

'How on earth?'

'Luck, really. You see, when the first one burst nothing came in at my particular window, but I could see what was happening in other places, so I opened my knife and put it handy on the sill, just in case. When one did come in with the next shower it fell across my shoulder, and I caught up the knife and slashed it just as it began to pull. There was about eighteen inches of it left behind. It just dropped off on to the floor, wriggled a couple of times, and then curled up. We posted it off with Johnny.'

'Ugh!' said Phyllis.

'In future,' I said, 'we, too, will carry knives.'

'Make sure they're sharp. It's mighty tough stuff,' Ted advised.

'If you can find another bit of one I'd like to have it for examination,' said Bocker. 'We decided that one had better go off to the experts. There's something very peculiar inded about those things. The fundamental is obvious enough, it goes back to some type of sea-anemone – but whether the things have been bred, or whether they have in some way been built-up on the basic pattern – ?' He shrugged without finishing the question. 'I find several points extremely disturbing. For instance, how are they made to clutch the animate even when it is clothed, and not attach themselves to the inanimate? Also, how is it possible that they can be directed on the route back to the water instead of simply trying to reach it the nearest way?

'The first of those questions is the more significant. It implies specialized purpose. The things are *used,* you see, but not like weapons in the ordinary sense, not just to destroy, that is. They are more like snares.'

We thought that over for a moment.

'You mean,' said Phyllis, 'the purpose was to catch and collect people, like – well, as if they were sort of – shrimping for us?'

145

'Something of the kind. Clearly the primary intention was capture – though whether as a means to something, or as an end in itself, one cannot say, of course.'

We digested that thought. I could have wished that Phyllis had dropped on some analogy other than shrimping. Presently Bocker went on:

'Ordinary rifle-fire doesn't appear to trouble either the "sea-tanks" or these millibrachiate things – unless there are vulnerable spots that were not found. Explosive cannon-shells can, however, fracture the covering. The manner in which it then disintegrates suggests that it is already under very strong stress, and not very far from breaking-point. We may deduce from that that in the April Island affair there was either a lucky shot, or a grenade was used. What we saw last night certainly explains the natives' talk of whales and jellyfish. These "sea-tanks" might easily, at a distance, be taken for whales. And regarding the "jellyfish" they weren't so far out - the things must almost without doubt be closely related to the coelenterates.

'As to the "sea-tanks" the contents seem to have been simply gelatinous masses confined under immense pressure – but it is hard to credit that this can really be so. Apart from any other consideration it would seem that there must be a mechanism of some kind to propel those immensely heavy hulls. I went to look at their trails this morning. Some of the cobblestones have been ground down and some cracked into flakes by the weight, but I couldn't find any track-marks, or anything to show that the things dragged themselves along by grabs as I thought might be the case. I think we are stumped there for the present.

'Intelligence of a kind there undoubtedly is, though it appears not to be very high, or else not very well co-ordinated. All the same, it was good enough to lead them from the water-front to the Square which was the best place for them to operate.'

'I've seen army tanks carry away house-corners in much the same way as they did,' I observed.

'That is one possible indication of poor co-ordination,' Bocker replied, somewhat crushingly. 'Now have we any observations to add to those I have made?' He looked round inquiringly.

Ted said, hesitantly:

'Well, I did have the impression that these jellyfish things were not all quite the same type. The later ones had a rather shorter range, and they didn't contract so quickly, either. One on the other side of the Square lay there for quite twenty seconds with the tentacles curling and twisting about before it started to pull in at all.'

Bocker turned to him.

'You're suggesting that the cilia were actually searching?'

'I'd not go as far as that. But, anyway, I got a picture of it on the hand-camera, so we'll be able to study it.'

'Yes. It's to be hoped we shall get quite a lot from those films. Anything else? Did anyone notice whether the shots appeared to have any effect at all on these tentacular forms?'

'As far as I could see, either the shooting was rotten, or the bullets went through without bothering them,' Ted told him.

'H'm,' said Bocker, and lapsed into reflection for a while.

Presently I became aware of Phyllis muttering.

'What?' I inquired.

'I was just saying "millibrachiate tentacular coelenterates",' she explained.

'Oh,' I said.

'The recorder kept on going to the end,' Ted observed to me, 'but I don't know that we shall get a lot from that. It's a pity we didn't have more of a plan. We ought to have had a mike fixed for you to give a running commentary.'

'I'm sure that's what EBC will say, too,' I agreed, 'but as it happened I was rather busy at the time. What I want to do now is to make a rather fuller and less hurried recording than this morning's version, but I'm damned if I can face Smithtown yet. Never under heaven was there such a concentrated pong.'

We continued to sit where we were, each of us mostly occupied with his own thoughts. It was quite a long time later that Bocker said reflectively:

'You know, I think that if I believed in God I should now be a very frightened man. Luckily, however, I am rather old-fashioned, so I don't, thank God.'

Phyllis's eyebrows rose.

'Why?' she said. 'I mean, why would you be frightened?'

'Because I should be a superstitious man – and superstitious men are always frightened when they are out of their depth with something new. I should be tempted to think that God proposed to teach me a lesson. That He was saying: "H'm. You think you're so clever. Little gods yourselves with all your atom-splitting and microbe-conquering. You think you rule the world, and possibly heaven, too. Very well, you conceited little mites, there's a lot about life and nature that you don't know. I'll just show you one or two new things and see how your conceit stands up to them. I have had to do it before." '

'However, as you don't believe that – ?' prompted Phyllis.

'I don't know. There have been lords of the earth before us. Some of them in a sounder position, too. There was a great variety of dinosaur types – which should have given them a broad chance of survival. All the human eggs, on the other hand, are pretty nearly in one basket.'

Nobody made any further comment. The four of us continued to sit on, looking out across a blandly innocent azure sea. . . .

*

Among the other papers I bought at London Airport was the current number of *The Beholder*. Though it is, I am aware, not without its merits and even well thought of in some circles, it leaves me with an abiding sense that it is more given to expressing its first prejudices than its second thoughts. Perhaps if it were to go to press a day later . . . However, the discovery in this issue of a leader entitled DOCTOR BOCKER RIDES AGAIN, did nothing to alter my impression. The text ran something after this fashion:

'Neither the courage of Dr Alastair Bocker in going forth to meet a submarine dragon, nor his perspicacity in correctly deducing where the monster might be met, can be questioned.

The gruesome and fantastically repulsive scenes to which the EBC treated us in our homes last Tuesday evening make it more to be wondered at that any of the party should have survived than that four of its members should have lost their lives. Dr Bocker himself is to be congratulated on his escape at the cost merely of a sprained ankle when his sock and shoe were wrenched off, and another member of the party on her even narrower escape.

'Nevertheless, horrible though this affair was, and valuable as some of the Doctor's observations may prove in suggesting counter-measures, it would be a mistake for him to assume that he has now been granted an unlimited licence to readopt his former role as the world's premier Fat Boy.

'We are alarmed, reasonably alarmed, at the damaging blows that attacks from beneath the sea have dealt to world trade, but we are confident that scientific research will before long find a means to restore to us the freedom of the seas. We are also distressed by the calamities that have fallen upon the inhabitants of certain islands, and we protest a disgust at its form which increases our sympathy for those who have experienced it. We do not, however, have any intention of responding to Dr Bocker's latest attempt to set our editorial flesh creeping; neither, we imagine, have our readers; nor, we hope, have any of the more thoughtful part of the population of this long-suffering island.

'It is our inclination to attribute his suggestion that we should proceed forthwith to embattle virtually the entire western coastline of the United Kingdom to the effect of recent unnerving experiences upon a temperament which has never shunned the sensational, rather than to the conclusions of mature consideration.

'Let us consider the cause of this panic-stricken recommendation. It is this: a number of small islands, all but one of them lying within the tropics, have been raided by some marine agency of which we as yet know little. In the course of these raids some hundreds of people – to an estimated total no larger than that of the number of persons injured on the roads in a few days – have lost their lives. This is unfortunate and regrettable, but scarcely grounds for the suggestion that we, thousands of miles from the nearest incident of the kind, should, at the taxpayer's expense, proceed to beset our whole shoreline with weapons and guards. This is a line of argument which would have us erect shockproof buildings in London on account of an earthquake in Tokio. . . . '

And so on. There wasn't a lot left of poor Bocker by the time they had finished with him. I did not show it to him. He would find out soon enough, for *The Beholder*'s readership had no use for the unique approach: it liked the popular view, bespokenly tailored.

Presently the helicopter set us down at the terminus, and Phyllis and I slipped away while pressmen converged on Bocker.

Dr Bocker out of sight, however, was by no means Dr Bocker out of mind. The major part of the Press had divided into pro- and anti- camps, and, within a few minutes of our getting back to the flat, representatives of both sides began ringing us up to put leading questions to their own advantage. After about five of these I seized on an interval to ring the EBC and tell them that as we were about to remove our receiver for a while they would probably suffer, and would they please keep a record of callers. They did. Next morning there was quite a list. Among those anxious to talk to us I noticed the name of Captain Winters, with the Admiralty number against it.

'Here's one that ought to have priority, I think,' I suggested. 'Would you like to deal with it?'

'Oh, dear! Can't I just be an invalid?' asked Phyllis. 'I really don't – ' then she saw where my finger was pointing. 'Oh, I see – well the Navy's a bit different, of course.'

She reported a little later:

'One of the Lordships wants to see us, and Captain Winters would be delighted if he may have the privilege of rewarding and reviving us with dinner afterwards. I said he should.'

'All right,' I agreed, and then took myself off to face a thirsty day of discussing and planning at EBC.

The Admiral, when we reached him, turned out to be a great deal more human and less awe-inspiring than his further approaches suggested. His greeting to Phyllis was, indeed, little short of avuncular. He asked concernedly after her injuries, and congratulated her upon her escape in a most protective manner. Then we all sat down. He glanced at a paper on his desk.

'Er – we have of course had Dr Bocker's report on the Escondida affair. It raises a large number of controversial points. In fact, he shows, if I may say so without offence, a generosity of hypothesis which appears to exceed the warrants of the observed facts to a degree quite remarkable in a scientist. I thought that a little talk with others who were present at the incident might – er – help to clarify the picture for us.'

I assured him that I understood the position well.

'All day long,' I told him, 'there has been a battle raging at EBC between the sponsor who backed the expedition, a government representative, EBC's Policy Panel, EBC's Audio-Assessment Department, the Director of Talks and Features, and several other people, about what Dr Bocker shall and shall not be allowed to say over the air. It's been heated, but a bit academic because Dr Bocker himself wasn't there and will certainly fight any amendments to his scripts that anybody tries to make, whatever they are.'

'There can be very little doubt of that, I think,' agreed the Admiral. He looked down at his paper again. 'Now he says here that these "sea-tank" things and the exuded objects which it pleases him to call "pseudo-coelenterata" are unaffected by rifle-fire, but that the "sea-tanks" completely disintegrate when hit by explosive cannon shell. You support that?'

'They explode – almost as thoroughly as a broken light-bulb implodes,' I told him.

'Leaving no identifiable fragments?'

'A lot of metal splinters and pieces which might have been anything. That's all.'

'Except the slime?'

'Yes. Except that, of course.'

Phyllis wrinkled her nose at the recollection of it.

'By the afternoon the sun had baked that dry, and it was like a hard varnish over everything,' she told him.

He nodded. 'Now these "pseudo-coelenterata" things. I'll read you what he says about them.' He did so, ending: 'Would you call that a fair description? Is there anything you would add?'

'No. It's accurate to my memory,' I said.

'I didn't see much, but the first part's accurate,' Phyllis agreed.

'Now would you say that both these forms were sentient?' he asked.

I frowned. 'That's a very difficult one, sir. In the most elementary sense of the word they both were – that is, they responded to certain external stimuli, and very strongly. But if you are meaning, did they show any degree of intelligence? – well, I simply can't tell you. There was intelligent *direction* of both forms undoubtedly. The sea-tanks followed an intelligent route into the Square, and disposed themselves advantageously when they got there. The other things took the same route back to the water when the straight line was obstructed by houses. But it would not be very difficult to make remote-control mechanisms that would obey directions of that kind.'

'Then you are aware of Dr Bocker's theory that these forms were, in fact, agents only; that is that the controlling mind was elsewhere and directed them by some means of communication at present unknown to us? What is your opinion on that?'

'Not very definite, sir. But I think Dr Bocker's theory is tenable. If you don't mind an analogy, the whole operation struck one as having more the style of trawling than of harpooning. My wife places it somewhat lower than that; she said "shrimping".'

'An undiscriminating instrument rather than a precise one?'

'Exactly, sir. It discriminated no further than to select the animate from the inanimate.'

'H'm,' said the Admiral. 'And neither of you has formed any idea how these sea-tanks may be propelled?'

We shook our heads. He looked down at his paper again for a moment.

'Very rarely, in my experience of him,' he observed, 'has Dr Bocker failed to equip himself with a brand-new cat when approaching pigeons. We now come to it. It is implicit in his use of the term '*pseudo*-coelenterata".

'If I understand him rightly, he suggests that these coelenterate forms are not only *not* coelenterates, but *not* animals, and probably *not*, in the accepted sense, living creatures at all.'

He raised questioning eyebrows. I nodded.

'It is his opinion that they may well be artificial organic constructions, *built* for a specialized purpose. He – let me see now, how does he put it? – ah, yes: "It is far from inconceivable that organic tissues might be constructed in a manner analogous to that used by chemists to produce plastics of a required molecular structure. If this were done and the resulting artifact rendered sensitive to stimuli administered chemically or physically, it could, temporarily at least, produce a behaviour which would, to an unprepared observer, be scarcely distinguishable from that of a living organism.

' "My observations lead me to suggest that this is what has been done: the coelenterate form being chosen, out of many others that might have served the purpose, for its simplicity of construction. It seems probable that the sea-tanks may be a variant of the same device. In other words, we were being attacked by organic mechanisms under remote, or predetermined, control. When this is considered in the light of the control which we ourselves are able to exercise over *in*organic materials; remotely, as with guided missiles, or predeterminedly, as with torpedoes, it should be less startling than it at first appears. Indeed, it may well be that once the technique of building up a natural form synthetically has been discovered, control of it would present less complex problems than many we have had to solve in our control of the inorganic."

'Now, Mr Watson, did you receive any impressions that would support such a view?'

I shook my head. 'Right out of my field, sir. Surely the report on the specimen ought to help there?'

'I have a copy of that – all jargon to me, but our advisers tell me that everything in it is so qualified and cautious as to be practically useless – except in so far as it shows that it is strange enough to baffle the experts.'

'Perhaps I'm being stupid,' Phyllis put in, 'but does it really matter a lot? From a practical point of view, I mean? The things have to be tackled the same way whether they are really living or pseudo-living, surely?'

'That's true enough,' the Admiral agreed. 'All the same, a speculation of that kind, if unsupported, has the effect of putting the whole report in a dubious light.'

We went on talking for a while, but little more of importance emerged, and shortly afterwards we were ushered from the presence.

'Oh – oh – oh!' said Phyllis painedly, as we got outside. 'I've a good mind to go straight round and shake Dr Bocker. He *promised* me he wouldn't say anything yet about that "pseudo" – business. He's just a kind of natural-born *enfant terrible,* it'd do him *good* to be shaken. Just wait till I get him alone.'

'It does weaken his whole case,' Captain Winters agreed.

'Weaken it! Somebody is going to hand this to the newspapers. They play it up hard as another Bockerism, the whole thing will become just a stunt – and that will put all the sensible people against whatever he says. And just as he was beginning to live some of the other things down, too! Oh, let's go and have dinner before I get out of hand.'

*

A bad week followed. Those papers that had already adopted *The Beholder's* scornful attitude to coastal preparations pounced upon the pseudo-biotic suggestions with glee. Writers of editorials filled their pens with sarcasm, a squad of scientists who had trounced Bocker before was now marched out again to grind him still smaller. Almost every cartoonist discovered simultaneously why his favourite political butts had somehow never seemed quite human.

The other part of the Press, already advocating effective coastal defences, let its imagination go on the subject of pseudo-living structures that might yet be created, and demanded still better defence against the horrific possibilities thought up by its staffs.

Then the sponsor informed EBC that his fellow directors considered that their product's reputation would suffer by being associated with this new wave of notoriety and controversy that had arisen around Dr Bocker, and proposed to cancel arrangements. Departmental Heads in EBC began to tear their hair. Time-salesmen put up the old line about any kind of publicity being good publicity. The sponsor talked about dignity, and also the risk that purchase of the product might be regarded as tacit endorsement of the Bocker theory, which, he feared, might have the effect of promoting sales-resistance in the upper income brackets. EBC parried with the observation that build-up publicity had already tied the names of Bocker and the product together in the public mind. Nothing would be gained from reining-in in midstream, so the firm ought to go ahead and get the best of its money's worth.

The sponsor said that his firm had attempted to make a serious contribution to knowledge and public safety by promoting a scientific expedition, not a vulgar stunt. Just the night before, for instance, one of EBC's own comedians had suggested that pseudo-life might explain a long-standing mystery concerning his mother-in-law, and if this kind of thing was going to be allowed, etc. . . . etc. . . . EBC promised that it would not contaminate their air in future, and pointed out that if the series on the expedition were dropped after the promises that had been made, a great many consumers in all income-brackets were likely to feel that the sponsor's firm was un-reliable. . . .

Members of the BBC displayed an infuriatingly courteous

sympathy to any members of our staff whom they chanced to meet.

People kept on popping their heads into the room where I was trying to work, and giving me the latest from the front; usually advising me to omit or include this or that aspect according to the way the battle was going at the moment. Through everything ran a nervous realization that the arch-rivals might come out with an eye-witness at any moment and ruin our thunder – the courteousness seemed suspiciously urbane. After a couple of days of the atmosphere there I decided to stay at home and do the work there.

But there was still the telephone bringing suggestions and swift changes of policy. We did our best. We wrote and re-wrote, trying to satisfy all parties. Two or three hurried conferences with Bocker himself were explosive. He spent most of the time threatening to throw the whole thing up because EBC too obviously would not trust him near a live microphone, and was insisting on recordings.

At last, however, the scripts were finished. We were too tired of them to argue any more. When the first of them did get on the air at last, it sounded to us like something misplaced from Mummy's Angel's Half-Hour. We packed hurriedly and departed blasphemously for the peace and seclusion of Corn-wall.

*

The first noticeable thing as we approached Rose Cottage, 268.6 miles this time, was an innovation.

'Good heavens!' I said. 'We've got a perfectly good one indoors. If I am expected to come and sit out in a draught there just because a lot of your compost-minded friends – '

'That,' Phyllis told me, coldly, 'is an arbour.'

I looked at it more carefully. The architecture was unusual. One wall gave an impression of leaning a little.

'Why do we want an arbour?' I inquired.

'Well, one of us might like to work there on a warm day. It keeps the wind off, and stops papers blowing about.'

'Oh,' I said.

With a defensive note, she added:

'After all, when one is bricklaying one has to build something.'

Logical enough, I supposed, but there was a haunting feeling that it did not start from quite the right premiss. I assured her that as arbours went, it was a very nice arbour. I had just not been expecting an arbour, that was all.

'It was not a kind conclusion to jump to,' she said, huffily.

There are times when I wonder whether the two of us are quite as well *en rapport* as I like to hope. The use of the word 'kind', for instance, in the circumstances . . . But I was able to assure her that I thought it very clever of her: and I did; I don't suppose I myself could have got one brick to stick to another.

It was a relief to be back. Hard to believe that such a place as Escondida existed at all. Still harder to believe in sea-tanks and giant coelenterates, pseudo or not. Yet, somehow, I did not find myself able to relax as I had hoped.

On the first morning Phyllis dug out the fragments of the frequently neglected novel and took them off, with a faintly defiant air, to the arbour. I pottered about, wondering why the sense of peace wasn't seeping in upon me quite as I had hoped. The Cornish sea still lapped immemorially at the rocks. It could thunder, it could menace, it could wreck good ships when it had a mind to; but these were old, natural hazards. They made places like Escondida seem frivolous, even in conception; such places belonged to a different world, one where it was not altogether surprising that freakish things should happen. But Cornwall was not frivolous. It was real and solid. The centuries passed over it unsensationally. The waves gnawed steadily at it, but slowly. When the sea killed its inhabitants it was because they had challenged it: not because it challenged them. It was hard indeed to imagine our home sea spawning such morbid novelties as had slid up the Caribbean beaches of Escondida. Bocker seemed, in recollection, like an impish sprite who had had a power of hallucination. Out of his range, the world was a more sober, better-ordered place. At least, so it appeared for the moment, though the extent to which it was not was increasingly borne in upon me during the next few days as I emerged from our particular concern to take a more general look at it.

The national air-lift was working now, though on a severe schedule of primary necessities. It had been discovered that two large air-freighters working on a rapid shuttle-service could bring in only a little less than the average cargo boat could carry in the same length of time, but the cost was high. In spite of the rationing system the cost of living had already risen by about two hundred per cent. The aircraft factories were working all round the clock to produce the craft which would bring the overheads down, but the demand was so great that the schedule of priorities was unlikely to be relaxed for a considerable time, possibly several years. Harbours were choked with the ships that were laid up either because the crews refused to work them, or the owners refused to pay the insurance rate. Dockers deprived of work were demonstrating and fighting for the guaranteed wages, while their union temporized and vacillated. Seamen, out of work through no fault of their own, joined them in demanding basic pay as a right. Airport staff pressed for higher pay. Cancellation of shipyard work brought thousands more demanding continuation of pay. Aircraft workers were threatening to come out in support. Reduced demand for steel reduced the demand for coal. It was proposed to close certain impoverished pits, whereat the entire industry struck, in protest.

The petrels of Muscovy, finding the climate bracing, declared through their accustomed London mouthpiece, and disseminated by all the usual channels, their view that the shipping crisis was largely a put-up job. The West, they declared, had seized upon and magnified a few maritime inconveniences as an excuse to carry out a vastly enlarged programme of air-power.

With trade restricted to essentials, half a dozen financial conferences were in almost permanent session. Ill-feeling and tempers were rising here and there where a disposition to make the delivery of necessities conditional on the acceptance of a proportion of luxuries was perceptible. There was undoubtedly some hard bargaining going on, and there would, equally without doubt, be some far-sighted concessions that the public would only learn about later on.

A few ships could still be found in which crews, at fortune-making wages, would dare the deep water, but the insurance rate pushed cargo prices up to a level at which only the direst need would pay, so that they were largely voyages of bravado.

Somebody somewhere had perceived in an enlightened moment that every vessel lost had been power-driven, and a ramp in sailing craft of every size and type had gone into operation all round the world. There was a proposal to mass-produce clipper ships, but little disposition to believe that the emergency would last long enough to warrant the investment.

In the backrooms of all maritime countries the boys were still hard at work. Every week saw new devices being tried out, some with enough success for them to be put into production – though only to be taken out of production again when it was shown that they had been rendered unreliable in some way, if not actually countered. Nevertheless, it was being recognized by a scientifically-minded age that even magicians may have sticky relays sometimes. That the boffins would come through with the complete answer one day was not to be doubted – and, always, it might be to-morrow.

From what I had been hearing, the general faith in boffins was now somewhat greater than the boffins' faith in themselves. Their shortcomings as saviours were beginning to oppress them. Their chief difficulty was not so much infertility of invention as lack of information. They badly needed more data, and could not get them. One of them had remarked to me: 'If you were going to make a ghost-trap, how would you set about it? – particularly if you had not even a small ghost to practise on.' They had become ready to grasp at any straw – which may have been the reason why it was only among a section of the boffins that Bocker's theory of pseudo-biotic forms received any serious consideration.

As for the sea-tanks, the more lively papers were having a

great time with them, so were the news-reels. Selected parts of the Escondida films were included in our scripted accounts on EBC. A small footage was courteously presented to the BBC for use in its news-reel, with appropriate acknowledgement. In fact, the tendency to play the things up to an extent which was creating alarm puzzled me until I discovered that in certain quarters almost anything which diverted attention from the troubles at home was considered worthy of encouragement. Sea-tanks were particularly suitable for this purpose; their sensation value was high, and unattended by those embarrassments which sometimes result from the policy of directing restive attention abroad.

Their depredations, however, were becoming increasingly serious. In the short time since we had left Escondida raids had been reported from ten or eleven places in the Caribbean area, including a township on Puerto Rico. A little further afield, only rapid action by Bermudan-based American aircraft had scotched an attack there. But this was small-scale stuff compared with what was happening on the other side of the world. Accounts, apparently reliable, spoke of a series of attacks on the east coasts of Japan. Raids by a dozen or more sea-tanks had taken place on Hokkaido and Honshu. Reports from further south, in the Banda Sea area, were more confused, but obviously related to a considerable number of raids upon various scales. Mindanao capped the lot by announcing that four or five of its eastern coastal towns had been raided simultaneously, an operation which must have employed at least sixty sea-tanks.

For the inhabitants of Indonesia and the Philippines, scattered upon innumerable islands set in deep seas, the outlook was very different from that which faced the British, sitting high on their Continental shelf with a shallow North Sea, showing no signs of abnormality, at their backs. Among the Islands, reports and rumours skipped like a running fire until each day there were more thousands of people forsaking the coasts and fleeing inland in panic. A similar trend, though not yet on the panic scale, was apparent in the West Indies.

Catching up on the news, the gravity of it came home to me

more strongly. I began to feel that I had been taking it all rather as the readers of the more irresponsible papers were still taking it. I started to see a far larger pattern than I had ever imagined. The reports argued the existence of hundreds, perhaps thousands of these sea-tanks – numbers that indicated not simply a few raids, but a campaign.

'They must provide defences, or else give the people the means to defend themselves,' I said. 'You can't preserve your economy in a place where everybody is scared stiff to go near the seaboard. You *must* somehow make it possible for people to work and live there.'

'Nobody knows where they will come next, and you have to act quickly when they do,' said Phyllis. 'That would mean letting people have arms.'

'Well, then, they should give them arms. Damn it, it isn't a function of the State to deprive its people of the means of self-protection.'

'Isn't it?' said Phyllis, reflectively.

'What do you mean?'

'Doesn't it sometimes strike you as odd that all our governments who loudly claim to rule by the will of the people are willing to run almost any risk rather than let their people have arms? Isn't it almost a principle that a people should not be allowed to defend itself, but should be forced to defend its Government? The only people I know who are trusted by their Government are the Swiss, and being landlocked they don't come into this.'

I was puzzled. The response was off her usual key. She was looking tired, too.

'What's wrong, Phyl?'

She shrugged. 'Nothing, except that at times I get sick of putting up with all the shams and the humbug, and pretending that the lies aren't lies, and the propaganda isn't propaganda, and the dirt isn't dirt. I'll get over it again. . . . Don't you sometimes wish that you had been born into the Age of Reason, instead of into the Age of the Ostensible Reason? I think that they are going to let thousands of people be killed by these horrible things rather than risk giving them powerful enough weapons to defend themselves. And they'll have rows of arguments why it is best so. What do a few thousands, or a few millions of people matter? Women will just go on making the loss good. But Governments are important – one mustn't risk them.'

'Darling –'

'There'll be token arrangements, of course. Small garrisons in important places, perhaps. Aircraft standing-by on call – and they will come along after the worst of it has happened – when men and women have been tied into bundles and rolled away by those horrible things, and girls have been dragged over the ground by their hair, like poor Muriel, and people have been pulled apart, like that man who was caught by two of them at once – *then* the aeroplanes will come, and the authorities will say they were sorry to be a bit late, but there are technical difficulties in making adequate arrangements. That's the regular kind of get-out, isn't it?'

'But, Phyl, darling –'

'I know what you are going to say, Mike, but I *am* scared. Nobody's really *doing* anything. There's no realization, no genuine attempt to change the pattern to meet it. The ships are driven off the deep seas; goodness knows how many of these sea-tank things are ready to come and snatch people away. They say: "Dear, dear! Such a loss of trade," and they talk and talk and talk as if it'll all come right in the end if only they can keep on talking long enough. When anybody like Bocker suggests *doing* something he's just howled down and called a sensationalist, or an alarmist. How many people do they regard as the proper wastage before they *must* do anything?'

'But they are trying, you know, Phyl –'

'Are they? I think they're balancing things all the time. What is the minimum cost at which the political set-up can be preserved in present conditions? How much loss of life will the people put up with before they become dangerous about it? Would it be wise or unwise to declare martial law, and at what stage? On and on, instead of admitting the danger and getting to work. Oh, I could – ' She stopped suddenly. Her expression changed. 'Sorry, Mike. I shouldn't have gone off the handle like that. I must be tired, or something.' And she took herself off with a decisive air of not wanting to be followed.

The outburst disturbed me badly. I hadn't seen her in a state anything like that for years. Not since the baby died.

The next morning didn't do anything to reassure me. I came round the corner of the cottage and found her sitting in that ridiculous arbour. Her arms lay on the table in front of her, her head rested on them, with her hair straying over the littered pages of the novel. She was weeping forlornly, steadily.

I raised her chin, and kissed her.

'Darling – darling, what is it – ?'

She looked back at me with the tears still running down her cheeks. She said, miserably:

'I can't do it, Mike. It won't work.'

She looked mournfully at the written pages. I sat down beside her, and put an arm round her.

'Never mind, Sweet, it'll come . . . '

'It won't, Mike. Every time I try, other thoughts come instead. I'm frightened.' She gave me a curiously intense look. I tightened my arm.

'There's nothing to be frightened about, darling.'

She kept on looking at me closely. 'You're not frightened?' she said, oddly.

'We're stale,' I said. 'We stewed too much over those scripts. Let's go over to the north coast, it ought to be good for surfboards to-day.'

She dabbed at her eyes. 'All right,' she said, with unusual meekness.

It was a good day. The wind and the waves and the exercise brought more colour into her cheeks, and neither of us pecked at our lunch. We reached the stage where I felt that I could hopefully suggest that she should see a doctor. Her refusal came pat. She was feeling a whole lot better. Everything would be all right in a day or two.

We idled the rest of the day away on a leisurely course which brought us back to Rose Cottage about nine-thirty in the evening. While Phyllis went to warm up some coffee, I turned on the radio. With a touch of disloyalty I tried the BBC first and got in on the early lines of a play in which it seemed likely that Gladys Young was going to be a possessive mother, so I turned to the EBC. I found it engaged in putting forth one of those highly monotonous programmes that it unblushingly calls variety. However, I let it run.

A plugged number finished. Somebody I had never heard of was introduced as my ever-popular old friend, So-and-So. There were a few preliminary runs on a guitar, then a voice began to sing:

> *Oh, I'm burning my brains in the backroom,*
> *Almost setting my cortex alight –*

It was a moment before my surprise registered, then I turned and stared incredulously at the set:

> *To find a new thing to go crack-boom!*
> *And blow up a xenobathite!*

There was a crash behind me. I turned to see Phyllis in the doorway, the coffee things on the floor at her feet. Her face was puckering, and she sagged. I caught her, and helped her to a chair. The radio was still going:

> *. . . technical journals,*
> *And now I'm just starting to pray.*

I leaned over and switched it off. They must have got the song somehow from Ted. Phyllis wasn't crying. She just sat there shaking all over.

*

'I've given her a sedative, so she'll sleep now. What she must have is a complete rest and a change,' said the doctor.

'That's what we're having,' I pointed out.

He regarded me thoughtfully.

'You, too, I think,' he said.

'I'm all right,' I told him. 'I don't understand this. She had a shock, and she was hurt, but that was right at the beginning of it. After that, she was unconscious. She seemed to get over it quite soon, and she really knows no more of the rest than anyone else who has seen the films. Though, of course, we have been rather steeping in it.'

He continued to look at me seriously.

'*You* saw it all,' he remarked. 'You dream about it, don't you?'

'It has given me a few bad nights,' I admitted.

He nodded. 'More than that. You've been going over it again and again in your sleep?' he suggested. 'Particularly you have been concerned with somebody called Muriel, and with a man who was torn to pieces?'

'Well, yes,' I agreed. 'But I haven't talked to her about it. I'd rather forget it.'

'Some people don't easily forget things like that. They are apt to break through when one is asleep.'

'You mean I've been talking in my sleep?'

'A lot, I gather.'

'I see. You mean that's why she – ?'

'Yes. Now I'm going to give you the address of a friend of mine in Harley Street. I want you both to go up to London to-morrow, and see him the next day. I'll fix it up for you.'

'Very well,' I agreed. 'You know, it wasn't the thing itself that worried me so much as the pressure of getting the scripts out afterwards. That's relaxed now.'

'Possibly,' he said. 'All the same, I think you should go and see him.'

There was something wrong, and I knew it. I didn't admit to the doctor, though I did to the Harley Street man, that it was more often Phyllis than Muriel that I saw being dragged along by her hair, and more often her than an unknown man that I saw being pulled to pieces. As a *quid pro quo* he told me that

Phyllis had been spending most of her nights listening to me and dissuading me from jumping out of the window to interfere in these imaginary happenings.

So I agreed to go out of circulation for a time.

*

Nirvana is for the few; nevertheless, the old manor house in Yorkshire to which my advice led me managed to induce a passable temporary substitute. The first few days without newspapers, without radio, without letters, had a purgatorially fretful quality, but after that came an almost physical sense of taut springs relaxing. As the feeling of urgency receded my values and perspective shifted. Exercise, open air, a complete change of pattern led to a feeling of having changed gear; the engine began to settle down to a more comfortable running-speed. There was a great simplification. One seemed to grow fresher and cleaner within, larger, too, and less pushable-around. There was a new sense of stability. A very comfortable, easy pattern it was; habit-forming, I imagine.

Certainly, in six weeks I had become addicted and might have continued longer had a twenty-mile thirst not happened to take me into a small pub close upon six o'clock one evening.

While I was standing at the bar with the second pint the landlord turned on the radio, the arch-rival's news-bulletin. The very first item shattered the ivory tower that I had been gradually building. The voice said:

'The roll of those missing in the Oviedo-Santander district is still incomplete, and it is thought by the Spanish authorities that it may never be completely definitive. Official spokesmen admit that the estimate of 3,200 casualties, including men, women, and children, is conservative, and may be as much as fifteen or twenty per cent below the actual figure.

'Messages of sympathy from all parts of the world continue to pour into Madrid. Among them are telegrams from San José, Guatemala, from Salvador, from La Serena, Chile, from Bunbury, Western Australia, and from numerous islands in both

the East and West Indies which have themselves suffered attacks
no less horrible, though smaller in scale, than those inflicted
upon the north Spanish coast.

'In the House to-day, the Leader of the Opposition, in giving
his party's support for the feelings of sympathy with the Spanish
people expressed by the Prime Minister, pointed out that the
casualties in the third of this series of raids, that upon Gijon
would have been considerably more severe had the people not
taken their defence into their own hands. The people, he said,
were entitled to defence. It was a part of the business of government to provide them with it. If a government neglected that
duty, no one could blame a people for taking steps for its self-
protection.

'It would be much better, however, to be prepared with an
organized force. Since time out of mind we had maintained
armed forces to deal with threats by other armed forces. Since
1829 we had maintained an efficient police-force to deal with
internal threats. But it appeared that we had now become so
administratively barren, so inventively infertile, so corporately
costive that we were unable to produce the means of giving the
dwellers upon our coasts that security to which their member-
ship of this great nation entitled them.

'It seemed to the members of the Opposition that the
Government, having failed to fulfil its election pledges, was
now about to belie the very name of its party by its reluctance to
consider means which would conserve even the lives of its
electors. If this were not so, then it would appear that the policy
of conservation was being carried to a length which scarcely
distinguished it from niggardliness. It was high time that
measures were taken to ensure that the fate which had over-
taken dwellers upon the littorals, not only in Spain, but in many
other parts of the world as well, could not fall upon the people
of these islands.

'The Prime Minister, in thanking the Opposition for its expression of sympathy, would assure them that the Government
was actively watching the situation. The exact steps that would,
if necessary, be taken would have to be dictated by the nature of

the emergency, if one should arise. These, he said, were deep waters: there was much consolation to be found in the reflection that the British Isles lay in shallow waters.

'The name of Her Majesty the Queen headed the list of subscribers to the fund opened by the Lord Mayor of London for the relief – '

The landlord reached over, and switched off the set.

'Cor!' he remarked, with disgust. 'Makes yer sick. Always the bloody same. Treat you like a lot of bloody kids. Same during the bloody war. Bloody Home Guards all over the place waiting for bloody parachutists, and all the bloody ammunition all bloody well locked up. Like the Old Man said one time: his bloody-self, "What kind of a bloody people do they think we are?" '

I offered him a drink, told him I had been away from any news for days, and asked what had been going on. Stripped of its adjectival monotony, and filled out by information I gathered later, it amounted to this:

In the past weeks the scope of the raids had widened well beyond the tropics. At Bunbury, a hundred miles or so south of Fremantle in Western Australia, a contingent of fifty or more sea-tanks had come ashore and into the town before any alarm was given. A few nights later La Serena, in Chile, was taken similarly by surprise. At the same time in the Central American area the raids had ceased to be confined to islands, and there had been a number of incursions, large and small, upon both the Pacific and Gulf coasts. In the Atlantic, the Cape Verde Islands had been repeatedly raided, and the trouble spread northward to the Canaries and Madeira. There had been a few small-scale assaults, too, on the bulge of the African coast.

Europe remained an interested spectator. *Ex Africa semper aliquid novi* may be translated, with a touch of freedom, as: 'Funny things happen in other places,' conveying that Europe, in the opinion of its inhabitants, is the customary seat of stability. Hurricanes, tidal waves, serious earthquakes, et cetera, are extravagances divinely directed to occur in the more exotic and less sensible parts of the earth, all important European damage being done traditionally by man himself in periodical frenzies. It was not, therefore, to be seriously expected that the danger would come any closer than Madeira – or, possibly, Rabat or Casablanca.

Consequently, when, five nights before, the sea-tanks had come crawling through the mud, across the shore, and up the slipways at Santander, they had entered a city that was not only unprepared, but also largely uninformed about them.

From the moment they were observed opinion split into two parties; roughly the modern and the classical. Someone in the former telephoned the garrison at the cuartel with the news that foreign submarines were invading the harbour in force; someone else followed up with the information that the submarines were landing tanks; yet another somebody contradicted that the submarines themselves were amphibious. Since something was certainly, if obscurely, amiss, the soldiery turned out to investigate.

Meanwhile, the sea-tanks had entered the streets. It was immediately clear to the more classically-minded citizens that, since the advancing objects were no known form of machine, their origin was likely to be diabolic, and they aroused their priests. The visitants were conjured in Latin to return to their Captain, the Father of Lies, in the Pit whence they had come.

The sea-tanks had continued their slow advance, driving the exorcising priests before them. The military, on their arrival, had to force their way through throngs of praying townspeople. In each of several streets patrols came to a similar decision: if this were foreign invasion, it was their duty to repel it; if it were diabolical, the same action, even though ineffective, would put them on the side of Right. They opened fire.

In the comisaría of police a belated and garbled alarm gave the impression that the trouble was due to a revolt by the troops. With this endorsed by the sound of firing in several places, the police went forth to teach the military a lesson.

After that, the whole thing had become a chaos of sniping, counter-sniping, partisanship, incomprehension, and exorcism, in the middle of which the sea-tanks had settled down to exude their revolting coelenterates. Only when daylight came and the sea-tanks had withdrawn had it been possible to sort out the confusion, by which time over two thousand persons were missing.

'How did there come to be so many? Did they all stay out praying in the streets?' I asked.

The innkeeper reckoned from the newspaper accounts that the people had not realized what was happening. They were not highly literate or greatly interested in the outer world, and until the first coelenterate sent out its cilia they had no idea what was going to happen. Then there was panic, the luckier ones ran right away, the others bolted for cover into the nearest houses.

'They ought to have been all right there,' I said.

But I was, it seemed, out of date. Since we had seen them in Escondida the sea-tanks had learnt a thing or two; among them, that if the bottom storey of a house is pushed away the rest will come down, and once the coelenterates had cleared up those trampled in the panic, demolition had started. The people inside had had to choose between having the house come down with them, or making a bolt for safety.

The following night, watchers at several small towns and villages to the west of Santander spotted the half-egg shapes crawling ashore at mid-tide. There was time to arouse most of the inhabitants and get them away. A unit of the Spanish air-force was standing-by, and went into action with flares and cannon. At San Vicente they blew up half a dozen sea-tanks with their first onslaught, and the rest stopped. Several more were destroyed on the second run; the rest started back to the sea. The fighters got the last of them when it was already a few inches submerged. At the other four places where they landed the defence did almost as well. Not more than three or four coelenterates were released at all, and only a dozen or so villagers caught by them. It was estimated that out of fifty or so sea-tanks engaged, not more than four or five could have got safely back to deep water. It was a famous victory, and the wine flowed freely to celebrate it.

The night after that there were watchers all along the coast ready to give the alarm when the first dark hump should break the water. But all night long the waves rolled steadily on to the beaches, with never an alien shape to break them. By morning it was clear that the sea-tanks, or those who sent them, had learnt a painful lesson. The few that had survived were reckoned to be making for parts less alert.

During the day the wind dropped. In the afternoon a fog came up, by the evening it was thick, and visibility no more than a few yards. It was somewhere about ten-thirty in the evening when the sea-tanks came sliding up from the quietly lapping waters at Gijon, with not a sound to betray them until their metal bellies started to crunch up the stone ramps. The few small boats that were already drawn up there they pushed aside or crushed as they came. It was the cracking of the timbers that brought men out from the waterside posadas to investigate.

They could make out little in the fog. The first sea-tanks must have sent coelenterate bubbles wobbling into the air before the men realized what was happening, for presently all was cries, screams, and confusion. The sea-tanks pressed slowly forward through the fog, crunching and scraping into the narrow streets, while, behind them, still more climbed out of the water. On the waterfront there was panic. People running from one tank were as likely to run into another. Without any warning a whip-like cilium would slash out of the fog, find its victim, and begin to contract. A little later there would be a heavy splash as it rolled with its load over the quayside, back into the water.

Alarm, running back up the town, reached the comisaría. The officer in charge put through the emergency call. He listened, then hung up slowly.

'Grounded,' he said, 'and wouldn't be much use even if they could take off.'

He gave orders to issue rifles and turn out every available man.

'Not that they'll be much good, but we might be lucky. Aim carefully, and if you do find a vital spot, report at once.'

He sent the men off with little hope that they could do more than offer a token resistance. Presently he heard sounds of firing. Suddenly there was a boom that rattled the windows, then another. The telephone rang. An excited voice explained that a party of dockworkers was throwing fused sticks of dynamite and gelignite under the advancing sea-tanks. Another boom rattled the windows. The officer thought quickly.

'Very well. Find the leader. Authorize him from me. Put your men on to getting the people clear,' he directed.

The sea-tanks were not easily discouraged this time, and it was difficult to sort out claims and reports. Estimates of the number destroyed varied between thirty and seventy; of the numbers engaged, between fifty and a hundred and fifty. Whatever the true figures, the force must have been considerable, and the pressure eased only a couple of hours before dawn.

When the sun rose to clear the last of the fog it shone upon a town battered in parts, and widely covered with slime, but also upon a citizenry which, in spite of some hundreds of casualties, felt that it had earned battle honours.

The account, as I had it first from the innkeeper, was brief, but it included the main points, and he concluded it with the observation:

'They reckons as there was well over a bloody 'undred of the damn things done-in them two nights. And then there's all those that come up in other places, too – there must be bloody thousands of the bastards a-crawlin' all over the bloody sea-bottom. Time something was bloody done about 'em, I say. But no. "No cause for alarm," says the bloody Government. Huh, we've had a basinful of that before. It'll go on being no bloody cause for bloody alarm until a few hundred poor devils somewhere 'as got their bloody selves lassoed by flying jellyfish. *Then* it'll be all emergency orders and bloody panic. You watch.'

'The Bay of Biscay's pretty deep,' I pointed out. 'A lot deeper than anything we've got around here.'

'So what?' said the innkeeper.

And when I came to think of it, it was a perfectly good question. The real sources of trouble were without doubt way down in the greater Deeps, and the first surface invasions had all taken place close to the big Deeps. But there were no grounds for assuming that sea-tanks *must* operate close to a Deep. Indeed, from a purely mechanical point of view, a slowly shelving climb should be easier for them than a steep one – or should it? There was also the point that the deeper they were the less energy they had to expend in shifting their weight. . . . Again the whole thing boiled down to the fact that we still knew too little about them to make any worthwhile prophecies at all. The innkeeper was as likely to be right as anyone else.

I told him so, and we drank to the hope that he was not. When I left, the spell had been rudely broken. I stopped in the village to send a telegram, and then went back to the Manor to pack my things, and tell them that I should be leaving the following day.

*

To occupy the journey by catching up on the world I bought a selection of daily and weekly newspapers. The urgent topic in most of the dailies was 'coast preparedness' – the Left demanding wholesale embattlement of the Atlantic seaboard, the Right rejecting panic-spending on a probable chimera. Beyond that, the outlook had not changed a great deal. The boffins had not yet produced a panacea (though the usual new device was to be tested), the merchant-ships still choked the harbours, the aircraft factories were working three shifts and threatening to strike, the C.P. was pushing a line of Every Plane is a Vote for War.

Mr Malenkov, interviewed by telegram, had said that although the intensified programme of aircraft construction in the West was no more than a part of a bourgeois-fascist plan by warmongers that could deceive no one, yet so great was the opposition of the Russian people to any thought of war that the production of aircraft within the Soviet Union for the Defence of Peace had been tripled. War was not inevitable.

Long analyses of this statement by the regular Kremlinologists conveyed the impression that the tripod, as well as a touch of the conversational style, of Delphi, had been transferred to Moscow.

The first thing I noticed when I let myself into the flat was a number of envelopes on the mat, a telegram, presumably my own, among them. The place immediately felt forlorn.

In the bedroom were signs of hurried packing, in the kitchen sink, some unwashed crockery. A half-written page in the typewriter in the sitting-room presented some cross-talk; as one of the speakers was called Perpetua, I recognized it for a part of the stand-by novel. I looked in the desk-diary, but the last entry was a week old, and said simply: 'Lamb chops.'

The precious notebook was there beside it. I don't usually look at that: it has a status slightly lower than personal letters, but still private. However, this was an exceptional occasion, and I wanted a clue if there was one, so I opened it. The last two entries read:

> *Ever since the phi etymological Mr Nash*
> *Turned the dictionary into a polysyllabical bit of hash,*
> *'S'no longer the lingo*
> *The Bard used to sing-oh.*

And:

> *Even if I should live a very, very long time*
> *I still shouldn't be very likely to find the rhyme*
> *That Ogden*
> *Got bogged on.*

More plaintive than constructive, I thought; certainly not instructive. I picked up the telephone.

It was nice of Freddy Wittier to sound genuinely pleased that I was about again. After the greetings and congratulations:

'Look,' I said, 'I've been so strictly incomunicado that I seem to have lost my wife. Can you elucidate?'

'Lost your what?' said Freddy, in a startled tone.

'Wife – Phyllis,' I explained.

'Oh, I thought you said "life". Oh, she's all right. She went off with Bocker a couple of days ago,' he announced cheerfully.

'That,' I told him, 'is not the way to break the news. Just what do you mean by "went off with Bocker"?'

'Spain,' he said, succinctly. 'They're laying bathy-traps there, or something. Matter of fact, we're expecting a dispatch from her any moment.'

'So she's pinching my job?'

'Keeping it warm for you – it's other people that'd like to pinch it. Good thing you're back.'

In the subsequent course of the conversation I learnt that Phyllis had stood her rest-cure for just one week, and then showed up again in London.

The flat was depressing, so I went round to the Club and spent the evening there.

The telephone jangling by the bedside woke me up. I switched on the light. Five a.m. 'Hullo,' I said to the telephone, in a five a.m. voice. It was Freddy. My heart gave a nasty knock inside as I recognized him at that hour.

'Mike?' he said. 'Good. Grab your hat and a recorder. There's a car on the way for you now.'

My needle was still swinging a bit.

'Car?' I repeated. 'It's not Phyl – ?'

'Phyl – ? Oh, Lord, no. She's okay. Her call came through about nine o'clock. Transcription gave her your love, on my instructions. Now get cracking, old man. That car'll be outside your place any minute.'

'But look here. – Anyway, there's no recorder here. She must have taken it.'

'Hell. I'll try to get one to the plane in time.'

'Plane – ?' I said, but the line had gone dead.

I rolled out of bed, and started to dress. A ring came at the door before I had finished. It was one of EBC's regular drivers. I asked him what the hell, but all he knew was that there was a special charter job laid on at Northolt. I grabbed my passport, and we left.

It turned out that I didn't need the passport. I discovered that when I joined a small, blear-eyed section of Fleet Street that was gathered in the waiting-hall drinking coffee. Bob Humbleby was there, too.

'Ah, the Other Spoken Word,' said somebody. 'I thought I knew my Watson.'

'What,' I inquired, 'is all this about? Here am I routed out of a warm though solitary bed, whisked through the night – yes, thanks, a drop of that would liven it up.'

The Samaritan stared at me.

'Do you mean to say you've not heard?' he asked.

'Heard what?'

'Bathies. Place called Buncarragh, Donegal,' he explained, telegraphically. 'And very suitable, too, in my opinion. Ought to feel themselves really at home among the leprechauns and banshees. But I have no doubt that the natives will be after telling us that it's another injustice that the first place in England to have a visit from them should be Ireland, so they will.'

It was queer indeed to encounter that same decaying, fishy smell in a little Irish village. Escondida had in itself been exotic and slightly improbable; but that the same thing should strike among these soft greens and misty blues, that the sea-tanks should come crawling up on this cluster of little grey cottages, and burst their sprays of tentacles here, seemed utterly preposterous.

Yet, there were the ground-down stones of the slipway in the little harbour, the grooves on the beach beside the harbour wall, four cottages demolished, distraught women who had seen their men caught in the nets of the cilia, and over all the same plastering of slime, and the same smell.

There had been six sea-tanks, they said. A prompt telephone-call had brought a couple of fighters at top speed. They had wiped out three, and the rest had gone sliding back into the water – but not before half the population of the village, wrapped in tight cocoons of tentacles, had preceded them.

The next night there was a raid further south, in Galway Bay . . .

By the time I got back to London the campaign had begun. This is no place for a detailed survey of it. Many copies of the official report must still exist, and their accuracy will be more useful than my jumbled recollections.

Phyllis and Bocker were back from Spain, too, and she and I settled down to work. A somewhat different line of work, for day-to-day news of sea-tank raids was now Agency and local correspondent stuff. We seemed to be holding a kind of E B C relations job with the Forces, and also with Bocker – at least, that was what we made of it. Telling the listening public what we could about what was being done for them.

And a lot was. The Republic of Ireland had suspended the past for the moment to borrow large numbers of mines, bazookas, and mortars, and then agreed to accept the loan of a number of men trained in the use of them, too. All along the west and south coasts of Ireland squads of men were laying minefields above the tidelines wherever there were no protecting cliffs. In coastal towns pickets armed with bomb-firing weapons kept all-night watch. Elsewhere, planes, jeeps, and armoured cars waited on call.

In the south-west of England, and up the more difficult west coast of Scotland similar preparations were going on.

They did not seem greatly to deter the sea-tanks. Night after night, down the Irish coast, on the Brittany coast, up out of the Bay of Biscay, along the Portuguese seaboard they came crawling in large or small raids. But they had lost their most potent weapon, surprise. The leaders usually gave their own alarm by blowing themselves up in the minefields; by the time a gap had been created the defences were in action and the townspeople had fled. The sea-tanks that did get through did some damage, but found little prey, and their losses were not infrequently one hundred per cent.

Across the Atlantic serious trouble was almost confined to the Gulf of Mexico. Raids on the east coast were so effectively discouraged that few took place at all north of Charleston; on the Pacific side there were few higher than San Diego. In general, it was the two Indies, the Philippines, and Japan that continued to suffer most; but they, too, were learning ways of inflicting enormous damage for very small returns.

Bocker spent a great deal of time dashing hither and thither trying to persuade various authorities to include traps among their defences. He had little success. It was agreed that a full knowledge of the enemy's nature would be a useful asset, but there were practical difficulties. Scarcely any place was willing to contemplate the prospect of a sea-tank, trapped on its fore-shore, but still capable of throwing out coelenterates for an unknown length of time, nor did even Bocker have any theories on the location of traps beyond the construction of enormous numbers of them on a hit-or-miss basis. A few of the pitfall type were dug, but none ever made a catch. Nor did the more hope-ful-sounding project of preserving any stalled or disabled sea-tank for examination turn out any better. In a few places the defenders were persuaded to cage them with wire-netting instead of blowing them to pieces, but that was the easy part of the problem. The question what to do next was not solved. Any attempt at broaching invariably caused them to explode in geysers of slime. Very often they did so before the attempt was made – the effect, Bocker maintained, of exposure to bright sunlight, though there were other views. Whatever the cause, it could not be said that anyone knew any more about their nature than when we first encountered them on Escondida.

It was the Irish who took almost the whole weight of the north-European attack which was conducted, according to Bocker, from a base somewhere in the Deep, south of Rockall. They rapidly developed a skill in dealing with them that made it a point of dishonour that even one should get away. Scotland suffered only a few minor visitations in the Outer Isles, with scarcely a casualty. England's only raids occurred in Cornwall, and they, too, were small affairs for the most part – the one exception was an incursion in Falmouth Harbour where a few did succeed in advancing a little beyond high-tide mark before they were destroyed; but much larger numbers, it was claimed, were smashed by depth-charges before they could even reach the shore.

Then, only a few days after the Falmouth attack, the raids ceased. They stopped quite suddenly, and, as far as the larger land-masses were concerned, completely.

A week later there was no longer any doubt that what some-one had nicknamed the Low Command had called the campaign off. The continental coasts had proved too tough a nut, and the attempt had flopped. The sea-tanks withdrew to less dangerous parts, but even there their percentage of losses mounted and their returns diminished.

A fortnight after the last raid came a proclamation ending the state of emergency. A day or two later Bocker made his comments on the situation over the air:

'Some of us,' he said, 'some of us, though not the more sensible of us, have recently been celebrating a victory. To them I suggest that when the cannibal's fire is not quite hot enough to boil the pot, the intended meal may feel some relief, but he has *not,* in the generally accepted sense of the phrase, scored a victory. In fact, if he does not do something before the cannibal has time to build a better and bigger fire, he is not going to be any better off.

'Let us, therefore, look at this "victory". We, a maritime people who rose to power upon shipping which plied to the furthest corners of the earth, have lost the freedom of the seas. We have been kicked out of an element that we had made our own. Our ships are only safe in coastal waters and shallow seas – and who can say how long they are going to be tolerated even there? We have been forced by a blockade, more effective than any experienced in war, to depend on air-transport for the very food by which we live. Even the scientists who are trying to study the sources of our troubles must put to sea in *sailing-ships* to do their work. Is *this* victory?

'What the eventual purpose of these coastal raids may have been, no one can say. It may be that those who referred to them as "shrimping" were not so far from the mark – that they have been trawling for us as we trawl for fish – it *may* be, though I do not think so myself; there is more to be caught more cheaply in the sea than on the land. But it may even have been part of an attempt to conquer the land – an ineffectual and ill-informed attempt, but, for all that, rather more successful than our attempts to reach the Deeps. If it was, then its instigators are now better informed about us, and therefore potentially more dangerous. They are not likely to try again in the same way with the same weapons, but I see nothing in what we have been able to do to discourage them from trying in a different way with different weapons. Do you?

'The need for us to find some way in which we can strike back at them is therefore not relaxed, but intensified.

'It may be recalled by some that when we were first made aware of activity in the Deeps I advocated that every effort should be made to establish understanding with them. That was not tried, and very likely it was never a possibility, but there can be no doubt that the situation which I had hoped we could avoid now exists – and is in the process of being resolved. Two intelligent forms of life are finding one another's existence intolerable. I have now come to believe that no attempt at rapprochement could have succeeded. Life in all its forms is strife; the better matched the opponents, the harder the struggle. The most powerful of all weapons is intelligence; any intelligent form dominates by, and therefore survives by, its intelligence: a rival form of intelligence must, by its very existence, threaten to dominate, and therefore threaten extinction. Any intelligent form is its own absolute; and there cannot be two absolutes.

'Observation has shown me that my former view was lamentably anthropomorphic; I say now that we must attack as swiftly as we can find the means, and with the full intention of complete extermination. These things, whatever they may be, have not only succeeded in throwing us out of their element with ease, but already they have advanced to do battle with us in ours. For the moment we have pushed them back, but they will return, for the same urge drives them as drives us – the necessity to

exterminate, or be exterminated. And when they come again,
if we let them, they will come better equipped. . . .

'Such a state of affairs, I repeat, is *not* victory. . . . '

*

I ran across Pendell of Audio-Assessment the next morning.
He gave me a gloomy look.

'We tried,' I said, defensively. 'We tried hard, but the Elijah
mood was on him.'

'Next time you see him just tell him what I think of him, will
you?' Pendell suggested. 'It's not that I mind his being right –
just that I never did know a man with such a gift for being right
at the wrong time, and in the wrong manner. When his name
comes on our programme again, if it ever does, they'll switch
off in their thousands. As a bit of friendly advice, tell him to
start cultivating the BBC.'

As it happened, Phyllis and I were meeting Bocker for lunch
that same day. Inevitably he wanted to hear reactions to his
broadcast. I gave the first reports gently. He nodded:

'Most of the papers take that line,' he said. 'Why was I con-
demned to live in a democracy where every fool's vote is equal
to a sensible man's? If all the energy that is put into diddling
mugs for their votes could be turned on to useful work, what a
nation we could be! As it is, at least three national papers are
agitating for a cut in "the millions squandered on research" so
that the taxpayer can buy himself another packet of cigarettes a
week, which means more cargo-space wasted on tobacco,
which means more revenue from tax, which the government
then spends on something other than research – and the ships go
on rusting in the harbours. There's no sense in it.'

'But those things down there have taken a beating,' Phyllis
pointed out.

'We ourselves have a tradition of taking beatings, and then
winning wars,' said Bocker.

'Exactly,' said Phyllis. 'We have taken a beating at sea, but
in the end we shall get back.'

Bocker groaned, and rolled his eyes. 'Logic –' he began, but I put in:

'You spoke as if you thought they might actually be more intelligent than we are. Do you?'

He frowned. 'I don't see how one could answer that. My impression is that they think in a quite different way – along other lines from ours. If they do, no comparison would be possible, and any attempt at it misleading.'

'You were quite serious about their trying again? I mean, it wasn't just propaganda to stop interest in the protection of shipping from falling off?' Phyllis asked.

'Did it sound like that?'

'No, but –'

'I meant it, all right,' he said. 'Consider their alternatives. Either they sit down there waiting for us to find a means to destroy them, or they come after us. Oh, yes, unless we find it very soon, they'll be here again – somehow. . . .'

Phase Three

SOMETHING checked us. Not with a jolt, but with a gentle yielding, and a slight rubbing sound. From where I sat in the stern of the dinghy, keeping a little way on, and steering with a muffled oar, I could see practically nothing in the darkness, but it did not feel as if we had hit the bank.

'What is it?' I whispered.

The little boat rocked as Phyllis clambered forward. There was a faint thud from some part of our gear dislodged. Presently her whisper came back:

'It's a net. A big one.'

'Can you lift it?'

She shifted. The dinghy rocked again, and then remained tilted for a moment. It relaxed back to an even keel.

'No. Too heavy,' she said.

I hadn't expected that kind of hold-up. A few hours before in daylight I had prospected the route with binoculars, from a church tower. I had observed that to the north-west there was a narrow gap between two hills, and beyond it the water widened out into a lake stretching further than I could see. It looked as if, once past that neck, one ought to be able to travel a considerable distance without coming too close to the shore. I traced the way to the gap and memorized it with care before I came down. The tide turned and began to rise before it was quite dark. We waited another half-hour, and then set off, rowing up on the flood. It had not been too difficult to find the gap, for the silhouette of the two hills showed faintly against the sky. I had moved to the stern to steer and let the tide carry us silently through. And now there was the net. . . .

I turned the craft so that the flow held us broadside against the barrier. I shipped the oar cautiously, felt for the net, and found it. It was made of half-inch rope with about a six-inch mesh, I judged. I felt for my knife.

'Hold on,' I whispered. 'I'll cut a hole.'

While I was in the act of opening the blade there came a crack, followed by a whoosh. A flare broke out above. The whole scene about us was suddenly visible, and there we sat in mid-stream, bathed in a hard, white light.

The lower hill, on the left, was covered with turf and a few bushes among wandering paths. To the right was a row of houses a few feet above the water-level. In front of them, and closer, was another row, built on a slant across the hillside. The house at the right-hand end was high enough for its whole roof to show above water. Its neighbours marched gradually deeper until they only showed chimney-pots, and finally nothing at all.

A rifle cracked somewhere in one of the houses in the upper row. I missed the flash, but the bullet phewed by, not far from our heads. I dropped my knife into the bottom of the dinghy, and put up my hands. A voice carried clearly from one of the dark windows:

'Get back where you came from, chum,' it advised.

I lowered my hands, looked at Phyllis, and shrugged.

'We only want to go through, to get home. We don't want to stay, or ask for anything,' she called back to the unseen man.

'That's what they all say. Where's home?' he asked.

'Cornwall,' she told him.

He laughed 'Cornwall! You've got a hope.'

'It's true,' she said.

'True it may be, but it's bloody impossible, too. *And* I've got my orders. It's get back or get hurt. So start moving.'

'But we've got enough food to –' Phyllis began.

I shook my head at her. From what I'd been told, the only chance had been to get through without being seen – and having food with one was not a thing to advertise.

'Okay,' I called wearily. 'We'll get back.'

There was no need for silence any more, so I tilted the outboard into the water, and wound the cord on it.

'You got sense – and better not try again,' advised the voice.

'I'm kind of old-fashioned – don't like shooting people that'll act reasonable. But there's others not so particular. So just keep going, chum.'

I pulled the cord, and she started. We pushed clear of the net, and then chugged off downstream, against the tide. The flare sank gradually behind us, and burnt out. Darkness, darker than before, closed in.

Phyllis clambered over the gear, and came to sit beside me. Her gloved hand found my knee, and pressed it.

'Sorry, darling,' I said.

'Can't be helped, Mike. We'll try again somewhere. Third time lucky, perhaps.'

'This time lucky,' I said. 'He shot to miss. He needn't have done that.'

'A net and a guard must mean that a lot of people have been trying this way. Where are we now?'

'I'm not sure. It's difficult to identify anything from the map. Must be somewhere in the Staines-Weybridge area, though. Seems a pity to go back now.'

'More of a pity to get shot,' said Phyllis.

We puttered along, keeping a look-out for obstacles by occasional flashes of a torch.

'If you don't know where we are, how do you know where we're heading?' Phyllis inquired.

'I don't,' I admitted. 'I'm just keeping going, like the gentleman said. It seems wise to get clear of his territory.'

Presently the moon rose and began to shine intermittently through gaps in the clouds. Phyllis pulled her coat more closely round her, and shivered a little.

'June,' she said. 'June – moon – spoon – soon. They used to sing about June nights on the river. Remember? Uh-huh. *Sic transit . . .*'

'From what I do remember they were a trifle optimistic, even then,' I replied. 'A wise man took rugs.'

'Oh?' said Phyllis. 'Who with?'

'Never you mind. *Autres temps, autres mondes.*'

'*Autre monde,*' indeed,' she said, looking round over the waste of water. 'We can't go on aimlessly like this, Mike. Let's find somewhere to get warm, and sleep.'

'All right,' I agreed, and put the tiller over a bit.

A mile or so away stood a mound, dotted with houses. One could not tell whether it was an island or not, but between it and us more houses, submerged to different degrees, protruded from the water. We selected a solid-looking white one, late-Georgian, judging from the visible upper storeys, and steered towards it.

The wood of the window-frame was too swollen to slide, so we had to push in the window with an oar before we could get inside. The torch showed a bedroom; very tasteful once, but now with a tidemark half-way up the walls. I squelched across the carpet and got the door open with a little difficulty. Outside on the landing the water was within a few inches of the top of the stairs. The floor above was all right, though. Quite comfortably furnished, too.

'This'll do,' Phyllis decided.

She lit a couple of candles, and started to rearrange things in the room she had chosen. I went down again, pulled our rolls of bedding and the other necessaries out of the dinghy, and made sure it was fastened securely, with enough slack for the tide.

When I got the stuff up Phyllis had already shed her coat and, looking business-like in a kind of windbreaker-suit, was lugging comfortable chairs in from another room. I got busy knocking away the stair-rail and breaking up the banisters for a fire.

The curtains were only cotton, so we covered them with blankets. It was not very likely that anyone would come to investigate a light, but if he did, and found the dinghy unguarded, he would certainly make off with it. Then we were able to settle down to stoking the fire and enjoying the growing warmth of the room.

Our supper consisted of biscuits, sausages cooked in the can and eaten off a fork, and tea made with bottled rainwater and condensed milk. Not an elegant meal, but in spite of the depressing thought that down in the depths of such a house, and safely out of our reach, there must be a lot of more exciting things to drink, we felt the better for it.

When it was done we extinguished the candles for economy's sake, piled on more wood, and lay back enjoying the blaze. For half a cigarette there was silence, then Phyllis said:

'Well, so far, so not very good. What now?'

It was a fair summary of my own state of mind.

'I don't like to admit it,' I said, 'but it does begin to look as if Cornwall may have to be cancelled.'

'That man was pretty scornful about it, wasn't he? But that might have been because he didn't believe us.'

'It sounded as if he foresaw a lot of obstacles in the way – with himself as the first,' I said. 'It seems likely that there are quite a lot of independent districts we should have to cross.'

'Even if we were to go back to London we should have to face getting out of it somehow, sooner or later – unless, of course, we get shot there. It's bound to go on getting worse all the time. In the country you can at least grow things. You do have a chance. But a city is a sort of desert of bricks and stones. Once you've used up what is there, you're done for.'

I considered Rose Cottage. There was some soil, of a kind – though it was not a region I should have chosen for attempting to live off the land. But it was clear that no one was going to welcome us on to good, lush land – if there was any left. And she was right about the barrenness of cities, once their reserves have been used up. I doubted any welcome in Cornwall, but Rose Cottage might offer just a chance – provided there was not someone already there, and that we could get there at all. . . .

We went on discussing the prospects in a desultory way for an hour or more without getting any further, and ended by gazing silently into the fire, devoid of further suggestions. Presently Phyllis yawned. We pulled the damp clothes from the beds, spread out on own bedding rolls with their waterproof covers on the mattresses, made up the fire again, put the shotgun handy, and then turned in.

Technically, I suppose, it was the morrow that brought us the new idea, though I have an abiding feeling that a morrow does not properly begin until breakfast-time, and this idea turned up at about one in the morning. It arrived with a bump that woke me.

I sat up with the sound of the thud still in my ears, thoroughly awakened and alert. The room was almost dark, for the fire had sunk to a few ashes. There came another, but lesser, thump on the wall outside, and then the sound of something scraping along it. I snatched up the shotgun, jumped out of bed, and whipped the blanket and curtain aside from the nearest window. There was plenty of flotsam, sheds, chicken-houses, furniture, logs, all kinds of smaller stuff that could have made the bump. On the other hand, it might have been made by somebody who had spotted the dinghy, and the loss of that would be disastrous.

I looked out. The moon was sinking now, but still bright. The dinghy still rode safely just below. The scraping came again, along the other wall. I scrambled back, and found the torch on the table between the beds.

'What's the matter?' inquired Phyllis's voice, but I was in too much of a hurry to answer. Gun in one hand and torch in the other, I ran to the next room. One of its windows faced north. I dropped the torch, raised the sash, and looked out over the levelled shotgun. Just below, there was a boat, a small, cabin motor-boat, nudging along the wall, and I was gazing down at the figure of a woman lying in her well. It was scarcely more than a glimpse, for at that moment the boat scraped to the corner of the house; the current swung her out and took her away. I caught up the torch.

'What is it?' Phyllis demanded as I pelted past the bedroom door.

'Boat,' I called back as I ran down the stairs.

The water on the next floor was waist-deep now, and icy, but I was in too much of a hurry to pay it a lot of attention. With the risen level it was difficult to get aboard the dinghy without upsetting her, but I managed it. Then, of course, the outboard had to go sulky. Not until the fourth or fifth attempt did it fire.

By that time I had lost sight of the drifting motor-boat, but I turned into the current, and chased after her.

It was only by chance that I did not miss her altogether and go charging on uselessly downstream. The current had carried her straight into a submerged spinney, and I had just a glimpse of her in the tangle of branches as I passed. Like any other boat nowadays she had been painted not for show but for discretion, and it was a near thing.

When I got aboard her I flashed the light in through the open doors of the little cabin. There was no one in there. The woman lying in the well had been shot twice, in the neck and in the chest, and must have died some hours before. I lifted her over the side, and let her go.

I could not hope to tow the boat back against both tide and current with the outboard, and I was growing too numb with cold to spend time trying to find out how to run her. The best course seemed to be to make sure that she would drift no further, and hope that no one else would see her before I could come back in daylight. It was a risk. A boat of any kind was beyond price, but the alternative was almost certainly pneumonia. Moreover, I daren't delay long, for once the moon had set it wouldn't be easy to find the house again.

Phyllis was warming a blanket for me in front of the rekindled fire. Freed of my wet pyjamas, and wrapped in that, I began to glow after a bit.

'A sea-going motor-boat?' Phyllis inquired, excitedly.

'Well, kind of high in the bows – not one of those car-on-water things. So I should think it's meant for sea. Small, though.'

'Don't be irritating. You know perfectly well what I mean. Could it get us to Cornwall?'.

'With our knowledge of the things, it's more a question of could *we* get *it* to Cornwall? – and there my opinion isn't worth any more than yours. We might try – at least it looks to me as if we might. See what you think when you've looked her over.'

I had no doubt whatever what she would think. But for decisive discouragement on my part we should probably have set out on an attempt to get along the coast in the little fibre-glass dinghy.

'I feel like making an offering, or something,' she said.

'Keep it until we find out whether she's sound. There could be a lot of snags yet,' I told her.

The warmth after the exposure was making me sleepy. I told her to wake me up when it began to get light, so that we could get across to the boat before anyone else should spot her.

Then I went to sleep with an easier mind than I had had for some weeks. I knew that whatever we should find in Cornwall it would be no picnic. On the other hand, London was a slowly-closing trap; a good place to get out of before it began to squeeze. . . .

*

Even though Bocker had been unaware of it when he gave his warning, the new method of attack had already begun, but it took six months more before it became apparent.

Had the ocean vessels been keeping their usual courses, it would have aroused general comment earlier, but with trans-atlantic crossings taking place only by air, the pilots' reports of unusually dense and widespread fog in the west Atlantic were simply noted. With the increased range of aircraft, too, Gander had declined in importance, so that its frequently fogbound state caused little inconvenience.

Checking reports of that time in the light of later knowledge I discovered that there were reports about the same time of unusually widespread fogs in the North-Western Pacific, too. Conditions were bad off the northern Japanese island of Hok-kaido, and said to be still worse off the Kuriles, further north. But since it was now some time since ships had dared to cross the Deeps in those parts information was scanty, and few were interested. Nor did the abnormally foggy conditions on the South American coast northward from Montevideo attract public attention.

The chilly mistiness of the summer in England was, indeed, frequently remarked, though more with resignation than surprise.

Fog, in fact, was scarcely noticed by the wider world-consciousness until the Russians mentioned it. A note from Moscow proclaimed the existence of an area of dense fog having its centre on the meridian 130° East of Greenwich, at, or about, the 85th parallel. Soviet scientists, after research, had declared that nothing of the kind was on previous record, nor was it possible to see how the known conditions in those parts could generate such a state, let alone maintain it virtually unchanged for three months after its existence had first been observed. The Soviet Government had on several former occasions pointed out that the Arctic activities of the hirelings of capitalist warmongers might well be a menace to Peace.

The territorial rights of the USSR in that area of the Arctic lying between the meridians 32° East and 168° West of Greenwich were recognized by International Law. Any unauthorized incursion into that area constituted an act of aggression. The Soviet Government, therefore, considered itself at liberty to take any action necessary for the preservation of Peace in that region.

The note, delivered simultaneously to several countries, received its most rapid and downright reply from Washington.

The peoples of the West, the State Department observed, would be interested by the Soviet Note. As, however, they had now had considerable experience of that technique of propaganda which had been called the pre-natal *tu quoque,* they were able to recognize its implications. The Government of the United States was well aware of the territorial divisions in the Arctic – it would, indeed, remind the Soviet Government, in the interests of accuracy, that the segment mentioned in the Note was only approximate, the true figures being: 32° – 4' – 35" East of Greenwich, and 168° – 49' – 30" West of Greenwich, giving a slightly smaller segment than that claimed, but since the centre of the phenomenon mentioned was well within this area the United States Government had, naturally, no cognizance of its existence until informed of it in the Note.

Recent observations had, curiously, recorded the existence of just such a feature as that described in the Note at a centre also close to the 85th Parallel, but at a point 79° West of Greenwich. By coincidence this was just the target-area jointly selected by the United States and Canadian Governments for tests of their latest types of long-range guided missiles. Preparations for these tests had already been completed, and the first experimental launchings would take place in a few days.

The Russians commented on the quaintness of choosing a target-area where observation was not possible; the Americans, upon the Slavonic zeal for pacification of uninhabited regions. Whether both parties then proceeded to attack their respective fogs is not on public record, but the wider effect was that fogs became news, and were discovered to have been unusually dense of late in a surprising number of places.

Had weather-ships still been at work in the Atlantic it is likely that useful data would have been gathered sooner, but they had been 'temporarily' withdrawn from service, following the sinking of two of them some time before. Consequently the first report which did anything to tidy up the idle speculations came from Godthaab, in Greenland. It spoke of an increased flow of water through the Davis Strait from Baffin Bay, with a content of broken ice quite unusual for the time of year. A few days later Nome, Alaska, reported a similar condition in the Bering Strait. Then from Spitsbergen, too, came reports of increased flow and lower temperatures.

That straightforwardly explained the fogs off Newfoundland and certain other parts. Elsewhere they could be convincingly ascribed to deep-running cold currents forced upwards into the warmer waters above by encounters with submarine mountain ranges. Everything, in fact, could be either simply or abstrusely explained, except the unusual increase in the cold flow.

Then, from Godhavn, north of Godthaab on the west Greenland coast, a message told of icebergs in unprecedented numbers and often of unusual size. Investigating expeditions were flown from American Arctic bases, and confirmed the report. The sea in the north of Baffin Bay, they announced, was crammed with icebergs.

'At about Latitude 77, 60° West,' one of the fliers wrote, 'we found the most awesome sight in the world. The glaciers which run down from the high Greenland Ice-Cap were calving. I have seen icebergs formed before, but never on anything like the scale it is taking place there. In the great ice-cliffs, hundreds of feet high, cracks appear suddenly. An enormous section tilts out, falling and turning slowly. When it smashes into the water the spray rises up and up in great fountains, spreading far out all around. The displaced water comes rushing back in breakers which clash together in tremendous spray while a berg as big as a small island slowly rolls and wallows and finds its balance. For a hundred miles up and down the coast we saw splashes starting up where the same thing was happening. Very often a berg had no time to float away before a new one had crashed down on top of it. The scale was so big that it was hard to realize. Only by the apparent slowness of the falls and the way the huge splashes seemed to hang in the air – the majestic pace of it all – were we able to tell the vastness of what we were seeing.'

Just so did other expeditions describe the scene on the east coast of Devon Island, and on the southern tip of Ellesmere Island. In Baffin Bay the innumerable great bergs jostled slowly, grinding the flanks and shoulders from one another as they herded on the long drift southward, through the Davis Strait, and out into the Atlantic.

Away over on the other side of the Arctic Circle, Nome announced that the southward flow of broken pack-ice had further increased.

The public received the information in a cushionly style. People were impressed by the first magnificent photographs of icebergs in the process of creation, but, although no iceberg is quite like any other iceberg, the generic similarity is pronounced. A rather brief period of awe was succeeded by the thought that while it was really very clever of science to know all about icebergs and climate and so on, it did not seem to be much good knowing if it could not, resultantly, do something about it.

Tuny, at a chance meeting with Phyllis, summed the attitude

up: 'I'm sure things like that must be frightfully interesting if one happens to be the kind of person who finds just being interested in things enough. What seems to me so feeble is that having found out all this they don't stop them doing it.'

'Well,' said Phyllis, 'stopping icebergs is probably pretty difficult –'

'I don't mean stopping icebergs, I mean stopping the Russians from making icebergs.'

'Oh,' said Phyllis, 'are they ? – making them, I mean ?'

'But of course! Just look at it logically,' Tuny told her. 'You don't get things like this suddenly happening for no reason at all. The Russians always seem to think they have more rights in the Arctic than anyone else although they were years after other people in getting to the North Pole, and I expect they're now claiming that they discovered it some time in the nineteenth century because they don't seem to be able to bear the thought that anybody else ever discovered anything, and – where was I ?'

'*I* was wondering why they should be making icebergs,' Phyllis said.

'Oh, yes. Well, that's all part of their general policy. I mean, everyone knows that their idea is to make trouble everywhere they can. And look at the wretched summer we've been having; things cancelled one after another, and now they're saying that Wimbledon may have to be washed out altogether. And the whole thing is due to these icebergs they keep on sending into our Gulf Stream. The scientists all know that, but nobody *does* anything about it. People are beginning to get fed-up with evasiveness, I can tell you. They want a strong line, and a clean-out that will stop this kind of thing. It's been allowed to go on much too long already. Surely they can blow them up, or something.'

'The Russians, or the icebergs ?' asked Phyllis.

'Well, I meant the icebergs. If they just blow them up and show the Russians it isn't going to work, they'll probably stop it.'

'But – er – are you quite *sure* the Russians are responsible for them ?' Phyllis said.

Tuny regarded her closely.

'I must say,' she remarked, 'it seems to me very odd indeed how concerned some people seem to be to justify the Russians on every possible occasion.' And shortly afterwards they parted.

Meanwhile, the interchange of Notes across the North Pole continued. Neither side particularized on the steps taken to deal with the offence in its own area, but the State Department admitted that its area of fog was, when undisturbed by wind, now greater than before; the Kremlin was less committal, but claimed no resounding successes.

The dreary summer passed into a drearier autumn. There seemed to be nothing anybody could do about it but accept it with a grumbling philosophy.

At the other end of the world spring came. Then summer, and the whaling season started – in so far as it could be called a season at all when the owners who would risk ships were so few, and the crews ready to risk their lives fewer still. Nevertheless, some could be found ready to damn the bathies, along with all other perils of the deep, and set out. At the end of the Antarctic summer came news, via New Zealand, of glaciers in Victoria Land shedding huge quantities of bergs into the Ross Sea, and suggestions that the great Ross Ice-Barrier itself might be beginning to break up. Within a week came similar news from the Weddell Sea. The Filchner Barrier there, and the Larsen Ice-Shelf were both said to be calving bergs in fantastic numbers. A series of reconnaissance flights brought in reports which read almost exactly like those from Baffin Bay, and photographs which might have come from the same region. Again the more sober illustrated weeklies ran rotogravure views of great masses plunging into seas already dotted for miles with gleaming bergs, and produced studies of individual bergs above such captions as 'Nature's Majesty: With Gothic pinnacles aspiring, a new Everest of the sea sets out upon her lonely voyage. The menacing beauty of this berg freshly calved by the David Glacier in the Ross Sea, is romantically caught by the camera. In many parts of the Antarctic coastline the production of such bergs has been so extensive that ice-shelves hitherto regarded as permanent have been shattered by their fall, and open water now replaces the frozen sea.'

The attitude of polite patronage towards Nature, and the reception, with well-bred congratulatory restraint, of the clever turns she put on to edify and amuse the human race might have continued unruffled for some months longer than it did, but for the urchin quality of Dr Bocker.

The Sunday Tidings, which had for some years been pursuing a policy of intellectual sensationalism, had never found it easy to maintain its supply of material. The stuff of mere emotional sensationalism, as used by its cheaper and less dignified contemporaries, lay thickly all around, easily malleable into shapes attractive to the constant human passions. Intellectual sensationalism, however, was a much more tricky business. In addition to avoiding the suggestion of sensationalism for sensationalism's sake, it required knowledge, research, careful timing, and, if possible, some literary ability. Inevitably, therefore, its policy was subject to lamentable gaps during which it could find nothing topical on its chosen level to disclose. It must, one fancies, have been a council of desperation over a prolonged hiatus of the kind which induced it to open its columns to Bocker.

That the Editor felt some apprehension over the result was discernible from his italicized note preceding the article in which he disclaimed, on grounds of fairmindedness, any responsibility for what he was now printing in his own paper.

With this auspicious beginning, and under the heading: *The Devil and the Deeps,* Bocker led off:

'Never, since the days when Noah was building his Ark, has there been such a well-regimented turning of blind eyes as during the last year. It cannot go on. Soon, now, the long Arctic night will be over. Observation will again be possible. Then, the eyes that should never have been shut *must* open. . . . '

That beginning I remember, but without references I can only give the gist and a few recollected phrases of the rest.

'This,' Bocker continued, 'is the latest chapter in a long tale of futility and failure stretching back to the sinkings of the *Yatsu-*

shiro, and the *Keweenaw,* and beyond. Failure which has already driven us from the seas, and now threatens us on the land. I repeat, *failure.*

'That is a word so little to our taste that many think it a virtue to claim that they never admit it. But blind stupidity is not one of the virtues; it is a weakness, and in this case it is a dangerous weakness, masked by a false optimism. All about us are unrest, inflating prices, whole economic structures changing – and, therefore, a way of life that is changing. All about us, too, are people who talk about our exclusion from the high seas as though it were some temporary inconvenience, soon to be corrected. To this smugness there is a reply; it is this:

'For over five years now the best, the most agile, the most inventive brains in the world have wrestled with the problem of coming to grips with our enemy – and they are still no closer to a solution than when they began. There is, on their present findings, nothing at all to indicate that we shall ever be able to sail the seas in peace again. . . .

'With the word "failure" so wry in our mouths it has apparently been policy to discourage any expression of the connexion between our maritime troubles and the recent developments in the Arctic and Antarctic. It is time for this attitude of "not before the children" to cease. I do not know, and I do not care, what kind of pressure has been preventing our more percipient men from pointing out this connexion; there are always cliques and factions anxious to keep the public in the dark "for its own good" – a "good" that is seldom far from the interests of the faction advocating it.

'I do not suggest that the root problem is being neglected; far from it. There have been, and are, men wearing themselves out to find some means by which we can locate and destroy the enemy in our Deeps. What I do say is that with them still unable to find a way, we now face the most serious assault yet.

'It is an assault against which we have no defences. It is not susceptible of direct attack. It can be checked only by our discovery of some means of destroying its High Command, in the Deeps.

'And what is this weapon to which we can oppose no counter?

'It is the melting of the Arctic ice – and a great part of the Antarctic ice, too.

'You think that fantastic? Too colossal? It is not, it is a task which we could have undertaken ourselves, had we so wished, at any time since we released the power of the atom.

'Because of the winter darkness little has been heard lately of the patches of Arctic fog. It is not generally known that, though two of them existed in the Arctic spring, by the end of the Arctic summer there were eight, in widely separated areas. Now, fog is caused, as you know, by the meeting of hot and cold currents of either air or water. How does it happen that eight novel, independent warm currents can suddenly occur in the Arctic?

'And the results? Unprecedented flows of broken ice into the Bering Sea, and into the Greenland Sea. In these two areas particularly, the pack-ice is hundreds of miles north of its usual spring maximum. In other places, the north of Norway, for instance, it is further south. And we ourselves had an unusually cold, wet winter.

'And the icebergs? We have all read a lot about them and seen a lot of pictures of them lately. Why? Obviously because there are a great many more icebergs than usual, but the question that no one has publicly answered is, *why* should there be more icebergs?

'Everyone knows where they are coming from. Greenland is a large island – greater than nine times the size of the British Isles. But it is more than that. It is also the last great bastion of the retreating ice-age.

'Several times the ice has come south, grinding and scouring, smoothing the mountains, scooping the valleys on its way until it stood in huge ramparts, dizzy cliffs of glass-green ice, vast slow-crawling glaciers, across half Europe. Then it went back, gradually, over centuries, back and back. The huge cliffs and mountains of ice dwindled away, melted, and were known no more – except in one place. Only in Greenland does that immemorial ice still tower nine thousand feet high, unconquered yet. And down its sides slide the glaciers which spawn the icebergs. They have been scattering their icebergs into the sea, season after season, since before there were men to know of it; but why, in this year, should they suddenly spawn ten, twenty times as many? There must be a reason for this. There is.

'If some means, or some several means, of melting the Arctic ice were put into operation, a little time would have to pass before its effects became mensurable. Moreover, the effects would be progressive; first a trickle, then a gush, then a torrent.

'I have seen "estimates" which suggest that if the polar ice were melted the sea-level would rise by one hundred feet. To call that an "estimate" is a shocking imposition. It is no more than a round-figure guess. It may be a good guess, or it may be widely wrong, on either side. The only certainty is that the sea-level would indeed rise.

'In this connexion I draw attention to the fact that in January of this year the mean sea-level at Newlyn, where it is customarily measured, was reported to have risen by two and a half inches.'

'Oh, dear!' said Phyllis, when she had read this. 'Of all the pertinaceous stickers-out-of-necks! We'd better go and see him.'

It did not entirely surprise us when we telephoned the next morning to find that his number was not available. When we called, however, we were admitted. Bocker got up from a desk littered with mail, to greet us.

'No earthly good your coming here,' he told us. 'There isn't a sponsor that'd touch me with a forty-foot pole.'

'Oh, I'd not say that, A. B., Phyllis told him. 'You will very likely find yourself immensely popular with the sellers of sandbags and makers of earth-shifting machinery before long.'

He took no notice of that. 'You'll probably be contaminated if you associate with me. In most countries I'd be under arrest by now.'

'Terribly disappointing for you. This has always been discouraging territory for ambitious martyrs. But you do try, don't you?' she responded. 'Now, look, A. B.,' she went on, 'do you really *like* to have people throwing things at you, or what is it?'

'I get impatient,' explained Bocker.

'So do other people. But nobody I know has quite your gift for going just beyond what people are willing to take at any given moment. One day you'll get hurt. Not this time because, luckily, you've messed it up, but one time certainly.'

'If not this time, then probably not at all,' he said. He bent a thoughtful, disapproving look on her. 'Just what do you mean, young woman, by coming here and telling me I "messed it up"?'

'The anti-climax. First you sounded as if you were on the point of great revelations, but then that was followed by a rather vague suggestion that somebody or something must be causing the Arctic changes – and without any specific explanation of how it could be done. And then your grand finale was that the tide is two and a half inches higher.'

Bocker continued to regard her. 'Well, so it is. I don't see what's wrong with that. Two and a half inches is a colossal amount of water when it's spread over a hundred and forty-one million square miles. If you reckon it up in tons –'

'I never do reckon water in tons – and that's part of the point. To ordinary people two and a half inches just means a very slightly higher mark on a post. After your build-up it sounded so tiddly that everyone feels annoyed with you for alarming them – those that don't just laugh, and say: "Ha! ha! These professors!"'

Bocker waved his hand at the desk with its load of mail.

'Quite a lot of people have been alarmed – or at least indignant,' he said. He lit a cigarette. 'That was what I wanted. You know well enough how it has been since the beginning of this business. At every stage the great majority, and particularly the authorities, have resisted the evidence as long as they could. This is a scientific age – in the more educated strata. It will therefore almost fall over backwards in disregarding the abnormal, and it has developed a deep suspicion of its own senses. Vast quantities of evidence are required before a theory based on scanty knowledge can be dislodged. Very reluctantly the existence of something in the Deeps was belatedly conceded. There has been equal reluctance to admit all the succeeding manifestations until they couldn't be dodged. And now here we are again, baulking at the newest hurdle.

'Ever since this business in the Arctic began, a number of people have been well aware of what must be going on – though not, of course, of how it is being done – but for one reason or another, not excluding Governmental pressure, they have been keeping quiet about it. I have myself.'

'That – er – doesn't sound quite – true to form,' I suggested.

He grinned briefly, and then went on:

'I misjudged it. Several of us did. When the purpose of the thing was clear, I doubted it. "This time," I said to myself, "they really have bitten off more than they can chew." There wasn't any point in alarming people unnecessarily. Things are bad enough already. So, as long as it was possible to hope that the attempt on the ice was going to fail, it was better to say nothing in public. A sort of semi-voluntary censorship.'

'But the Americans – ?'

'Same attitude – if anything a bit more so. Business is their national sport, and, like most national sports, semi-sacred. A still bigger slump than they have been having since the shipping troubles started wouldn't help anyone. So we all watched and waited.

'We've not been altogether idle, though. The Arctic Ocean is deep, and even more difficult to get at than the others, so there was some bombing where the fog-patches occurred, but the devil of it is there's no way of telling results.

'Also, a group of us put it to the Admiralty that there were only two ways the things could be getting into the Arctic. They wouldn't be using the Bering Sea route past Alaska because that would give them something like a couple of thousand miles in shallow water. So they must be coming up our way, between Rockall and Scotland. By cutting through one ridge south of the Faeroes they could have fairly deep water right the way up to the Polar Basin. Now, by that route there are two narrow passes they would have to use. We and the Norwegians got together over that, and between us we put down quite a lot of bombs east of Jan Mayen Island, and another lot further north, between Greenland and Spitsbergen. They may have done something, but, again, you can't tell. At best it can only have meant a bit of delay, because the trouble still went on, and new fog-patches started up.

'In the middle of all this the Muscovite, who seems to be constitutionally incapable of understanding anything to do with the sea, started making trouble. The sea, he appeared to be arguing, was causing a great deal of inconvenience to the West; therefore it must be acting on good dialectically materialistic principles, and I have no doubt that if he could contact the Deeps he would like to make a pact with their inhabitants for a brief period of dialectical opportunism. Anyway, he led off, as you know, with accusations of aggression, and then in the back-and-forth that followed began to show such truculence that the attention of our Services became diverted from the really serious threat to the antics of this oriental clown who thinks the sea was only created to embarrass capitalists.

'Thus, we have now arrived at a situation where the "bathies", as they call them, far from falling down on the job as we had hoped, are going ahead fast, and all the brains and organizations that should be working flat out at planning to meet the emergency are congenially fooling around with those ills they have, and ignoring others that they would rather know not of. There are times when one fails to see why God thought it necessary to devise the ostrich.'

'So you decided that the time had come to force their hands by – er – blowing the gaff?' I asked.

'Yes – but not alone. This time I have the company of a number of eminent and very worried men. Mine was only the opening shot at the wider public on this side of the Atlantic. My weighty companions who have not already lost their reputations over this business are working more subtly. As for the American end, well, just take a look at *Life* and *Collier's* this next week. Oh, yes, something is going to be done.'

'What?' asked Phyllis.

He looked at her thoughtfully for a moment, then shook his head slightly.

'That, thank God, is someone else's department – at least, it will be when the public forces them to admit the situation.'

'But what *can* they do?' Phyllis repeated.

He hesitated. Then he said: 'This is between ourselves. Not a word of it have you heard from me. The only possible thing that I can see for them to do is to organize salvage. To make sure that certain things and people are not lost. That, I have no doubt, they will start to do immediately the reality of the danger has been accepted. The rest will have to take their chance – and I'm afraid that for most of us it won't be much of a chance.'

'Like preparations for a war – move great works of art and important people away to safe places?' suggested Phyllis.

'Exactly – almost too exactly.'

Phyllis frowned. 'Just what do you mean by that, A. B. ?'

He shook his head. 'That they will think in terms of ordinary war – and I don't trust the sense of values that will operate. Art treasures? Yes, no doubt they will try to preserve them, but at the cost of what else? Call me a Philistine, if you like, but Art really only became Art in the last two centuries. Essentially, before that, it was furniture for improving one's home. Well, we seemed to get along all right although we lost the Crô-Magnon art for some thousands of years, but should we have done so if it had been the knowledge of fire that we had lost?

'And "important people"? Who is important? Some Norman, or pre-Norman, blood must run in the veins of every Englishman of three generations' standing, but I have no doubt that those who can trace it back by a list of names on paper will be considered to have prior claims to survival. Certain eminent intellectuals are likely to be tolerated, too, on the strength of honours earned in the days when they had fresh ideas. How many will be among the élite because they still have ideas, remains to be seen. As for the ordinary man, much his wisest course would be to enlist in a regiment with a famous name. There'll be a use for him.'

'Come off it, A.B. It's many years now since you even *looked* like a cynical undergraduate,' said Phyllis.

Bocker grinned, and then wiped the grin off just as suddenly: 'All the same, it is going to be a very bloody business,' he said, seriously.

'What I want to know –' Phyllis and I began, simultaneously.

'Your turn, Mike,' she offered.

'Well, mine is; how do you think the thing's being done? Melting the Arctic seems a pretty formidable proposition.'

'There've been a number of guesses. They range from an incredible operation like piping warm water up from the tropics, to tapping the Earth's central heat – which I find just about as unlikely.'

'But you have your own idea?' I suggested, for it seemed improbable that he had not.

'Well, I think it *might* be done this way. We know that they have some kind of device that will project a jet of water with considerable force – the bottom sediment that was washed up into surface currents in a continuous flow pretty well proved that. Well then, a contraption like that, used in conjunction with a heater, say an atomic reaction pile, ought to be capable of generating a quite considerable warm current. The obvious snag there is that we don't know whether they have atomic fission or not. So far, there's been no indication that they have – unless you count our presenting them with at least one atomic bomb that didn't go off. But if they *do* have it, I think that might be an answer.'

'They could get the necessary uranium?'

'Why not? After all, they have forcibly established their rights, mineral and otherwise, over more than two-thirds of the world's surface. Oh, yes, they could get it, all right, if they know about it.'

'And the iceberg angle?'

'That's less difficult. In fact, there is pretty general agreement that if one has a vibratory type of weapon that can cause a ship to fall to pieces, there ought to be no great difficulty in causing a lump of ice – even a considerable sized lump of ice – to crack.'

'And nobody knows of anything we can do about it?'

'It boils down to this, we simply don't *think* the same way. When you consider it, practically all our strategy of defence or attack is based on our ability to deliver or resist missiles of one kind or another – whereas they don't seem to be interested in missiles at all; at least, you could scarcely call a pseudo-coelenterate a missile. Another thing, and this is one of those that keeps the backroom boys stumped, is that they don't use iron or any ferrous metals – which knocks out a whole range of possible magnetic approaches.

'In war, you have at least a rough idea of the way your enemy must be thinking, so you can put up appropriate counter-thoughts, but with these brutes it's nearly always some slant we haven't explored. If they drove those sea-tanks with any kind of engine known to us we could have picked them up well offshore, and destroyed them – but whatever does make them go, it obviously isn't an engine in our sense of the term, at all. The answer, as with the coelenterates, is probably up some biological avenue that we simply haven't discovered to exist, so how the devil do we start understanding it, let alone produce an opposing form? We've only got the weapons we know – and they're not the right ones for this job. Always the same funda-mental trouble – how the hell do you find out what is going on five miles down?'

'Suppose we can't find a way of hindering the process, how long do you think it'll take before we are in real trouble?' I asked him.

He shrugged. 'I've absolutely no idea. As far as the glaciers and the ice-cap are concerned, it presumably depends on how hard they work at it. But directing warm currents on pack-ice would presumably show only small results to begin with and then increase rapidly, very likely by a geometrical progression. Worse than useless to guess, with no data at all.'

'Once this gets into people's heads, they're going to want to know the best thing to do,' Phyllis said. 'What would you advise?'

'Isn't that the Government's job? It's because it's high time they thought about doing some advising that we have blown the gaff, as Mike put it. My own personal advice is too impracticable to be worth much.'

'What is it?' Phyllis asked.

'Find a nice, self-sufficient hilltop, and fortify it,' said Bocker, simply.

*

The campaign did not get off to the resounding start that Bocker had hoped. In England, it had the misfortune to be adopted by the Nethermore Press, and was consequently regarded as stunt territory wherein it would be unethical for other journalistic feet to trespass. In America it did not stand out greatly among the other excitements of the week. In both countries there were interests which preferred that it should seem to be no more than a stunt. France and Italy took it more seriously, but their governments' political weight in world councils was lighter. Russia ignored the content, but explained the purpose; it was yet another move by cosmopolitan-fascist warmongers to extend their influence in the Arctic.

Nevertheless, official indifference was slightly breached, Bocker assured us. A Committee on which the Services were represented had been set up to inquire and make recommendations. A similar Committee in Washington, D.C., also inquired in a leisurely fashion until it was brought up sharply by the State of California.

The average Californian was not greatly worried by a rise of a couple of inches in the tide-level; he had been much more delicately stricken. Something was happening to his climate. The average of his seaboard temperature had gone way down, and he was having cold, wet fogs. He disapproved of that, and a large number of Californians disapproving makes quite a noise. Oregon, and Washington, too, rallied to support their neighbour. Never within the compass of their statistical records had there been so cold and unpleasant a winter.

It was clear to all parties that the increased flow of ice and cold water pouring out of the Bering Sea was being swept eastward by the Kuro Siwo current from Japan, and patent to at least one of the parties that the amenities of the most important State in the Union were suffering gravely. Something *must* be done.

In England the spur was applied when the April spring-tides overflowed the Embankment wall at Westminster. Assurances that this had happened a number of times before and was devoid of particular significance were swept aside by the triumphant we-told-you-so of the Nethermore Press. A hysterical Bomb-the-Bathies demand sprang up on both sides of the Atlantic, and spread round the world. (Except for the intransigent sixth.)

Foremost, as well as first, in the Bomb-the-Bathies movement, the Nethermore Press inquired, morning and evening: 'WHAT IS THE BOMB FOR?'

'Billions have been spent upon this Bomb which appears to have no other destiny but to be held up and shaken threateningly, or, from time to time, to provide pictures for our illustrated papers. Having made it, we were too scared to use it in Korea; now, it seems, we are too scared to use it on the Bathies. The first reluctance was understandable, the present one is unforgivable. The people of the world, having evolved and paid for this weapon, are now forbidden to use it against a menace that has sunk our ships, closed our oceans, snatched men and women from our very shores, and now threatens to drown us. Procrastination and ineptitude has from the beginning marked the attitude of the Authorities in this affair . . . ' and so on, with the earlier bombings of the Deeps apparently forgotten by writers and readers alike.

'Working up nicely now,' said Bocker when we saw him next.

'It seems pretty silly to me,' Phyllis told him, bluntly. 'All the same old arguments against the indiscriminate bombing of Deeps still apply.'

'Oh, not that part,' Bocker said. 'They'll probably drop a few bombs here and there with plenty of publicity and no results. No, I mean the planning. We're now in the first stage of stupid suggestions like building immense levees of sandbags, of course; but it is getting across that something has got to be done.'

It got across still more strongly after the next spring-tides. There had been strengthening of the sea defences everywhere. In London the riverside walls had been reinforced and topped for their whole length with sandbags. As a precaution, traffic had been diverted from the Embankment, but the crowds turned out to throng it and the bridges, on foot. The police did their best to keep them moving, but they dawdled from one point to another, watching the slow rise of the water, waving to the crews of passing tugs and barges which presently were riding above the road-level. They seemed equally ready to be indignant if the water should break through, or disappointed if there were an anti-climax.

They were not disappointed. The water lapped slowly above the parapet and against the sandbags. Here and there it began to trickle through on to the pavements. Firemen, Civil Defence, and Police watched their sections anxiously, rushing bags to reinforce wherever a trickle enlarged, shoring up weak-looking spots with timber struts. The pace gradually became hotter. The bystanders began to help, dashing from one point to another as new jets started up. Presently there could be little doubt what was going to happen. Some of the watching crowd withdrew, but many of them remained, in a wavering fascination. When the breakthrough came, it occurred in a dozen places on the north bank almost simultaneously. Among the spurting jets a bag or two would begin to shift, then, suddenly, came a collapse, and a gap several yards wide through which the water poured as if over a weir.

From where we stood on top of an EBC van parked on Vauxhall Bridge we were able to see three separate rivers of muddy water pouring into the streets of Westminster, filling basements and cellars as they went, and presently merging into one flood. Our commentator handed over to another, perched on a Pimlico roof. For a minute or two we switched over to the BBC to find out how their crew on Westminster Bridge was faring. We got on to them just in time to hear Bob Humbleby describing the flooded Victoria Embankment with the water now rising against New Scotland Yard's own second line of defences. The television boys didn't seem to be doing too well; there must have been a lot of bets lost on where the breaks-through would occur, but they were putting up a struggle with the help of telephoto lenses and portable cameras.

From that point on, the thing got thick and fast. On the south bank water was breaking into the streets of Lambeth, South-wark, and Bermondsey in a number of places. Up river it was seriously flooding Chiswick; down river Limehouse was get-ting it badly, and more places kept on reporting breaks until we lost track of them. There was little to be done but stand by for the tide to drop, and then rush the repairs against its next rise.

The House outquestioned any quiz. The replies were more assured than assuring.

The relevant Ministries and Departments were actively tak-ing all the steps necessary, claims should be submitted through Local Councils, priorities of men and material had already been arranged. Yes, warnings had been given, but unforeseen factors had intruded upon the hydrographers' original calculations. An Order in Council would be made for the requisition of all earth-moving machinery. The public could have full confidence that there would be no repetition of the calamity; the measures already put in hand would insure against any further extension. Little could be done beyond rescue-work in the Eastern Counties at present, that would of course continue, but the most urgent matter at the moment was to ensure that the water could make no further inroads at the next high-tides.

The requisition of materials, machines, and manpower was one thing; their apportionment, with every seaboard commun-ity and low-lying area clamouring for them simultaneously, quite another. Clerks in half a dozen Ministries grew pale and heavy-eyed in a welter of demands, allocations, adjustments, redirections, misdirections, subornments, and downright thefts. But somehow, and in some places, things began to get done. Already, there was great bitterness between those who were chosen, and those who looked like being thrown to the wolves.

Phyllis went down one afternoon to look at progress of work on the riverside. Amid great activity on both banks a superstructure of concrete blocks was arising on the existing walls. The sidewalk supervisors were out in their thousands to watch. Among them she chanced upon Bocker. Together they ascended to Waterloo Bridge, and watched the termite-like activity with a celestial eye for a while.

'Alph, the sacred river – and more than twice fives miles of walls and towers,' Phyllis observed.

'And there are going to be some deep but not very romantic chasms on either side, too,' said Bocker. 'I wonder how high they'll go before the futility comes home to them.'

'It's difficult to believe that anything on such a scale as this can be really futile, but I suppose you are right,' said Phyllis.

Bocker waved a hand at it.

'The basis of all this is an assurance by that old fool Stackley, who is a geographer who knows damn-all about oceans, that the overall rise cannot be more than ten or twelve feet at the most. Heaven knows what he bases it on: a desire to create full employment, by the look of it. Some departments have accepted that as the authentic dope. They seem to think they can muddle through this thing as they muddle through their wars. Others, thank God, have a bit more sense. However, this isn't being interfered with because it is felt that some kind of show is necessary for morale.'

'I've had to speak to you about this undergraduate attitude before, A. B.,' said Phyllis. 'What *is* being done that's useful?'

'Oh, they're working out plans,' Bocker said, with deliberate vagueness.

They continued to regard the medley of men and machinery down below for a time.

'Well,' Bocker remarked, at length, 'there must be at least one figure among the shades who is getting a hell of a good laugh out of this.'

'Nice to think there's even one,' Phyllis said. 'Who?'

'King Canute,' said Bocker.

We were having so much news of our own at that time that the effects in America found little room in newspapers already straitened by a paper shortage. Newscasts, however, told that they were having their own troubles over there. California's climate was no longer Problem Number One. In addition to the difficulties that were facing ports and seaboard cities all over the world, there was bad coastline trouble in the south of the United States. It ran almost all the way around the Gulf from Key West to the Mexican border. In Florida, owners of real estate began to suffer once again as the Everglades and the swamps spilt across more and more country. Across in Texas a large tract of land north of Brownsville was gradually disappearing beneath the water. Still worse hit were Louisiana, and the Delta. The enterprise of Tin Pan Alley considered it an appropriate time to revive the plea: 'River, Stay 'Way from My Door,' but the river did not – nor, over on the Atlantic coast, did other rivers, in Georgia and the Carolinas.

But it is idle to particularize. All over the world the threat was the same. The chief difference was that in the more developed countries all available earth-shifting machinery worked day and night, while in the more backward it was sweating thousands of men and women who toiled to raise great levees and walls.

But for both the task was too great. The more the level rose, the further the defences had to be extended to prevent outflanking. When the rivers were backed up by the incoming tides there was nowhere for the water to go but over the surrounding countryside. All the time, too, the problems of preventing flooding from the rear by water backed up in sewers and conduits became more difficult to handle. Even before the first serious inundation which followed the breaking of the Embankment wall near Blackfriars, in October, the man in the street had suspected that the battle could not be won, and the exodus of those with wisdom and the means had already started. Many of them, moreover, were finding themselves forestalled by refugees from the eastern counties and the more vulnerable coastal towns elsewhere.

Some little time before the Blackfriars breakthrough a confidential note had circulated among selected staff, and contracted personnel such as ourselves, at EBC. It had been decided as a matter of policy in the interests of public morale, we learnt, that, should certain emergency measures become necessary, etc., etc., and so on, for two foolscap pages, with most of the information between the lines. It would have been a lot simpler to say: 'Look. The gen is that this thing's going to get serious. The BBC has orders to stay put, so for prestige reasons we'll have to do the same. We want volunteers to man a station here, and if you care to be one of them, we'll be glad to have you. Suitable arrangements will be made. There'll be a bonus, and you can trust us to look after you if anything does happen. How about it?'

Phyllis and I talked it over. If we had had any family, we decided, the necessity would have been to do the best we could by them – in so far as anyone could possibly know what might turn out to be best. As we had not, we could please ourselves. Phyllis summed up for staying on the job.

'Apart from conscience and loyalty and all the proper things,' she said. 'Goodness knows what is going to happen in other places if it does get really bad. Somehow, running away seldom seems to work out well unless you have a pretty good idea of what you're running to. My vote is for sticking, and seeing what happens.'

So we sent our names in, and were pleased to find that Freddy Whittier and his wife had done the same.

After that, some clever departmentalism made it seem as if nothing were happening for a while. Several weeks passed before we got wind of the fact that EBC had leased the top two floors of a large department-store near Marble Arch, and were working all-out to have them converted into as near a self-supporting station as was possible.

'I should have thought,' said Phyllis, when we acquired this information, 'that somewhere higher, like Hampstead or Highgate, would have been better.'

'Neither of them is quite London,' I pointed out. 'Besides,

EBC probably gets it for a nominal rent for announcing each
time: "This is the EBC calling the world from Selvedge's."
Goodwill advertising during the interlude of emergency.'

'Just as if the water would just go away one day,' she said.

'Even if they don't think so, they lose nothing by letting
EBC have it,' I pointed out.

By that time we were becoming highly level-conscious, and
I looked the place up on the map. The seventy-five foot contour
line ran down the street on the building's western side.

'How does that compare with the arch-rival?' wondered
Phyllis, running her finger across the map.

Broadcasting House appeared to be very slightly better off.
About eight-five feet above mean sea-level, we judged.

'H'm,' she said. 'Well, if there is any calculation behind our
being on the top floors, they'll be having to do a lot of moving
upstairs, too. Gosh,' she added, glancing over to the left of the
map. 'Look at their television-studios! Right down on the
twenty-five foot level. There'll be a lot of helter-skelter back to
Ally-Pally, I should think.'

In the weeks just before the breakthrough London seemed to
be living a double life. Organizations and institutions were
making their preparations with as little ostentation as possible.
Officials spoke in public with an affected casualness of the need
to make plans 'just in case', and then went back to their offices
to work feverishly on the arrangements. Announcements continued to be reassuring in tone. The men employed on the jobs
were for the most part cynical about their work, glad of the
overtime pay, and curiously disbelieving. They seemed to
regard it as a stunt which was working nicely to their benefit;
imagination apparently refused to credit the threat with any
reality outside working hours. Even after the breakthrough,
alarm was oddly localized with those who had suffered. The
wall was hurriedly repaired, and the exodus was still not much
more than a trickle of people. Real trouble came with the next
spring-tides.

There was plenty of warning this time in the parts likely to
be most affected. The people took it stubbornly and phleg-

matically. They had already had experience to learn by. The main response was to move possessions to upper storeys, and grumble loudly at the inefficiency of authorities who were incapable of saving them the trouble involved. Notices were posted giving the times of high-water for three days, but the suggested precautions were couched with such a fear of promoting panic that they were little heeded.

The first day passed safely. On the evening of the highest water a large part of London settled down to wait for midnight and the crisis to pass, in a sullenly bad-tempered mood. The buses were all off the streets, and the Underground had ceased to run at eight in the evening. But plenty of people stayed out, and walked down to the river to see what there was to be seen from the bridges. They had their show.

The smooth, oil surface of the river crawled slowly up the piers of the bridges and against the retaining walls. The muddy water flowed upstream with scarcely a sound, and the crowds, too, were almost silent, looking down on it apprehensively. There was no fear of it topping the walls; the estimated rise was twenty-three feet, four inches, which would leave a safety margin of four feet to the top of the new parapet. It was pressure that was the source of anxiety.

From the north end of Waterloo Bridge where we were stationed this time, one was able to look along the top of the wall, with the water running high on one side of it, and, to the other, the roadway of the Embankment, with the street lamps still burning there, but not a vehicle or a human figure to be seen upon it. Away to the west the hands on the Parliament clock-tower crawled round the illuminated dial. The water rose as the big hand moved with insufferable sloth up to eleven o'clock. Over the quiet crowds the note of Big Ben striking the hour came clearly downwind.

The sound caused people to murmur to one another; then they fell silent again. The hand began to crawl down, ten past, a quarter, twenty, twenty-five, then, just before the half-hour, there was a rumble somewhere upstream; a composite, crowd-voice sound came to us on the wind. The people about us craned their necks, and murmured again. A moment later we saw the water coming. It poured along the Embankment towards us in a wide, muddy flood, sweeping rubbish and bushes with it, rushing past beneath us. A groan went up from the crowd. Suddenly there was a loud crack and a rumble of falling masonry behind us as a section of the wall, close by where the *Discovery* had formerly been moored, collapsed. The water poured through the gap, wrenching away concrete blocks so that the wall crumbled before our eyes and the water poured in a great muddy cascade on to the roadway. . . .

Before the next tide came the Government had removed the velvet glove. Following the announcement of a State of Emergency came a Standstill Order, and the proclamation of an orderly scheme of evacuation. There is no need for me to write here of the delays and muddles in which the scheme broke down. It is difficult to believe that it can have been taken seriously even by those who launched it. An unconvincing air seemed to hang over the whole affair from the beginning. The task was impossible. Something, perhaps, might have been done had only a single city been concerned, but with more than two-thirds of the country's population anxious to move on to higher ground, only the crudest methods had any success in checking the pressure, and then not for long.

But, though it was bad here, it was still worse elsewhere. The Dutch had withdrawn in time from the danger areas, realizing that they had lost their centuries-long battle with the sea. The Rhine and the Mass had backed up in flood over square miles of country. A whole population was trekking southward into Belgium or south-east into Germany. The North German Plain itself was little better off. The Ems and the Weser had widened out, too, driving people southward from their towns and farms in an increasing horde. In Denmark every kind of boat was in use ferrying families to Sweden and the higher ground there.

For a little time we managed to follow in a general way what was happening, but when the inhabitants of the Ardennes and Westphalia turned in dismay to save themselves by fighting off the hungry, desperate invaders from the north, hard news disappeared in a morass of rumour and chaos. All over the world the same kind of thing must have been going on, differing only in its scale. At home, the flooding of the Eastern Counties had already driven people back on the Midlands. Loss of life was small, for there had been plenty of warning. Real trouble started on the Chiltern Hills where those already in possession organized themselves to prevent their being swamped by the two converging streams of refugees from the east and from London.

Within London, too, the same pattern was taking shape on a smaller scale. The dwellers in the Lea Valley, Westminster, Chelsea, Hammersmith, left their homes for the most part belatedly and reluctantly, but as the water continued to rise and forced them to move the obvious direction to take was towards the heights of Hampstead and Highgate, and as they approached those parts they began to encounter barricades in the streets, and, presently, weapons. Where they were stopped they looted, and searched for weapons of their own. When they had found them they sniped from upper windows and rooftops until they drove the defenders off their barricades and could rush them.

To the south, similar things were happening at Sydenham and Tooting Bec. Districts which were not yet flooded began to catch the panic. Although at high tide the water barely reached the fifteen foot contour as yet, the orderly mood which the Government had striven to maintain was broken. It was largely succeeded by the conviction that position was going to be nine points of survival, and the wise thing to do was to make sure of that position as soon as possible. The dwellers on the high ground took the same view, reinforced by determination to defend themselves and their property.

Over the untouched parts of Central London a mood of Sunday-like indecision hung for several days. Many people, not knowing what else to do, still tried to carry on as nearly as usual. The police continued to patrol. Though the Underground was flooded plenty of people continued to turn up at their places of work, and some kinds of work did continue, seemingly through habit or momentum, then gradually lawlessness seeped inwards from the suburbs and the sense of breakdown became inescapable. Failure of the emergency electric supply one afternoon, followed by a night of darkness, gave a kind of *coup de grâce* to order. The looting of shops, particularly foodshops, began, and spread on a scale which defeated both the police and the military.

We decided it was time to leave the flat and take up our residence in the new EBC fortress.

From what the short-waves were telling us there was little to distinguish the course of events in the low-lying cities anywhere – except that in some the law died more quickly. It is outside my scope to dwell on the details; I have no doubt that they will be described later in innumerable official histories.

EBC's part during those days consisted largely in duplicating the BBC in the reading out of Government instructions hopefully intended to restore a degree of order: a monotonous business of telling those whose homes were not immediately threatened to stay where they were, and directing the flooded-out to certain higher areas and away from others that were said to be already overcrowded. We may have been heard, but we could see no visible evidence that we were heeded. In the north there may have been some effect, but in the south the hugely disproportionate concentration of London, and the flooding of so many rails and roads, ruined all attempts at orderly dispersal. The numbers of people in motion spread alarm among those who could have waited. The fe ling that unless one reached a refuge ahead of the main crowd there might be no place at all to go was catching – as also was the feeling that anyone trying to do so by car was in possession of an unfair advantage. It quickly became safer to walk wherever one was going – though not outstandingly safe at that. It was best to go out as little as possible.

The existence of numerous hotels, and a reassuring elevation of some seven hundred feet above normal sea-level were undoubtedly factors which influenced Parliament in choosing the town of Harrogate, in Yorkshire, as its seat. The speed with which it assembled there was very likely due to the same force as was motivating many private persons – the fear that someone else might get in first. To an outsider it seemed that a bare few hours after Westminster was flooded, the ancient institution was performing with all its usual fluency in its new home. Questions were being asked regarding the Bomb-the-Bathies policy in the Arctic, and whether it was not an observed fact that the extensive use of hydrogen and other fissile-material bombs in that region was hastening the disintegration of the ice-fields without producing any patently deterrent effects on the originators of the trouble? Were we not, in fact, working there to our own disadvantage?

The First Lord thought this was probably so. The House had taken the decision to bomb, against expert advice.

In answer to a further question the Foreign Secretary stated that a cessation of bombing now by our forces would make little difference since his information was that the Russians were delivering a greater weight of bombs in their sector than we were in ours – or, rather, than our American Allies were, with ourselves. Asked the reason for this sudden Kremlin right-about, he replied:

'From sources which it would be unwise to disclose we understand that the Russians are showing a greater appreciation of the situation than they have hitherto. It appears that floods in Karelia and the marshes south of the White Sea are extensive, and growing worse rapidly. Further to the east lies an inlet of the Arctic Sea called the Gulf of Ob. To the south of it stretches an immense area of marshland now in the process of inundation. If the rise in the water-level continues it is likely that we shall see the formation in Central Russia of a great inland sea, possibly larger than Hudson Bay – a feature doubtless more familiar to members of this House than is the Gulf of Ob.'

We began to hear a lot of Harrogate and district, and it became obvious that a great deal of preparation had been done in the area. For one thing, our own centre of EBC administration was established there in a resuscitated military camp, though, according to our informants at such a distance from the town that the only leisure occupation was to spy by telescope upon the arch-rival concern situated similarly, but on the other side of a valley.

As for ourselves, we began to shake down into a routine. Our living-quarters were on the top floor. Offices, studios, technical equipment, generators, stores, etc., on the floor beneath. A great reserve of diesel-oil and petrol filled large tanks in the basement, whence it was pumped as necessary. Our aerial systems were on roofs two blocks away, reached by bridges slung high over the intervening streets. Our own roof was largely cleared to provide a helicopter landing, and to act as a rainwater catchment. As we gradually developed a technique for living there we decided it was pretty well found.

Even so, my recollection is that nearly all spare time in the first few days was spent by everyone in transferring the contents of the provision department to our own quarters before it should disappear elsewhere.

There seems to have been a basic misconception of the role we should play. As I understand it, the idea was that we were to preserve, as far as possible, the impression of business as usual, and then, as things grew more difficult, the centre of EBC would follow the administration by gradual stages to Yorkshire. This appears to have been founded upon the assumption that London was so cellularly constructed that as the water flowed into each cell it would be abandoned while the rest carried on much as usual. As far as we were concerned bands, speakers, and artists would all roll up to do their stuff in the ordinary way until the water lapped our doorsteps – if it should ever reach as far – by which time they would presumably have changed to the habit of rolling up to the Yorkshire station instead. The only provision on the programme side that anyone had made for things not happening in this naïve fashion was the transfer of our recorded library before it became actually necessary to save it. A dwindling, rather than a breakdown, was envisaged. Curiously, quite a number of conscientious broadcasters did somehow manage to put in their appearances for a few days. After that, however, we were thrown back almost entirely upon ourselves and the recordings. And, presently, we began to live in a state of siege.

*

I don't propose to deal in detail with the year that followed. It was a drawn-out story of decay. A long, cold winter during which the water lapped into the streets faster than we had expected. A time when armed bands were roving in search of untouched food-stores, when, at any hour of the day or night, one was liable to hear a rattle of shots as two gangs met. We ourselves had little trouble; it was as if, after a few attempts to raid us, word had gone round that we were ready to defend, and with so many other stores raidable at little or no risk we might as well be left until later.

When the warmer weather came there were noticeably fewer people to be seen. Most of them, rather than face another winter in a city by now largely plundered of food and beginning to suffer epidemics from lack of fresh water and drainage, were filtering out into the country, and the shooting that we heard was usually distant.

Our own numbers had been depleted, too. Out of the original sixty-five we were now reduced to twenty-five, the rest having gone off in parties by helicopter as the national focus became more settled in Yorkshire. From having been a centre we had declined to the state of an outpost maintained for prestige.

Phyllis and I discussed whether we would apply to go, too, but from the description of conditions that we prised out of the helicopter pilot and his crew the EBC Headquarters sounded congested and unattractive, so we decided to stay for a while longer, at any rate. We were by no means uncomfortable where we were, and the fewer of us that were left in our London eyrie, the more space and supplies each of us had.

In late spring we learnt that a decree had merged us with the arch-rival, putting all radio communication under direct Government control. It was the Broadcasting House lot that were moved out by a swift airlift since their premises were vulnerable while ours were already in a prepared state, and the one or two BBC men who stayed came over to join us.

News reached us mainly by two channels: the private link with EBC, which was usually moderately honest, though discreet; and broadcasts which, no matter where they came from, were puffed with patently dishonest optimism. We became very tired and cynical about them, as, I imagine, did everyone else, but they still kept on. Every country, it seemed, was meeting and rising above the disaster with a resolution which did honour to the traditions of its people.

By midsummer, and a cold midsummer it was, the town had become very quiet. The gangs had gone; only the obstinate individuals remained. They were, without doubt, quite numerous, but in twenty thousand streets they seemed sparse, and they were not yet desperate. It was possible to go about in relative safety again, though wise to carry a gun.

The water had risen further in the time than any of the estimates had supposed. The highest tides now reached the fifty-foot level. The flood-line was north of Hammersmith and included most of Kensington. It lay along the south side of Hyde Park, then to the south of Piccadilly, across Trafalgar Square, along the Strand and Fleet Street, and then ran northeast up the west side of the Lea Valley; of the City, only the high ground about St Paul's was still untouched. In the south it had pushed across Barnes, Battersea, Southwark, most of Deptford, and the lower part of Greenwich.

One day we walked down to Trafalgar Square. The tide was in, and the water reached nearly to the top of the wall on the northern side, below the National Gallery. We leant on the balustrade, looking at the water washing around Landseer's lions, wondering what Nelson would think of the view his statue was getting now.

Close to our feet, the edge of the flood was fringed with scum and a fascinatingly varied collection of flotsam. Further away, fountains, lamp-posts, traffic-lights, and statues thrust up here and there. On the far side, and down as much as we could see of Whitehall, the surface was as smooth as a canal. A few trees still stood, and in them sparrows chattered. Starlings had not yet deserted St Martin's church, but the pigeons were all gone, and on many of their customary perches gulls stood, instead. We surveyed the scene and listened to the slip-slop of the water in the silence for some minutes. Then I asked:

'Didn't somebody or other once say: "This is the way the world ends, not with a bang but a whimper?"'

Phyllis looked shocked. ' "*Somebody or other!*" she exclaimed. 'That was Mr Eliot!'

'Well, it certainly looks as if he had the idea that time,' I said.

'It's the job of poets to have the idea,' she told me.

'H'm. It might also be that it is the job of poets to have enough ideas to provide a quotation for any given set of circumstances, but never mind. On this occasion let us honour Mr Eliot,' I said.

Presently Phyllis remarked: 'I thought I was through a phase now, Mike. For such a long time it kept on seeming that something could be done to save the world we're used to – if we could only find out what. But soon I think I'll be able to feel: "Well, that's gone. How can we make the best of what's left?" – all the same, I wouldn't say that coming to places like this does me any good.'

'There aren't places like this. This is – was – one of the uniques. That's the trouble. And it's a bit more than dead, but not yet ready for a museum. Soon, perhaps, we may be able to feel, "Lo! All our pomp of yesterday is one with Nineveh and Tyre" – soon, but not quite yet.'

'You seem to be on unusually happy terms with other people's Muses to-day. Whose was that?' Phyllis inquired.

'Well,' I admitted, 'I'm not sure whether you would class her as a muse at all – more, perhaps, of a bent. Mr Kipling's.'

'Oh, poor Mr Kipling. Of course he had a Muse, and she probably played a jolly good game of hockey, too.'

'Cat,' I remarked. 'However, let us also honour Mr Kipling.'

There was a pause. It lengthened.

'Mike,' she said, suddenly, 'let's go away from here – now.'

I nodded. 'It might be better. We'll have to get a little tougher yet, darling, I'm afraid.'

She took my arm, and we started to walk westward. Halfway to the corner of the Square we paused at the sound of a motor. It seemed, improbably, to come from the south side. We waited while it drew closer. Presently, out from the Admiralty Arch swept a speedboat. It turned in a sharp arc and sped away down Whitehall, leaving the ripples of its wake slopping through the windows of august Governmental offices.

'Very pretty,' I said. 'There can't be many of us who have accomplished that in one of our waking moments.'

Phyllis gazed along the widening ripples, and abruptly became practical again.

'I think we'd better see if we can't find one of those,' she said. 'It might come in useful later on.'

*

The rate of rise continued to increase. By the end of the summer the level was up another eight or nine feet. The weather was vile and even colder than it had been at the same time the previous year. More of us had applied for transfer, and by mid-September we were down to sixteen.

Even Freddy Whittier had announced that he was sick and tired of wasting his time like a shipwrecked sailor, and was going to see whether he could not find some useful work to do. When the helicopter whisked him and his wife away, they left us reconsidering our own position once more.

Our task of composing never-say-die material on the theme that we spoke from, and for, the heart of an empire bloody but still unbowed was supposed, we knew, to have a stabilizing value even now, but we doubted it. Too many people were whistling the same tune in the same dark. A night or two before the Whittiers left we had had a late party where someone, in the small hours, had tuned-in a New York transmitter. A man and a woman on the Empire State Building were describing the scene. The picture they evoked of the towers of Manhattan standing like frozen sentinels in the moonlight while the glittering water lapped at their lower walls was masterly, almost lyrically beautiful – nevertheless, it failed in its purpose. In our minds we could see those shining towers – they were not sentinels, they were tombstones. It made us feel that we were even less accomplished at disguising our own tombstones; that it was time to pull out of our refuge, and find more useful work. Our last words to Freddy were that we would very likely be following him before long.

We had still, however, not reached the point of making definite application when he called us up on the link a couple of weeks later. After the greetings he said:

'This isn't purely social, Mike. It is disinterested advice to those contemplating a leap from the frying-pan – don't!'

'Oh,' I said, 'what's the trouble?'

'I'll tell you this. I'd have an application in for getting back to you right now – if only I had not made my reasons for getting out so damned convincing. I mean that. Hang on there, both of you.'

'But –' I began.

'Wait a minute,' he told me.

Presently his voice came again.

'Okay. No monitor on this, I think. Listen, Mike, we're overcrowded, underfed, and in one hell of a mess. Supplies of all kinds are right down, so's morale. The atmosphere's like a lot of piano-strings. We're living virtually in a state of siege here, and if it doesn't turn into active civil war in a few weeks it'll be a miracle. The people outside *are* worse off than we are, but seemingly nothing will convince them that we aren't living on the fat of the land. For God's sake keep this under your hat, but stay where you are, for Phyl's sake if not for your own.'

I thought quickly.

'If it's as bad as that, Freddy, and you're doing no good, why not get back here on the next helicopter. Either smuggle aboard – or maybe we could offer the pilot a few things he'd like?'

'All right. There certainly isn't any use for us here. I don't know why they let us come along. I'll work on that. Look for us next flight. Meanwhile good luck to you both.'

'Good luck to you, Freddy, and our love to Lynn – and our respects to Bocker, if he's there and nobody's slaughtered him yet.'

'Oh, Bocker's here. He's now got a theory that it won't go much over a hundred and twenty-five feet, and seems to think that's good news.'

'Well, considering he's Bocker, it might be a lot worse. 'Bye. We'll be looking forward to seeing you.'

We were discreet. We said no more than that we had heard the Yorkshire place was already crowded, so we were staying. A couple who had decided to leave on the next flight changed their minds, too. We waited for the helicopter to bring Freddy back. The day after it was due we were still waiting. We got through on the link. They had no news except that it had left on schedule. I asked about Freddy and Lynn. Nobody seemed to know where they were.

There never was any news of that helicopter. They said they hadn't another that they could send.

The cold summer drew into a colder autumn. A rumour reached us that the sea-tanks were appearing again for the first time since the waters had begun to rise. As the only people present who had had personal contact with them we assumed the status of experts – though almost the only advice we could give was always to wear a sharp knife, and in such a position that it could be reached for a quick slash by either hand. But the sea-tanks must have found the hunting poor in the almost deserted streets of London, for presently we heard no more of them. From the radio, however, we learnt that it was not so in some other parts. There were reports soon of their reappearance in many places where not only the new shore-lines, but the collapse of organization made it difficult to destroy them in effectively discouraging numbers.

Meanwhile, there was worse trouble. Overnight the combined EBC and BBC transmitters abandoned all pretence of calm confidence. When we looked at the message transmitted to us for radiation simultaneously with all other stations we knew that Freddy had been right. It was a call to all loyal citizens to support their legally elected Government against any attempts that might be made to overthrow it by force, and the way in which it was put left no doubt that such an attempt was already being made. The thing was a sorry mixture of exhortation, threats, and pleas, which wound up with just the wrong note of confidence – the note that had sounded in Spain and then in France when the words must be said though speaker and listener alike knew that the end was near. The best reader in the service could not have given it the ring of conviction.

The link could not, or would not, clarify the situation for us. Firing was going on, they said. Some armed bands were attempting to break into the Administration Area. The military had the situation in hand, and would clear up the trouble shortly. The broadcast was simply to discourage exaggerated rumours and restore confidence in the Government. We said that neither what they were telling us, nor the message itself inspired us personally with any confidence whatever, and we should like to know what was really going on. They went all official, curt, and cold.

Twenty-four hours later, in the middle of dictating for our radiation another expression of confidence, the link broke off, abruptly. It never worked again.

*

Until one gets used to it, the situation of being able to hear voices from all over the world, but none which tells what is happening in one's own country, is odd. We picked up enquiries about our silence from America, Canada, Australia, Kenya. We radiated at the full power of our transmitter what little we knew, and could later hear it being relayed by foreign stations. But we ourselves were far from understanding what had happened. Even if the H.Q.'s of both systems, in Yorkshire, had been over-run, as it would appear, there should have been stations still on the air independently in Scotland and Northern Ireland at least, even if they were no better informed than ourselves. Yet, a week went by, and still there was no sound from them. The rest of the world appeared to be too busy keeping a mask on its

own troubles to bother about us any more – though one time
we did hear a voice speaking with historical dispassion of
'l'écroulement de l'Angleterre'. The word *écroulement* was not
very familiar to me, but it had a horribly final sound. . . .

*

The winter closed in. One noticed how few people there were
to be seen in the streets now, compared with a year ago. Often
it was possible to walk a mile without seeing anyone at all.
How those who did remain were living we could not say.
Presumably they all had caches of looted stores that supported
them and their families; and obviously it was no matter for
close enquiry. One noticed also how many of those one did see
had taken to carrying weapons as a matter of course. We ourselves adopted the habit of carrying them – guns, not rifles –
slung over our shoulders, though less with any expectation of
needing them than to discourage the occasion for their need
from arising. There was a kind of wary preparedness which was
still some distance from instinctive hostility. Chance-met men
still passed on gossip and rumours, and sometimes hard news
of a local kind. It was by such means that we learnt of a quite
definitely hostile ring now in existence around London; how
the surrounding districts had somehow formed themselves into
miniature independent states and forbidden entry after driving
out many who had come there as refugees; how those who did
try to cross the border into one of these communities were fired
upon without questions.

'It's going to be bad later on,' was the opinion of most of
those I spoke to. 'Just now pretty well all those who are left
still have a few cases of this and that stowed away, and the chief
worry is stopping the other fellow from finding out where it is.
But later on the worry is going to be the other way round; finding out where the chaps who do have some left are hiding it –
and that's going to be nasty.'

In the New Year the sense of things pressing in upon us grew
stronger. The high-tide mark was now close to the seventy-five
foot level. The weather was abominable, and icy cold. There

seemed to be scarcely a night when there was not a gale blowing from the south-west. It became rarer than ever to see anyone in the streets, though when the wind did drop for a time the view from the roof showed a surprising number of chimneys smoking. Mostly it was wood smoke, furniture and fitments burning, one supposed; for the coal stores in power-stations and railway yards had all disappeared the previous winter.

From a purely practical point of view I doubt whether any-one in the country was more favoured or as well found as our group. The food originally supplied together with that ac-quired later made a store which should last sixteen people for some years. There was an immense reserve of diesel-oil, and petrol, too. Materially we were better off than we had been a year ago when there were more of us. But we had learnt, as had many before us, about the bread-alone factor, one needed more than adequate food. The sense of desolation began to weigh more heavily still when, at the end of February, the water lapped over our doorsteps for the first time, and the building was filled with the sound of it cascading into the basements.

Some of the party grew more worried.

'It *can't* come very much higher, surely. A hundred feet *is* the limit, isn't it?' they were saying.

It wasn't much good being falsely reassuring. We could do little more than to repeat what Bocker had said; that it was a guess. No one had known, within a wide limit, how much ice there was in the Antarctic. No one was quite sure how much of the northern areas that appeared to be solid land, tundra, was in fact simply a deposit on a foundation of ancient ice; we just had not known enough about it. The only consolation was that Bocker now seemed to think for some reason that it would not rise above one hundred and twenty-five feet – which should leave our eyrie still intact. Nevertheless, it required fortitude to find reassurance in that thought as one lay in bed at night, listen-ing to the echoing splash of the wavelets that the wind was driving along Oxford Street.

One bright morning in May, a sunny, though not a warm morning, I missed Phyllis. Enquiries eventually led me on to the roof in search of her. I found her in the south-west corner gazing towards the trees that dotted the lake which had been Hyde Park, and crying. I leant on the parapet beside her, and put an arm round her. Presently she stopped crying. She dabbed her eyes and nose, and said:

'I haven't been able to get tough, after all. I don't think I can stand this much longer, Mike. Take me away, please.'

'Where is there to go? – if we could go,' I said.

'The cottage, Mike. It wouldn't be so bad there, in the country. There'd be things growing – not everything dying, like this. There isn't any hope here – we might as well jump over the wall here if there is to be no hope at all.'

I thought about it for some moments.

'But even if we could get there, we'd have to live,' I pointed out, 'we'd need food and fuel and things.'

'There's – ' she began, and then hesitated and changed her mind. 'We could find enough to keep us going for a time until we could grow things. And there'd be fish, and plenty of wreckage for fuel. We could make out somehow. It'd be hard – but, Mike, I can't stay in this cemetery any longer – I can't.

'Look at it, Mike! Look at it! We never did anything to deserve all this. Most of us weren't very good, but we weren't bad enough for this, surely. And not to have a chance! If it had only been something we could fight – ! But just to be drowned and starved and forced into destroying one another to live – and by things nobody has ever seen, living in the one place we can't reach!

'Some of us are going to get through this stage, of course – the tough ones. But what are the things down there going to do then? Sometimes I dream of them lying down in those deep dark valleys, and sometimes they look like monstrous squids or huge slugs, other times as if they were great clouds of luminous cells hanging there in rocky chasms. I don't suppose that we'll ever know what they really look like, but whatever it is, there they are all the time, thinking and plotting what they can do to finish us right off so that everything will be theirs.

'I dream about that sea-bottom; the great wide plains down there where it is always always raining teeth and scales and bits of bone and shells and millions and millions of tiny plankton creatures, on and on for centuries. There are ranges of mountains rising out of the plains, and in some places huge precipices split by winding gullies, and the things down below send the sea-tanks in regiments across the plains, and the regiments break into strings which go into the gullies, and come winding up in search of us in long, long processions; out of the gullies into the shallow water, and then through the towns which have gone under the sea, still searching for us and hunting us.

'Sometimes, in spite of Bocker, I think perhaps it is the things themselves that are inside the sea-tanks, and if only we could capture one and examine it we should know how to fight them, at last. Several times I have dreamt that we have found one and managed to discover what makes it work, and nobody's believed us but Bocker, but what we have told him has given him an idea for a wonderful new weapon which had finished them all off.

'I know it all sounds very silly, but it's wonderful in the dream, and I wake up feeling as if we had saved the whole world from a nightmare – and then I hear the sound of the water slopping against the walls in the street, and I know it isn't finished; it's just going on and on and on . . .

'I can't stand it here any more, Mike. I shall go mad if I have to sit here doing nothing any longer while a great city dies by inches all round me. It'd be different in Cornwall, anywhere in the country. I'd rather have to work night and day to keep alive than just go on like this. I think I'd rather die trying to get away than face another winter like last.'

I had not realized it was as bad as that. It wasn't a thing to be argued about.

'All right, darling,' I said. 'We'll go.'

*

Everything we could hear warned us against attempting to get away by normal means. We were told of belts where everything had been razed to give clear fields of fire, and there were booby-traps and alarms, as well as guards. Everything beyond those belts was said to be based upon a cold calculation of the number each autonomous district could support. The natives of the districts had banded together and turned out the refugees and the useless on to lower ground where they had to shift for themselves. In each of the areas there was acute awareness that another mouth to feed would increase the shortage for all. Any stranger who did manage to sneak in could not hope to remain unnoticed for long, and his treatment was ruthless when he was discovered – survival demanded it. So it looked as though our own survival demanded that we should try some other way.

The chance by water, along inlets that must be constantly widening and reaching further, looked better. Our search for a speedboat had been disappointing. We had discovered nothing better than the fibre-glass dinghy. Into that I began to stow supplies that I hoped might at least serve to buy us safe transit.

We delayed a little in the hope that the weather would turn warmer, but by late June we gave up the hope, and set out up-river.

*

But for the luck of our finding that sturdy little motor-boat, the *Midge,* I don't know what would have happened to us. I rather think we should have tried up-river again, and quite likely got ourselves shot. The *Midge,* however, changed the whole outlook. The following day, we took her back to London. Navigation of the more deeply flooded streets was a strain. Only unreliable memories could tell us whether the lamp-standards ran in the middle of the street, or at the sides, and we went cautiously, in constant alarm lest we should hole the boat upon one of them. Shallower parts we could take faster. At Hyde Park Corner we hove-to a couple of hours, waiting for the tide, and then ran safely up into Oxford Street on the flood.

An uneasy feeling that some of the others might wish to get away, too, and press to come with us now that we had more room, turned out to be baseless. Without exception they considered us crazy. Most of them contrived to take one of us aside at some time or another to point out the wilful improvidence of giving up warm, comfortable quarters to make a certainly cold and probably dangerous journey to certainly worse and probably intolerable conditions. They helped to fuel and store the *Midge* until she was inches lower in the water, but not one of them could have been bribed to set out with us.

Our progress down the river was cautious and slow, for we had no intention of letting the journey be more dangerous than was necessary. Our main recurrent problem was where to lay up for the night. We were sharply conscious of our probable fate as trespassers, and also of the fact that the *Midge* with her contents was tempting booty. Our usual anchorages were in the sheltered streets of some flooded town. Several times when it was blowing hard we lay up in such places for several days. Fresh water, which we had expected to be the main problem, turned out not to be difficult; one could almost always find some still in the tanks in the roof-spaces of a partly submerged house. Overall, the trip which used to clock at 268.8 (or .9) by road took us slightly over a month to make.

Round the corner and into the Channel the white cliffs looked so normal from the water that the flooding was hard to believe – until we looked more closely at the gaps where the towns should have been. A little later, we were right out of the normal, for we began to see our first icebergs.

We approached the end of the journey with caution. From what we had been able to observe of the coast as we came along there were often encampments of shacks on the higher ground. Where the land rose steeply there were often towns and villages where the higher houses were still occupied though the lower were submerged. What kind of conditions we might find at Penllyn in general and Rose Cottage in particular, we had no idea.

I took the *Midge* carefully into the Helford River, with shotguns lying to hand. Here and there a few people on the hillsides stopped to look down at us, but they neither shot, nor waved. It was only later that we found they had taken her to be one of the few local boats that still had the fuel to run.

We turned north from the main river. With the water now close on the hundred-foot level the multiplication of waterways was confusing. We lost our way half a dozen times before we rounded a corner on an entirely new inlet and found ourselves looking up a familiar steep hillside at the cottage above us.

People had been there, several lots of them, I should think, but though the disorder was considerable the damage was not great. It was evidently the consumables they had been after chiefly. The standbys had vanished from the larder to the last bottle of sauce and packet of pepper. The drum of oil, the candles, and the small store of coal were gone, too.

Phyllis gave a quick look over the debris, and disappeared down the cellar steps. She re-emerged in a moment and ran out to the arbour she had built in the garden. Through the window I saw her examining the floor of it carefully. Presently she came back.

'That's all right, thank goodness,' she said.

It did not seem a moment for great concern about arbours. 'What's all right?' I inquired.

'The food,' she said. 'I didn't want to tell you about it until I knew. It would have been too bitterly disappointing if it had gone.'

'What food?' I asked, bewilderedly.

'You've not much intuition, have you, Mike? Did you really think that someone like me would be doing all that bricklaying just for fun? I walled-off half the cellar full of stuff, and there's a lot under the arbour, too.'

I stared at her. 'Do you mean to say – ? But that was ages ago! Before the flooding even began.'

'But not before they began sinking ships so fast. It seemed to me it would be a good thing to lay in stores before things got difficult, because it quite obviously was going to get difficult later. I thought it would be sensible to have a reserve here, just in case. Only it was no good telling you, because I knew you'd just get stuffy about it.'

I sat down, and regarded her.

'Stuffy?' I inquired.

'Well, there are some people who seem to think it is more ethical to pay black-market prices than to take sensible precautions.'

'Oh,' I said. 'So you bricked it in yourself?'

'Well, I didn't want anybody local to know, so the only way was to do it myself. As it happened, the food airlift was much better organized than one could have expected, so we didn't need it, but it will come in useful now.'

'How much?' I asked.

She considered. 'I'm not quite sure, but there is a whole big vanload here, and then there's all the stuff we've got in the *Midge,* too.'

I could see, and do see, several angles to the thing, but it would have been churlishly ungrateful to mention them just then, so I let it rest, and we busied ourselves with tidying up and moving in.

It did not take us long to understand why the cottage had been left unoccupied. One had only to climb to the crest to see that our hill was destined to be an island. Four months later it became one.

Here, as elsewhere, there had been first the cautious retreat as the water started to rise, and, later, the panicky rush to stake a claim on the high ground while there was still room there. Those who remained, and still remain, are a mixture of the obstinate, the tardy, and the hopeful who are continually thinking that the water will not come much further. A feud between those who stayed and those who went is well established. The uplanders will allow no newcomer into their strictly rationed territory: the lowlanders carry guns and set traps to discourage raids upon their fields. It is said, though I do not know with how much truth, that conditions here are good compared with Devon and other places further east, since a large part of the population, once it took to flight, decided to keep on towards the lusher areas beyond the moorlands. There are fearful tales about the guerilla warfare between starving bands that goes on in Devon, Somerset, and Dorset, but here one hears shooting only occasionally, and only on a small scale.

The thoroughness of our isolation, beyond occasional bits of hearsay, has been one of the difficult things to bear. The radio set which might have told us something of how the rest of the world, if not our own country, was faring, failed a few weeks after we reached here, and we have neither the means of testing it, nor of replacing the necessary parts.

Luckily, our island offers little temptation, so we have not been molested. The people about here grew enough food last summer to keep themselves going with the help of fish, which are plentiful. Also, our status is not entirely that of strangers, and we have been careful to make no demands or requests. I imagine we are supposed to be existing on fish and what stores we brought aboard the *Midge* – and that what is likely to be left of those by now would not justify the trouble of a raid on us. It might have been a different story had the crops been poorer last summer . . .

*

I started this account at the beginning of November. It is now the end of January. The water continued to rise slightly, but since about Christmastime there has been no increase that we can measure. We are hoping that it has reached its limit. There are still icebergs to be seen in the Channel, but it seems to us that they are fewer than they were.

There are still not infrequent raids by sea-tanks, sometimes singly, but more usually in fours or fives. As a rule, they are more of a nuisance than a danger, for the people living close to the water post watchers to give the alarm. The sea-tanks avoid any climbing, and seldom venture more than a quarter of a mile from the water's edge; when they find no victims they soon go away again.

By far the worst thing we have had to face has been the bitter cold of the winter. Even making allowance for the difference in our circumstances, we think that it has been a great deal colder than last. Our inlet has been frozen over for many weeks, and in calm weather the sea itself freezes well out from the shore. But mostly it is not calm weather; for days on end there have been gales when everything is covered with ice from the spray carried inland. We are lucky to be sheltered from the full force of the south-west, but it is bad enough.

We have now quite decided that when the summer comes we must try to get away. Possibly we could last out here another winter, but it would leave us less well provisioned, and less fit to face a journey that will have to be made sometime. We may, we hope, be able to find in what is left of Plymouth, or Devonport, fuel to replace that which we used in coming here; but, in any case, we intend to rig a mast so that if we are warned-off, or if there is no fuel to be found, we shall be able to continue southward under sail when our present supplies give out.

Where to? We don't know yet. Somewhere warmer, where it will be easier to grow things and start again. Perhaps we shall find only bullets where we try to land, but even that will be better than slow starvation in bitter cold.

Phyllis agrees. 'We shall be taking "a long shot, Watson; a very long shot!"' she says. 'But, after all, what is the good of our having been given so much luck already if we don't go on using it?'

May 24th

I amend the foregoing. We shall *not* be going south. This MS. will *not* be left here in a tin box on the chance of somebody finding it some day, as I had intended; it will go with us. Perhaps it may even be read by a number of people after all, for this is what has happened:

We had the *Midge* pulled up on shore, and were working to get her ready for the journey. Phyllis was painting, and I still had the engine apart, trying to get the valve-timing back right, when a dinghy came tacking into our inlet, with only one man aboard her. As he came closer I recognized him as a local whom I used to see about when times were normal, and had come across once or twice since. I did not know his name. But there was nothing to bring anyone up the inlet except us. I took a look at the gun, just to make sure it was handy. He kept on on a tack that brought him a little above us, and then turned into the wind.

'Ahoy, there!' he hailed. 'Your name Watson?' We told him it was. 'Good,' he called. 'Got a message for you.'

He shortened his sheet, put the rudder over, and ran straight towards us. Then he dropped his sail and let the dinghy run right on to the heather. He jumped out, pulled her up a bit, and then turned to us.

'Michael and Phyllis Watson? Used to be with EBC?' he asked.

We admitted it, wonderingly.

'They been putting your names out on the wireless,' he said.

We stared at him blankly. At last:

'Who – who has?' I said, unsteadily.

'Council for Reconstruction they call themselves,' he told us. 'They've been putting out a broadcast every night for a week or ten days now. Every time they end up with a list of people they're trying to find. Your names were among 'em last night – "believed to be in the neighbourhood of Penllyn, Cornwall" – so I reckoned you'd better know about it.'

'But – but who are they? What do they want?' I asked him.

He shrugged. 'Some party that's trying to straighten this lot out a bit. Good luck to 'em, I say, whoever they are. It's more than time somebody did.'

Phyllis went on staring at him. She was looking a little pale.

'Does that mean it's – all over?' she said.

The man looked at her and then turned to regard the water spread over former fields, the new inlets that reached back into the land, the abandoned homes washed through by every tide.

'No,' he said, decisively, 'that's not what it means. But trying to make the best of it is going to be a lot better than just putting up with it.'

'But what is it about us? What do they want?' I asked.

'They just said they want you in London – if you think you can make it safely. If you can't, you're to stand by for instructions later on. They give lists of names of people that they want to go to London, or Malvern, or Sheffield, or one or two other places – not many for London, but yours was.'

'They don't say anything about what it's for?'

He shook his head. 'There's not really a lot they have said yet, but they're going to be dropping small radio-sets with batteries soon, and later on some transmitters, too. For the present they're telling people to form groups for local government until communications get working properly.'

Phyllis and I looked thoughtfully at one another for some moments.

'I think I can see what we're going to be wanted for,' I said.

She nodded. We let the idea sink in for a bit, then I turned back to the man.

'Come on,' I said, nodding towards the cottage. 'There's a bottle or two up there that I've been keeping in case of something special. This seems to be it.'

Phyllis linked her arm in mine, and we went up the hill together.

'We want to know more about it,' I said, putting down my half-empty glass.

'There's not much yet,' he repeated. 'But what there is sounds like the turn all right, at last. Remember that fellow Bocker? They had him on talking a night or two ago – and a bit more cheerful than he used to be, too. Giving what he called a general survey of the position, he was.'

'Tell us,' said Phyllis, beside me. 'Dear A. B. being cheerful ought to have been worth hearing.'

'Well, the main things are that the water's finished rising – could've told him that ourselves, near six months ago, but I suppose there'll be people some places that haven't heard of it yet. A big lot of the best land's gone under, but all the same he reckons that if we get organized we ought to be able to grow enough, because they think the population's down to between a fifth and an eighth of what it was – could be even less.'

'All that?' said Phyllis, staring at him incredulously. Surely – ?'

'Sounded as if we've been pretty lucky round here compared with most parts,' the man told her. 'Pneumonia, mostly, he said, it was. Not much food, you see; no resistance, no medical services, no drugs, and three hellish winters – it's taken 'em off like flies.'

He paused. We were silent, trying to grasp the scale of it, and what it would mean. I got little beyond telling myself the obvious – that it was going to be a very different world from the old one. Phyllis saw a little further:

'But shall we even get a fair chance to try?' she said. 'I mean, the Bathies are still there. Suppose they have something else that they've not used yet – ?'

The man shook his head. He gave a twisted grin of satisfaction.

'Oh, he talked about them, too, Bocker did. Reckons that this time they've really had it.'

'How?' I asked.

'According to him, they've got hold of some kind of thing that'll go down in the Deeps. It puts out ultra-something – not ultra-violet; a sort of noise, only you can't hear it.'

'Ultrasonics?' I suggested.

'That's it. Sounds queer to me, but he says the waves it puts out'll kill under water.'

'It's right enough,' I told him. 'There were a whole lot of people working on that four or five years ago. The trouble was to get a transmitter that'd go down there.'

'Well, he says they've done it now – and who do you think? – the Japs. They reckon they've cleared a couple of small Deeps already. Anyway, the Americans seem to think it works all right, 'cause they're making some, too, to use round the West Indies way.'

'But they have discovered what Bathies *are* ... What they look like?' Phyllis wanted to know.

He shook his head. 'Not so far as I know. All Bocker said was that a lot of jelly stuff came up, and went bad quickly in the sunlight. No shape to it. Not the pressure to hold the things together, see? So what a Bathy looks like when it's at

239

home is still anybody's guess – and likely to stay that way.'

'What they look like when they're dead is good enough for me,' I said, filling up the glasses once more. I raised mine. 'Here's to empty Deeps, and free seas again.'

*

After the man had left, we went out and sat side by side in the arbour, looking out at the view that had changed so greatly. For a little time neither of us spoke. I took a covert glance at Phyllis; she was looking as if she had just had a beauty treatment.

'I'm coming to life again, Mike,' she said.

'Me, too,' I agreed. 'Though it isn't going to be a picnic life,' I added.

'I don't care. I don't mind working hard when there's hope. It was having no more hope that was too much for me.'

'It's going to be a very strange sort of world, with only a fifth or an eighth of us left,' I said, meditatively.

'There were only five million or so of us in the first Elizabeth's time – but we counted,' she said.

We sat on. There was planning, as well as the reorientation, to be done.

'As soon as we can get the *Midge* ready?' I asked. 'I think we've still more more than enough fuel to take us that far.'

'Yes. As soon as we can,' she told me.

She went on sitting, with her elbows on her knees and her chin on her hands, looking far away. It was getting chilly again as the sun sank. I moved closer and put my arm round her.

'What is it?' I asked.

'I was just thinking. . . . Nothing is really new, is it, Mike? Once upon a time there was a great plain, covered with forests and full of wild animals. I expect our ancestors hunted there. Then one day the water came in and drowned it all – and there was the North Sea. . . .

'I think we've been here before, Mike. . . . And we got through last time . . .'